A Shifter Vengeance Novel

Never Mind

SILAS REAMES

Copyright © 2024 Silas Reames
All rights reserved

The characters and events portrayed in this book are fictitious. Any similarity to real persons, living or dead, is coincidental and not intended by the author.

No part of this book may be reproduced, or stored in a retrieval system, or transmitted in any form or by any means, electronic, mechanical, photocopying, recording or otherwise without express written permission of the publisher.

Ebook ISBN-13: 978-1-961057-20-3
Paperback ISBN-13: 978-1-961057-21-0

Cover by: Deranged Doctor Designs
Published by: Night Loch Publishers LLC

1

WE NEED THE BRUTE SQUAD

Nahum lugs the last duffel out of the house and over to a black SUV parked by the curb.

"That's all of it. Everything I could think of that we might need. Unless you've changed your mind and want to stop by the vampsion for more stuff?" He raises a brow at me, but I shake my head. In any other moment, I'd be ensnared by the dragon's purple eyes and their small flecks of gold, but we've got a mission.

"No time. We'll call and debrief Hugh on the way. He can send whatever we need, or better yet bring it himself."

"Cellphone!" Nahum blurts, running back into my house for the forgotten item.

Late last night, or early this morning, depending on what you consider the time when everyone's asleep and no one has any business being awake, I was dragged out of bed by the defensive shields around my house going off. I'd been expecting a visit from the Bone Reader, and an explanation of some very mysterious things that have been happening—my intuition increasing, my new Rizik abilities, or the fact that a dying valkywolf became a goddess instead of a permanent cemetery resident after she was attacked by zombies.

Instead, I'd been met by a group made up of mostly friends, and one new face, telling me that those of us in the supernatural community have a major problem.

Actually, I suppose it's technically a *minor* problem.

Namely, someone is kidnapping the magical minors. There have been reports of supernatural kids going missing in northern California. Recently I've had my paws full juggling a series of debts and revenge-based missions, but now I've got everything else settled and can turn my full attention to this case. The perpetrators have taken Lynx's triplets, and the feline shifter is a wreck. They've also nabbed multiple bear cubs under the care of the local bear king, Rex. I owe both those shifters for having my back, but I also admire each of them. I'd help them no matter what. It's the perfect time to get back to my enforcer roots and down to business.

This is what I'm good at.

This is what I've spent hundreds of years perfecting.

Focus on the bad guys. Tune out the distractions. Seek justice, and vengeance, which go hand in hand a lot more than people like to think.

My to-do list is ready to go.

1. Rescue the kids.
2. Kill whoever is responsible for their disappearance.

Easy peasy. I like to keep my plans simple. They manage to find a way to become chaotic all on their own without me helping them along.

I jump, claws extending when the SUV horn blares twice. I let out a low growl. It's early enough that the neighbors aren't up yet, and I'm sure someone will complain. Then again, Sacramento is full of nightly noise.

"Would you two get a move on!" Todd yells from the driver's seat, window rolled down as he leans out. The bear shifter is often more laid back than I am, but Lynx is his best friend. The triplets just kidnapped are his godkids. In his fur, Todd looks like an impossibly large brown grizzly with caramel face markings, but right now he's in his skin. His amber eyes are flashing. Todd's hands are gripping the steering wheel so tight he's going to break the damn thing if he's not careful.

"Maybe"—I keep my voice lower and calmer than normal as I approach the shifter—"I should drive."

"Why? I'm perfectly capable of—finally!" He snarls as Nahum runs back out to the vehicle.

Todd moves a hand to punch the trunk button for our luggage, and I see finger-shaped indentations on the steering wheel.

I clear my throat, staring at them pointedly.

The bear growls, opening the door and stomping onto the road. Todd's wearing a fitted t-shirt today, his deep brown, muscled arms on full display as he stalks to the passenger seat. Claws extend from his fingers for a moment before he pulls them back. My intuition picks up on all the internal rage and helplessness.

He wants these perpetrators caught even worse than I do.

Todd shoots me a glare as he slides his tall form into the passenger seat.

"Fine! You drive, then, if you're so calm. You weren't feeling this way when it was your life on the line."

I reel back from him, but I don't take it personally. Now that I've come back from the Underworld I can read the motivations behind emotions as well as the feelings themselves.

Lucky for me, and lucky for the bear.

"You don't mean that. You know I take every enforcer case seriously, and that I'll treat this one with all the effort it deserves. You're just hurting and you don't know how else to express yourself. This isn't your fault, Todd."

He's halfway to a new growl when his shoulders slump and his face falls. Tears well in his eyes.

"I don't regret helping you, Never. We needed to stop Mizor. But if I'd been here instead ..."

I understand. It's more than inconvenient when multiple evil forces decide to act at once. I had to stop the elf; he was on a murderous rampage. That doesn't make me any happier than the bear that it drew us away from a case that's gotten out of control.

"We will get them back, Todd. Every single kid."

"In what kind of condition? Be realistic, Never. You've been captured by beings with ill intent before. Think of what happened to you. What do you think it would have been like if you'd been a child? Barely able to handle shifting, let alone control your abilities enough to fight back."

I am thinking about it. It's all I've thought about since he and the others popped up on my lawn overnight. It's why I'm rushing off with more haste than I ever have when only my life was on the line.

My friends have been there for me through mate-mad exes, a duplicitous Bone Reader, a corrupt government overthrow, and an old enemy returning to kill me, just to name a few.

This time, I'm going to be the one they can lean on. I'm going to be the support.

Maybe not the level-headed and calm support they would like, but I will be the vengeful and furious support they need.

Todd slams the door on his side of the SUV as I get settled in the driver's seat. With a scowl, he reaches up for that little handle above his window that I refer to as the "oh shit" handle. My friends sometimes refer to it by its formal name, "Oh shit someone gave Never the keys," but my version is shorter.

Nahum takes the seat behind me, reaching up to grip my

shoulder as I start the vehicle, back up, and peel out of my driveway.

We will get them back, he promises me in my mind.

I don't say anything in response.

He's said it all.

As far as I'm concerned, it's our only option.

From the passenger side of the car, a sulky Todd rattles off directions. We'll be taking the car to a small airport, where a Magikai jet will be meeting us. That will be the quickest way to get to the nearest Magikai compound and rendezvous with the rest of the team.

We're getting our crew, and we're going hunting.

2

I AM THE BRUTE SQUAD

After parking the SUV in the lot of a tiny airport I've never heard of, and loading the duffels, we get ourselves secured in the seats of the plane.

Todd looks out the window as the wheels go up, then back at Nahum and me.

"We'll be in Arizona shortly; then we can get up to speed on the rest of the case."

My personal feelings? It's a stupid delay. We don't need anyone else. The Magikai could have sicced the three of us on the guilty party or parties and followed us whenever it was convenient for them. Namely, when all the work was already done for them.

But that's bitterness and impatience speaking.

Since my friends and I overthrew Amun, the supernatural-selling previous leader of the Magikai, things have shifted. The remaining representatives have formed multiple committees genuinely intent on helping their community.

I'd give them a round of applause if their newfound "let's all hold hands and get along on this group project" attitude wasn't slowing us down.

At least it's a short flight. Not even two hours, wheels up to wheels down.

Nahum, Todd and I barely have time to work on strategy before the pilot the Magikai lent us is announcing our descent.

"It's agreed, then. We work with whomever we're assigned, but we're prepared to break off from the group if necessary," Todd confirms.

Nahum nods, and I do the same, throwing a stray piece of silver hair over my shoulder.

"I still vote we try to get Nadia to defect with us, if it comes to that."

My former intuitive protégé has gone government-mode, but I have faith in her commitment to the greater good. Surely she'll help us out if we need to go rogue in order to save the kids.

I stare out the window as we prepare for landing. I haven't been back to the Arizona wilderness since just after overthrowing the previous Head Representative and sending the government into chaos. I'm not sorry to have broken up a secret auction ring where both criminals and innocents were bought and sold, but that doesn't mean I left everyone in an easy spot. The remaining representatives and enforcers have been scrambling to track down any lingering individuals involved in the crimes while cobbling together this new system. I had been asked to head up one of the committees, but I declined. I'm not sure they appreciated the way I left, either.

I met the Bone Reader last Halloween for a mission of my own and never returned. Oh well, water under the bridge. I'm here now, and they're in no position to complain.

The wheels of the plane touch down and we slide to a halt on a red-dirt runway in the desert. Through the window I spot Ji-hwan off the side of the runway, waving at us. The black and white spotted Were and the rest of the individuals who showed up on my lawn to recruit us won't have beat us back by much.

He's eager and running toward us as soon as we get the door opened.

"You can leave your bags in the plane. We won't be staying here long," Ji-hwan informs us as we step onto the dirt.

The three of us follow him across the training grounds and to the Magikai representative offices.

"Things were getting cheerier around here, but this latest case has downed the mood considerably," Ji-hwan says as we pass by the canvas tent walls and cement slabs that make up most of the enforcer trainee housing. The trainees are just getting started for the day, emerging and heading to the mess for breakfast.

"It's not just the kids being taken, although that was a gut-punch for all of us. It's the dead enforcers that have popped up every time we send groups after whoever is doing this. The three in northern California are just the latest in a string of failures," Ji-hwan continues.

And here I thought my home state was ground-zero for this debacle.

"Sounds like we need to get the rest of the story," I state, casting glances to either side of me at the trainees walking by. I ignore a small pang in my chest. The previous head of the enforcers was a wolf shifter named Brutus. A real pain in the ass and a bit of a jerk. I like to think I was a good influence. He was starting to shape up into a really nice guy when one of my schemes got him killed.

Damien did promise me that, as god of the Underworld, he'd make sure the shifter was taken care of in the afterlife, but that's not buoying my mood much at the moment. The whole scene is just a reminder that the people close to me tend to die, or at least get hurt. If not that, they turn out to be villains.

My track record isn't stellar.

I shake off my regrets as we enter the air-conditioned and

glass-walled building that makes up the Magikai headquarters on US soil. A very welcome amenity in the desert, not that it's that hot out here in February.

Ji-hwan wastes no time leading us past several empty offices, including one they've kept reserved for me, should I ever choose to join a committee as an official representative. There's still a placard with my name hanging next to the door.

Ji-hwan stops and gestures us into a large boardroom on the second floor of the building.

I sigh in relief when I smell coffee. It's bound to be absolute gutter-swill from a huge tub of grounds, but I'll take anything at this point.

"You made it!" Nadia smiles as she hands me a foam cup wafting steam. I beam at the petite Were and chug half the cup.

Yep, as expected. Swill.

I down the rest and go for seconds.

After Nahum and Todd are offered cups as well, Ji-hwan ushers us to the table in the center of the room, where several magicals are already waiting.

Nadia turns and makes her way to her seat as well. Her curled, deep brown hair is clipped back on each side to keep it out of her eyes. I knew my little Wereling had risen in the ranks of the Magikai, but I'm surprised when she stands up at the head of the oval table to make introductions.

"Everyone, this is Never. She's an intuitive Were and experienced enforcer, and also responsible for figuring out what the former Head Representative was up to and freeing all the captured supernaturals he'd been keeping. The dragon with her is Nahum ..." She hesitates, but the dragon fills in where she leaves off.

"I'm Never's mate. I'm a nightmare dragon, and an empath. Feel free to put me on the front lines of this operation." Admitting to people he doesn't know well that he can send them into their worst nightmares and not be killed could be read as a power play, or as helpful. He means it as the second, but several eyes around the table go wide as fear and tension permeate the room.

Todd is introduced, and then another representative I've met before steps up to address the table.

"I'm Sky, a wind elf and representative for the Great Plains supernaturals. Before this kidnapper or kidnappers made their way to the West Coast, they were working in our region of the US. I'm as invested as the rest of you. We've lost two children among the elves, not to mention a few peryton youths and a lightning bird pre-teen. During the last abduction in the region, before whoever is behind this moved on, a few of our enforcers set up a stakeout to try to catch the criminals. We'd gotten parental consent to utilize a group of the kids as bait. We had them completely protected."

Sky's breath hitches before she continues.

"Or so we thought. It didn't work. We ended up with three enforcers seriously injured, one dead, and two more children taken. An alicorn and another lightning bird."

I let out a low whistle. Alicorns aren't exactly falling from trees. Not that any of these captured magical beings are. The Great Plains region has a lot of flying supernaturals. My best guess? Wide open skies, plenty of flat, open land to act as a runway, and the windy and tornadic conditions as a draw for flying thrill-seekers.

Sky sits, pale shoulders slumped and utterly defeated as her blue eyes stare at the floor.

"Then the Magikai had our most recent loss. Four enforcers attacked, and only one survivor, and we still haven't identified the culprit. We knew it was time to get more help."

It's like Ji-hwan said, then. Whoever is doing this has been location-hopping.

The next two people to speak are familiar to me as well.

Rex, king of the Sacramento bear sleuth, stands and introduces himself. Lynx, one of my close friends and father of the missing triplets, rises next. I'm shocked he has the wherewithal to introduce himself under the current circumstances. His eyes are bloodshot, his hair disheveled like he's been pulling chunks of it out. He's sniffling, but he makes it through and then sits, leaving the floor to our next guest.

"I'm Jackal," the next individual, whom I've only met once —on my lawn—stands up. He's got light brown eyes and skin that's a pattern of deeply tanned, warm-toned skin and pale white. Jackal is the first shifter I've met with Vitiligo. He's also got a British accent. "Hyena shifter, and not technically an enforcer or representative at all. My sister is one, though, and her daughter is one of the kidnapped children. Nadia and the committee have deputized me, as I guess you all would say over here. I may not have been an enforcer back home, but I do have plenty of relevant skills. Also, I've got no compunctions about killing, if that's what it takes to get these kids back."

He sits, and I feel the eagerness to get started hitting my intuition in waves, along with the desire for violence he admitted to having. Without knowing him well at all, I can already tell I wouldn't want to be whoever has his niece. He's on my short-list for useful allies.

Next in line are Occam and Parsim, a pair of warlock twins whose accents suggest they're here from France. Their story confirms it.

"These scoundrels have stolen children all the way from Paris to Nice, and we will not leave until these crimes are stopped," one of the twins vows.

They're identical, and I can already tell I'm going to have a devil of a time telling them apart. Where Todd and his brother have a few physical differences in height, bulk, and eye color, these two are a dead ringer for each other. Both brothers have blue eyes, brown hair, straight noses and a perpetual sneer as they look at the rest of us.

The next individual greets everyone with an equally French "*Bonjour,*" but it quickly becomes apparent the speaker doesn't hail from Paris or anywhere close.

"Scrub. I'm a lutin and representative from Louisiana." The very petite lutin, wearing what appear to be hand-sewn shoes and a small red cap, glares around the table as though daring anyone to question his stature or commitment to this agenda. He also manages to cut an entire syllable out of the word *Louisiana* during his introduction.

"We been big big mad about all this down in the bayou."

He goes on to describe the capturing of multiple lutin children, a few wolf shifter cubs, and, the most personally offensive of all ...

"They done took a Rougarou, just like you two." The lutin points at me, and then Ji-hwan. It's the Cajun term for Were, and my hackles start to rise as fur threatens to erupt.

A kidnapped Were? Not again.

As the others talk, I'm creating a mental catalog. If their dates and information are accurate, I'm beginning to sense a pattern. Then again, my mind gets sidetracked on the best of days, and this is a terrible day. I'll have to run my theory by someone else before I blurt it out to everyone.

After the lutin goes, a harpy named Flare stands up to speak. His hair is brown and disheveled, as if he flew directly into the room. His eyes are an amber that's a bit more orange-tinted than Todd's, and he's wearing only a pair of tattered shorts, leaving his tanned chest bare and the legs, ending in feathers and talons, on full display as he recounts missing children from his assigned post in the Pacific.

Last to speak is an intriguing-looking individual with a turtle shell on her back, black hair, green eyes, and facial features that hit somewhere between human and tortoise.

"Chelone, here as a representative of the Greek supernaturals."

I started this meeting annoyed at the time spent introducing what, in my mind, were too many cooks in the kitchen. As Chelone finishes up a story of missing chimera and minotaur kids, I realize we're actually a much smaller group than we should be for this size of job.

Sky stands.

"By our count, there are between two and three hundred missing children from around the globe. And we are the ones entrusted with getting them back. We may all have personal attachments to our own regions, or our own species, but I ask that we work together for the good of all these children. In addition to what you've heard firsthand here today, we've received communications from representatives in Australia, China, and Madagascar with similar news. And that's just the start of it."

She fills us in on the remaining missing kids not accounted for by the other representatives.

These kidnappers have been busy. They've worked their way across the globe. How did I not know about this until it had reached a near-worldwide problem?

"The good news is, the western portions of the USA and Canada would be the last regions hit," Sky finishes.

She takes her seat, and Nadia stands.

"The bad news is, we still don't know who or how many people we're dealing with. We have no idea of the purpose of taking these kids. The villains responsible could circle back and keep going, or after they finish in the Northwest they could be done with their mission. If that's the case, we may be running out of time. If we don't catch them soon, the kids could disappear forever."

Everyone's emotions slam into me. The severity of our situation. The stakes.

These kids need us.

When I desperately needed someone in my past, no one came to my rescue.

I won't let that happen to these kids.

We're stopping whoever's responsible before they can find a new hunting ground, or worse, disappear without a trace.

3

BUTTING HEADS

Fourteen magicals are crammed into a Magikai jet built for no more than twelve, and it's upping the tension.

According to Sky, we're heading to the last place the enforcers and representatives had a run-in with our mysterious kidnappers. Back to the wilderness. Per the representative, our destination is the base of the Saint Elias Mountains, which range over portions of Canada and Alaska.

See what I mean about how I could have skipped a trip to Arizona? If they'd let me leave directly from my home in Sacramento, I'd already be at the site! One thing that hasn't changed about the Magikai is the mind-numbingly convoluted procedures they use for everything.

I'm in no better mood than anyone else.

"Stop fidgeting so much! You're making me nervous!" one of the warlocks complains to his brother. I still can't tell the two apart. Maybe once I know their keys.

Each witch and warlock tends to use the magic that doesn't cost them anything much more than they use other spells, so I'm sure they'll each reveal theirs soon enough.

"I can't help it! Some of us aren't going to levitate our way out of here if this thing comes crashing down."

There's mention of a key already. But it's no use if I can't tell which name the levitation goes with.

"Occam, Parsim, stop it. You know the rest of us would get you out if something happened to the jet." Sky glares at the bickering enforcers.

Great. No closer to knowing my allies, except that one of them has a fear of flying. Between my foul mood and my impatience, my mouth gets the best of me.

"Oh sure, they'd be fine, as long as you didn't decide to drop one of them like a rock," I grumble to myself.

"What was that?" Sky shoots me a glare, and Nadia stands up in the aisle.

"Sky, you know she didn't mean anything by it. Let it go."

I very much did mean something by it, and as a fellow intuitive, Nadia knows that. She's just trying to keep the peace. I'm trying to be the supportive one on this trip, but I don't have to like the elf who almost killed the closest thing I have to a Were sister, even if the two of them have set aside their differences.

Sky backs down, and I can feel trace amounts of guilt coming from her direction.

Good. At least she knows where she stands.

In the wrong.

I don't escalate the situation with the elf, and I let the others bicker and debate around me until their noise and emotions are about to make me scream.

It takes roughly twenty minutes.

"Enough!"

I'm not the one yelling. Go figure.

Lynx unbuckles and stands up, one hand fisted into his hair and the other waving at everyone in the jet.

"Do you think that, just once, you self-important idiots could stow it? My kids are out there somewhere! In the hands of some madman, or a group of villains, or some abominable creature. We don't even know who or what has them! And all you are doing is sitting around here sniping at one another! No wonder the Magikai aren't efficient. It's no surprise to me that it took Never investigating for Amun's deeds to be brought out into the open. The rest of you would never have noticed because you were too busy looking in the mirror and thinking only about yourselves!"

The feline shifter is huffing, his breaths coming in short bursts. The red-rimmed and wild-eyed look is doing nothing for his composure, but everyone is riveted regardless.

"This isn't about us. This isn't about our comfort, or our egos, or whether you wanted to take a car instead of the jet. This is about the kids. Could we just focus on them? Please!"

The *please* tacked on at the end is shouted in a hoarse voice, and then he collapses back into his seat, sobbing and hyperventilating at the same time.

Todd puts an arm around his friend, patting his shoulder and shooting a menacing glare at the other occupants.

"Why are we even going back to this location?" Chelone demands, ignoring Lynx's request completely. I put her in my 'instantly dislike' column. "We lost multiple good enforcers there. I vote we turn this jet around and head back to headquarters and to the drawing board. If anyone asked me—"

"Stuff it in your shell! If you all could have gotten anything done shut in a boardroom, this case would be closed by now. Any good enforcer would know, and clearly you're not one of them, that you've got to follow the information." I snap my teeth at the odd, shell-bearing supernatural.

Ah yes, that calm support you were mentioning to me, Nahum teases in my mind.

All right, I might have been a bit over-optimistic when I swore to the dragon that, for once, I'd be the relaxed voice of reason.

Clearly that's already out the window. At least the relaxed bit.

His voice in my head calms me down enough to keep my promise of being reasonable. It's not about bickering with a team I never would have picked out. It's about solving a case.

"Based on what you all shared earlier, whoever is doing this has managed to make it all around the globe without being caught, and we're down to the last pocket they haven't hit yet. Even then, we can't check every single city, town, and barren wilderness in the Pacific Northwest. That means the best and most recent information we have is wherever they last were, and we try to look for clues there. It may very well be dangerous, but that's supposed to be our job. The rest of you can head on home after you drop me off, if that's what you'd like, but I'm staying."

One by one, Nahum, Todd, Rex, a weepy Lynx, Ji-hwan, and then Nadia echo my plans to stay regardless of the group decision. I give a decisive nod and the Wereling flashes me a smile. Jackal adds his voice to the list of individuals determined to stay and investigate, but I don't know him well enough to trust him like I do the others.

"That settles it. We land where the other enforcers died, unless any of you has a better idea?"

The warlocks shake their head at me; Chelone scowls and pouts but keeps her trap shut. The other Magikai members are staring at their shoes, or out the window, or anywhere that isn't the demanding and crazed Were. I can feel what they think of me, and now I know why.

Thanks, Bone Reader, really appreciating that trip to the Underworld. Before, I just guessed at why people didn't like me. Now, I get to know. These beings have all heard of my results, but they've also heard of my methods. I suppose forcing your way out of the Underworld, insulting Fae royals, setting a few places on fire, and shoving their former boss out a window isn't exactly considered the by-the-book method for getting things done.

Hell's bells. As if they could do any better.

Nahum glares at them all from his spot near the front. He's sitting in the small seat that would typically be reserved for the cabin crew.

"Don't any of you have any useful information? What was happening just before you had to abandon the last search? What went wrong that got those other enforcers killed?"

Sky shrugs, the feathers attached to her forearms fluttering.

"We don't know for sure what happened in the last few hours before the enforcers died. The Magikai had gotten reports of another missing child, and luckily we were already on the trail and near the area. We'd realized there was a pattern to the locations. Within a few hours we arrived at the kidnapping site, and we split up to look. The group that got attacked never called for help. We'd set up check-in times with each other, and these enforcers missed theirs. At that point, we went back, looking for them. When we arrived, the only enforcer still alive insisted that his fellow enforcers attacked him."

Even worse than I'd feared.

"You're saying we could have a mole. Or multiple moles." They can't have caught everyone working with Amun, and anyone willing to sell people in an underground auction ring doesn't rate too far above my estimation of individuals who would take kids.

Nadia fixes me with a hard stare, her brown eyes boring into my singular blue.

"We'd vetted everyone, Never. *I* had vetted everyone looking for the kids. At least all the people searching in the USA with us. If they really were double agents or moles of some kind, they fooled my intuition entirely."

I tilt my head. It would be hard to do but not impossible. I don't want to admit it in front of the others, but intuition isn't foolproof. Just last year I got a magic-canceling collar slapped around my neck by the vampire who ruled the coven that is now mine, thanks to some white lies and trickery that got around my intuition.

If it hadn't been for my friends, I'd have been a vampire slave instead of their ruler. I shake the thought out of my head, and Jackal clears his throat.

"We don't have a whole lot of options here. The new plan is the old plan. We get to the site, comb for clues, and then spread out in groups if we need to search further. Our investigation was cut short last time when bodies started dropping. This time, we need to keep going until we find what we're after," Jackal insists. He's leaned back in his seat with his arms over his chest. He doesn't even bother to open his eyes as he addresses everyone, appearing for all purposes as though he's mid-nap.

I wish we already had a clue, I complain to Nahum in his mind.

At least they made it this far. A murder scene is better than nothing. Technically, that is a clue.

My dragon, ever the optimist.

The others continue debating, but in the end no one has a better idea than Jackal's. I copy his move and pretend to nap for the duration.

Everyone pushes out of the plane without delay as soon as we land. I've dealt with plenty of unruly shifters and supernaturals before, but in the past couple of years I've worked alongside people I enjoy, for the most part.

We're not even a day into this endeavor, and it's cementing my decision to keep myself as far away from politics as possible. Of course, that would leave me without a job if I quit being an enforcer, but I'm sure someone's in the market for a private-pay vigilante. At this point, to be fair, I'm not sure I'm really that employed anyway. I haven't taken a formal job in what feels like ages.

My nose picks up the fresh scent of trees and clean air. I scan the area, letting out a low whistle. They've set us down on the Canadian side of the border, and it's undeniably breathtaking. We're at the base of the mountains, and though the snowy peaks dominate the skyline, we're in a small clearing amid towering aspens.

We may not be on the Alaskan side, but we're still awfully close to B.R.'s territory. On the one hand, he recently reminded me I still owe him my bones. The way he figures it, I'm obligated to help him with his pesky siblings. On the other hand, I'm willing to set aside my problems with him if it means helping kids. And he's close.

I just hope it doesn't come to that.

Jackal steps up beside me.

One thing I immediately like about the misnamed hyena shifter: his emotions aren't making me want to scrape my own skin off yet. He's just as concerned as everyone else, but he's keeping himself away from the drama.

The others talk a big game, but I can recognize a fellow malcontent. Jackal isn't intimidated by these blustering representatives and enforcers any more than I am. He's only scared of not finding his niece.

Sky waves us on, and we trudge into the dense trees. Not far from our landing point, we all come to a stop. We're in another semi-clearing, but this one isn't natural. There are broken and bent trees. Chunks torn out of trunks. Blood stains the bark and the ground, and that's just for starters. Humans are bound to notice this.

"Worse than you pictured?" the hyena asks, still at my side.

"It's definitely something," I allow. "Is there a magically protected perimeter?"

He nods.

The whole area in front of us is scorched. Great portions of the ground have been blackened, and some of the trees have been disintegrated all the way down to their roots. There's a few bits of crispy, crackly grass that are brown and still clinging to the ashen soil, but that's about it. It looks like we're in the center of a bomb blast.

"We had witches set a deterrent spell on the perimeter right away," Nadia informs me. "Once we're done here, we'll hire someone who can compel forest rangers to think there's been a fire."

At least human interference isn't something we'll have to worry about.

"What do you think?"

The Wereling is looking at me expectantly. Am I in charge of this mess?

Time to find out.

"Let's get to looking, then. Lynx, you've got the best eyes. You and Todd scan the trees and hills nearby for any clues. Ji-hwan, Nadia and I can sniff around," I add.

We'll have the best noses.

"I'll help with that. Bear noses are nothing to sniff at, you know."

I just stare at Rex, unable to process that he's actually made a joke.

I'd just as soon work only with those I trust, but that's not an option.

Sky volunteers to scan from the skies, along with Flare.

"Occam, Parsim, do … whatever it is you can do," I finish lamely.

Their sneers turn into smirks for just a moment.

"I," one twin announces, "can levitate myself and other things. Observe." He begins floating several feet off the ground, his hands gesturing at broken branches and rocks that join him in the sky.

"Occam, get down from there," his brother chastises. Well, at least now I know Occam is the floater.

The second twin doesn't acknowledge me verbally, but he gestures to a large tree at the edge of the scorched area, and it shrinks to the size of something that could fit in a small terrarium; then he makes it grow again.

"Parsim will help us remove any obstacles, or enlarge any evidence for better examination," Sky volunteers as the warlocks wander northeast by themselves to lift and look under things.

"Jackal, Scrub, you two check the scorched area itself. Maybe there's something here that was missed."

"I guess that leaves me and the turtle shifter," Nahum states, walking over to Chelone.

"I'm not a turtle shifter," Chelone tells the dragon, although she has yet to clarify exactly what she actually is, unless she really is an ancient and cursed being who pissed off the wrong gods. There's a legend that alludes to such a thing.

Nahum shoots me a look as they walk south into the trees.

My own emotions are mixed as I watch him go. The dragon proposed to me, as part of a deal, barely a week ago. We've both agreed to table that discussion for the time being. After all, there is absolutely nothing romantic about our current circumstances or this case.

Half of me is anxious about it. Fated mates are one thing, but a wedding is such a human celebration, and my last celebration ended so poorly. Half of me is actually looking forward to it, because the dragon is one of the few things in my life I am sure about.

"Coming, oh fearless leader?" Rex calls.

I shake my head, wandering back over to Rex.

"Right. Let's each take a direction and span out. Nadia, east. Rex, west. Ji-hwan, south. I'll take north."

The relative quiet as I walk farther into the woods, and

farther away from the others, is welcome. What I wouldn't give to have my own crew working on this instead of a motley bunch of Magikai annoyances.

Speaking of annoyance, I'm more than a little miffed when the first half-hour of searching yields nothing useful, and then everything hits at once.

"I think we found something!"

I whip my head around, recognizing the voice of one of the twins. I turn to head back to the charred clearing when a scent slams into my nose.

"Shifter," I murmur to myself, sucking more air up my snout.

No. Surely not.

"Lynx! Todd! Rex! Get over here!"

I found something, I add in Nahum's mind.

On my way.

Hurry!

Without waiting to see if the others are on my tail, I barrel into the woods.

I've scented a kid.

4

THE FIRST GOOD THING

My claws tear through grass and dirt, ripping up chunks of ground as I speed through the trees, following the scent.

Wait. Make that *scents*.

There's multiple shifters. Multiple kids? Or one kid, and a kidnapper? I know I'm smelling a youthful shifter, but I can't tell if that's masking an adult.

I'm not slowing down until I find out.

The others heard you. Rex and Lynx are gaining on you, Nahum informs me as a shadow passes overhead.

Good. There's someone with the kid.

Nahum growls in my mind.

My sense of smell is superior to that of both wolves and wolf shifters, and while I can smell clearly I'm still a couple of miles out.

I don't yell back to the males as I get closer. No sense in giving away our position. Instead, I go against all my instincts and slow down, swinging wide to approach what I smell from the side. I'm all for barreling into a fight, but even I am not going to risk a kid just to look like a badass.

As I make my way to the source of the smell, there's a soft whimpering coming from a cluster of fallen trees that have been shoved together as a sort of makeshift shelter.

I try not to even breathe too loudly, raising a clawed hand as I come up on the side of the entrance. I'm bringing it down to rip the top off the shelter when the whimpering rises to a wail and Lynx and Rex burst through the trees behind me, Todd hot on their tails.

"Kiko!" Lynx yells, rushing the shelter.

Shit on a shortcake.

No wonder I was so drawn to the scent.

It's one of the triplets.

I pull back the trees shielding the shifters. Lynx is yowling and baring his fangs at whoever has his child but skids to a halt when I reveal what's waiting in the shelter.

A bear shifter. A black bear with amber fur at the edge of his paws. He roars at us from where he stands over the baby feline shifter.

The bear's not even knee-high. I lean down close and he turns and swipes at me with both front paws. I jump back, and as Lynx lunges for his child, the bearling roars at him again, pulling his lips back from his pint-sized fangs.

"Arthur?"

The bearling stops, snapping his mouth closed and tilting his head at the sound of Rex's voice.

"Arthur, is that you?"

"Well, they got the name right," I mutter to myself.

It means *bear*, and it's associated with a certain king who pulled a certain sword from a certain stone. If ever I've seen kingly behavior, it's a pint-sized shifter standing up to several huge threats to protect an even smaller shifter.

"It's okay, Arthur, we're here to help. This is the boy's father. You can let him take the baby." Rex keeps his voice soft and relaxed as he coaxes the small shifter to surrender Lynx's child.

Lynx is trembling but hasn't inched closer to the bear cub. My intuition is rattling across my skin as it picks up how hard he's working to not charge the bearling standing over his son.

As Arthur gently steps away from the feline, careful with his paws, Lynx surges forward and my intuition is hit with a landslide of relief.

He scoops the bawling baby shifter into his arms, transforming back to his skin and cradling the child to his chest.

"It's all right. I'm right here."

Arthur is standing halfway between the father-son reunion and the king of the Sacramento bears, uncertain and out of place.

"My mom?" Arthur squeaks, looking much younger than before as he asks after his mother.

"Back with the sleuth, safe and sound. We'll take you to her right now," Rex assures the little one.

That's enough for Arthur. He goes running toward the larger shifter, nuzzling up against his fur. Rex puts a protective paw over him.

At moments like this, I can see why the bear king is so popular with his sleuth, even when he can be a bit rough around the edges. Although he's nothing compared to me in that department. It's only in the past year or so that I've embraced, well, embracing.

Once Rex and Todd have Arthur calmed down and Kiko has stopped squalling, we head back toward our temporary home base. No two children have ever been so thoroughly protected. Lynx's arms are wrapped around his son, and Arthur is actually walking under Rex's bulk. With me leading the way, Nahum overhead, and Todd bringing up the rear, no one could hope to steal these kids back.

We'll have to sweep the area where you found them for any clues, the dragon reminds me.

And question Arthur, but we need to get them away from here first.

I can feel his agreement. The area has to be traumatizing for poor Artie. It would be for me. My need to gather clues and go after the rest of the kids is held at bay by the immediate need—to take care of the two small shifters we have managed to save.

On our return to the charred clearing, the rest of the group is gathered around the warlock brothers, deep in discussion. At the sight of us, they break away and rush the group.

Before they reach us, Nahum lands, slamming into the ground and pitting himself between the surge of new magicals and the kids with their guardians. As a dragon, Nahum is on the smaller side, clocking in at just a foot or two taller than me in my fur, but that wingspan? Be still my heart. He snaps the appendages open, blocking the kids from view.

I step around him and address the others.

"We've found two of the children. A bear cub, and one of Lynx's triplets, but—"

"What about the others? Did you see anyone else?" Jackal demands, moving to shove one of the wings aside. Nahum pushes him back.

"Are they all right?" Nadia asks.

"Are they hurt?" Sky echoes her.

"What did they say about whoever took them?" Flare demands, his talons clicking together and his own wings twitching in agitation.

Nahum flexes his wings, managing to make their coverage stretch even further.

"We're all excited, but let's consider how that cub is likely feeling. I understand the Magikai, and the parents, need answers. But"—he swivels his scaled head to look at each member of the group in turn—"what we are not going to do is further traumatize a child. Only the cub is old enough to tell us anything. I say we relay any questions to Rex, who can ask the cub himself. The top priority needs to be getting these kids home, not interrogating them."

The smallest amount of fog lingers, floating out from between his fangs, to underscore his point.

"The dragon's right. This is about the kids. We should tell the Were and dragon what we found, anyway. Then we can get our questions together and send them through Rex. The cub's not likely to open up to an unfamiliar adult," Jackal states. He's a surprising voice of reason, given his emotions. He wants answers badly, and it's tied to worry over his niece.

When no one moves, Jackal backs away from the dragon and gestures for the others to follow.

Nahum relaxes his wings as everyone else copies the hyena shifter.

Todd taps me on the shoulder.

"I won't push Arthur, but I'm going to go help him and my brother." It's not a request, and I don't treat it like one. His motivation is strictly to help make sure that the kids are comfortable. He won't stress them out.

"Tell Lynx and your brother that they should take the jet back. This crew may not like it, but it's the quickest way. If a need arises, the rest of us will just have to travel the old-fashioned way and use our legs."

Todd bares his teeth, but I can tell he's trying to smirk.

"Works for me. Now, get over there and figure out what the twins found. I don't want to be left out of the loop. Convince them to let us take the jet, and we'll get out of here."

I throw him a mock salute before walking off.

"That's not going to help us!" Jackal is arguing as I approach.

One of the twins holds an item aloft.

"You're nothing but negative. This could be a huge break for us!" Parsim argues back. At least I assume it's Parsim, because he points a finger at the object and it begins to grow.

"A jacket?" I question as I stare up at the engorged puffer. It's appropriate for roaming around the woods. It looks warm and waterproof but not too heavy. I lift my snout and sniff.

Whoever wore it wasn't fully human. My guess is witchy or warlocky, but that could be because the twins have been handling the thing.

Parsim shrinks it back down as we cluster together.

"This jacket, if you'll all notice, is missing a good portion of one of the sleeves." Occam holds out the sleeve in question, and sure enough, it's been ripped or bitten through. Bits of down feather alternative are loose at the edges.

"Care to guess?" Occam holds it out to me, and I lean and sniff again.

"Bear shifter?" It's a shot in the dark. My nose is good, but it's possible it's a real bear that was at work. Although in that case I'd expect there to be quite a few more tears. If only the attacker had managed to bite off a bone, I'd summon B.R. out to help us, no matter the cost.

But there's no bone, just a bit of blood.

Parsim and Occam nod in tandem as I guess bear.

"We think the cub must have done it when he got away. That means our kidnapper wore this, and *that* means this belongs to them as well."

Occam reaches down and plucks a hair off the inside of the jacket hood. Without needing to be asked, Parsim enlarges it. It's chestnut and has just the slightest wave. As the brother shrinks it down, I can see it's of medium length. I try doing some mental imagery of how it would look still attached to someone's scalp. Maybe down to their chin? Hard to know for sure.

"This is the kind of clue we've been after. We'll all take the jet back, and when we get to Arizona we can send the hair for

DNA testing. That could give us a starting point!" Parsim announces, well pleased with himself.

Hell's bells.

Moon save me from over-important warlocks and Magikai members who have no idea how to run a proper investigation.

"Won't work," I quip.

The twins turn to me with identical glares.

"Who died and put you in charge?" Occam demands.

I open my mouth, fully prepared to remind them that I did throw the former Head Representative out of a penthouse window, but I'm saved—or prevented, depending on how you look at it—from an argument by Sky, of all people.

"We will send the hair off. After all, our DNA lab analysis is better than the humans' would be."

The twins high-five, and I add them to the list of magicals I have no desire to work with ever again.

Sky holds a finger up in their direction.

"But, Never is also right. Who among us is registering our assets, let alone our DNA, in any sort of system. No one lie. We all do it. I can't be the only one with spells and the like protecting my personal information. Only an amateur kidnapper would have their DNA just available in the system with no magical protection. And whoever this is, they aren't an amateur. The testing is just for the sake of being thorough."

She's right. The paperwork for all the property I own, my bank statements—all legal. But all magically obscured. There's almost no way this individual hasn't done something similar with something as important as their DNA.

"It's still worth a shot," Parsim grumbles.

Chelone nudges him.

"The pocket," she whispers, too loud for shifter ears. She's eager. The twins' moods lift as well.

"Yeah. We found one more thing."

Occam holds the jacket as his brother reaches into one of

the zippered pockets and tugs out a large chunk of weathered stone with a bit of lichen coating it. One edge is rough and broken, but a side of it is smooth and arched, like it's been carved that way. There's faded lettering on it.

"No idea what it means, but maybe we could test it as well. My brother and I did sense magic on it."

"We need reinforcements. Someone who would be able to look at an old rock like that and puzzle out what it's from," Nadia suggests.

A whirring sound above us is growing louder and louder as it closes in.

"Speaking of reinforcements," Nadia yells over the growing din. "Everyone should probably get under the trees and out of the way!"

A large black helicopter lowers into the scorched clearing as we make for the trees.

Once it has touched down, the engine is shut off and the blades whir to a slow stop.

Two passengers bail out of the side. Both are familiar.

Aggie, my favorite stripper witchling, hops out the left side. Hugh, the magical history and language expert who would be the first person I'd recommend to examine some old hunk of stone, steps out of the other.

The pilot of the Magikai jet has just been relaxing inside the craft, only here for transport. The helicopter pilot, however, removes his headset and gets out to join the group.

I recognize his face as well.

Feral. Founding vampire of terror and kick-assery, although that title is one I made up and not his formal moniker. And, in a situation where I'd like to put the unholy fear of any deity still out there into our kidnapper, exactly the guy I would have called.

Things are actually looking up.

5

SEPARATION STATION

The trio of supernaturals marches up to us. They almost look intimidating, striding in our direction with a helicopter in their wake, except for the witchling. Aggie waves frantically at me before breaking the line and running in my direction. My intuition picks up on both excitement and nervous energy. She's happy to be here with us but somber about the reason.

"You didn't really think you could get away with leaving us at home, did you?" she teases, nudging me good-naturedly once she's close enough, and after she's wrapped me into a hug.

"Lady Never. I rather thought we were past this habit of yours where you sprint off into danger while leaving the rest of us behind," Hugh chides with a stern finger wagging.

"She didn't have a lot of notice. This was time-sensitive and she *did* call you at the vampsion to let you know what we were up to," Nahum reminds the Were.

Hugh fixes him with a stare, but then shrugs.

"True. And, fortunately for you all, I am a master of reading between the lines when it comes to the vampire lady's instructions. When I called the Magikai headquarters to follow up, they were kind enough to patch me through to Nadia, who provided your coordinates."

Nadia thumps Hugh on the back, grinning conspiratorially at him.

"My instincts paid off! Now we've got someone to check out our first clue, Aggie for backup, and while I wasn't expecting Feral, he's a welcome addition. *Yo si que soy una dura,*" Nadia congratulates herself.

She *is* good, but it means I've got two potentially empty properties with who knows what level of defense.

"And just who is watching my vampsion?" I demand.

"Chrys, obviously. And she agreed to do it for quite a low fee," Hugh informs me.

"I'll just bet she did," I mutter as he shuffles off to where the warlocks are waiting with their stone clue. I'd be more sour if Chrys and Hugh hadn't been running the vampsion almost by themselves since I inherited the darned place.

I take another look at the vamp-turned-Were. He's gesticulating wildly, holding the stone up to the light and gasping as Parsim enlarges it again so Hugh can see it in greater detail. I'll leave them to it. Hugh will let us know once he's found something. I turn back to the Founder, holding my hand out for Feral to shake.

"What about your castle? I wouldn't have expected you'd step away from it so soon after clearing the grounds of your resident serial killer."

Feral's emotions wash over me, then swirl around me, lingering in the air.

All his regrets. All the weight of his choices and his guilt.

"Truthfully, I don't know what will happen to CoED in the long run."

The Council of Evil Dignitaries named themselves as a joke. They're made up of individuals who were maligned by members of the human race or magical community, but they weren't evil. At least, not most of them. While I brought the killer in their midst down, it took the power of all my friends together and resulted in the death of quite a few people.

On top of that, we'd had a bunch of compelled and coerced shifters and other supernaturals we'd had to sort through. Feral's staff and the vamps at my vampsion had to be rescued.

It had been, as the kids of several years back might say, a hot mess. A clusterfuck of the highest order. And, as the elf responsible has only just been offed, Feral is still deep in the muck of fixing the organization.

"What about your newest residents?" I ask.

The Sewing Circle, a group of supernatural beings with a genetic variant that made them look like grandparents, complete with wrinkles and grey hair, had decided to stay at the CoED castle rather than return to Fae.

Feral smiles, and while it doesn't reach his eyes, the suffocating negative emotions ease just a bit, giving me room to breathe.

"Honestly? They're the only thing keeping us together. Rose and Gladys have taken over supervision of any cooking duties. Those two witches can put together a meal. The banshee's been wandering the grounds with Aethra. The harpy is quite taken with her."

The harpy is someone I'd never quite made up my mind on, but after what she'd been through I wasn't going to begrudge her any friendships.

"Cynthia and Tom have been spending most of their time outside on the grounds, keeping those up. Hexia's helped some with the gardening, since she hoards the plants. She's made herself most useful as a counselor to the staff, though."

I step back when he delivers that news. Hexia is a golden dragon who turn up the power of the sun, and the castle staff is mostly vampires. Those two things don't mix without a staggering amount of vampscreen.

"What about Eon?" I ask after the Founder of Cunning.

"Sulking in his rooms. He can't believe someone else got the jump on him and used his abilities to compel so many others. Ayuna and the remaining other Founders are gone for now as well, tending to business elsewhere. Odessa and I are running things," Feral confides, naming the gorgon. At least his partner in leadership has a solid head on her shoulders. Quite a few heads, since her hair is made up entirely of snakes.

Sad about Ayuna, though. She's a blood charmer. I temporarily had her powers and was quite useless, but she's a master. She'd come in handy against kidnappers. I'm considering having a call put in for more backup when Hugh yells.

"You're all going to want to see this!"

Nahum and the others make their way over to the twins and Hugh. Even Rex and Lynx make their way to the group, along with the children.

Only I hang back. I grab Feral's arm, without too much force.

"One more thing. The Bone Reader?" I can't help asking.

B.R. screwed me over quite spectacularly, but my intuition can't get over his reasoning. He does care about me, and he needs me. Whatever is coming for us all has even the Bone Reader worried.

That should be enough to terrify the rest of us.

Feral shakes his head, a lock of black hair falling across his forehead before he sweeps it away.

"He's kept away for the most part. The only contact he's had with me has been to tell me as much, that he'd be keeping to himself."

I can't decide if I'm reassured or not. In large part because Feral's emotions are so confused about it. The Bone Reader is nothing if not a meddler and a manipulator of the highest order. He wouldn't miss out on rebuilding an organization he helped lead unless he had something bigger going on, further confirming that whatever the Bone Reader told me is coming is something we should indeed be very worried about.

For a later time, though. The kids come first.

We join the rest of the group in time to hear part of Hugh's explanation.

"Yes, I really am quite certain. I'd have to look at some photographs or see the site itself to confirm, of course, but the signs are all there."

"Whatcha got, Sherlock?" I ask.

"Well, Lady Never, unless I'm very much mistaken, what we are looking at is part of a gravestone. Some hundreds of years old, I would guess, based upon the weathering pattern and its condition."

He stares back at the piece in question before settling on his answer and giving a nod.

"Yes, a few hundred years old at least."

"And you can tell all this because of the second lifetime you spent as an archaeologist somewhere?"

The Were rolls his eyes at me.

"Oh, ye of little faith. You're well aware that I studied old languages for the museum prior to my forced entrance into vampire life and then my eventual Were turning. Old grave markers can be a fascinating aspect of that. How they were used, what was said on them, when language started to shift."

I'll take his word for it. Hanging around the dead is not my idea of a good time. I'm not scared of graveyards, but they're not a hot spot or hangout for me, either. I'm not a zombie or a necromancer, after all.

"What, then, do we need to explore every cemetery around the globe? Because that's not much help," Flare snaps, clicking his talons together.

The harpy is already more annoying than my limited patience can tolerate.

I move to obscure Hugh, snarling at the offensive representative on instinct. I'm more satisfied than I'll admit out loud when he recoils.

Still got it, folks.

Hugh lets out an over-dramatic sigh, slapping a hand to his forehead.

"Of course not. If you really wanted, you could run a scientific analysis on the stone and lichen to determine the region from which it might originate. Or—"

We all lean in a bit closer, waiting on the Were's pronouncement. Hugh flashes a triumphant smile in Flare's direction when, he too, leans closer.

"Or?" I prod my vampsion historian.

"Or you just follow your nose. I'm admittedly no expert, having spent less than a year as a Were myself, but that jacket smells like someone. Follow the trail."

The twins scoff, swiping the bit of headstone back.

"What trail? Everything around here is scorched by magic, and it's made it impossible to pick up anything, with the exception of the kids your friends found."

An idea pulls at the back of my mind. Then it gives a full tug.

"The kids! That's right. I smelled them at the edge of all this. If our kidnapper left on foot, and I know it's a big if, maybe we could pick them up along the perimeter."

Their emotions hit me before their voices do. The thing about intuition is I never need things to go to a vote. I can already tell if I've won over the majority before anyone says a word. In this case, a couple of the representatives will be displeased, but I'm going to win.

The deal is sealed as Rex clears his throat.

"Arthur has informed me that they were initially moved in vehicles but had been on foot once reaching the woods. There were sleds and wagons, with the older children pulling the younger ones. We're not lucky enough to have a kidnapper who revealed their ultimate destination, but he stated they were headed up into the mountains. He's also confirmed there were several adults with them."

The bear cub is still in his fur. Rex has put his skin back on, but Todd is all grizzly. Arthur is standing behind one of Todd's massive legs, shielding himself from view.

I'm itching to ask more, but I agree with what Nahum told the others earlier. We aren't going to re-traumatize a kid.

"Arthur has stated that only one of the adults spoke to them. A tall man with brownish hair, although, given Arthur's size, tall may be relative. The other adults with them never spoke, and they were cloaked and masked."

That means we've got a whole group of bad guys. Not ideal, except it means there's plenty of evil to go around when we get to the mauling and maiming portion of this mission. In other words, my favorite part.

From underneath Todd's legs, Arthur lets out a squeaky grunt.

"That's right," Todd adds. "There was also one other supernatural who joined them temporarily. When the Magikai were on the trail here, Arthur says the other individual appeared from a cloud of red smoke and provided directions to those guarding and moving the children. When the visitor disappeared into the red smoke and the adults were distracted, Arthur saw his opportunity. He attacked one of the cloaked figures but was scared when they started firing some kind of magic at him. When he was knocked back, he fell into the arms of the one man who spoke to them. On instinct, Arthur bit at the man's arm, then grabbed the child he'd been holding and ran."

It's a miracle they both made it. Many would say unharmed, although I wouldn't consider what they've endured a lack of harm. I might rather classify it as: no lasting *physical* injuries.

I step into the middle of the group.

"New plan. First and most important step: get the kids back home and to safety. Next most important step: follow the scent. Equally as important step: figure out where this gravestone came from. That step will be for Hugh to puzzle over. Now then, let's get these kids home. We could lend them the Magikai jet?"

My intuition is hit by reluctance from several of the surrounding representatives, loath to give up their transportation out of here. They're still nervous, and since we are standing in a spot where their colleagues were killed, it's hard to blame them, but I manage.

After all, it's for the kids.

"I can fly a chopper."

"What?" I turn as Lynx speaks, my jaw hanging wide.

He smirks, for one second revealing a bit of his old self before frowning again and holding Kiko closer to his chest.

"There's plenty you don't know about me. You forget that Todd and I were very successful enforcers even before you came along."

"That's right." Todd stands by his friend, and when he offers a very large paw, Lynx gives it a half-hearted fistbump. "We have skills."

"Color me impressed." I could make one of my typical jokes or barbs, but I wouldn't dream of it in Lynx's current state.

Once their precious jet is off the table, the others are quick to agree.

"The jet stays here, then. The rest of us will fan out on the perimeter until and if we can find the scent. If we can't, we test the stone and the hair," Sky instructs.

"Todd, Never, Aggie?" Lynx beckons us over to the helicopter.

Rex is already in the chopper, seated next to Arthur. After a moment's hesitation, Lynx hands his son to the bear king before turning back to us.

"I need to go home. I need to make sure, I *have* to see for myself, that Kiko stays safe. And I won't feel that way until he's in Fiona's arms. But my other kids." He gets choked up for a moment, throwing a hand out when Aggie steps forward. "No. I need to finish this. Ever since we all worked on the Jeweled Claw case together, you all have become more than just coworkers or friends. You're my family, and as my family, I am trusting you with this. Bring my kids home. No matter what the Magikai rules say. No matter what it takes. Do not let these people get away."

"We won't stop until we've found them," Todd promises.

"We'll make sure your babies are safe," Aggie adds.

"And whoever has taken these children will pay. You have my word on that," I finish.

He sniffles, wiping a hand over his nose. Normally, snot is the one thing I can't handle, but I don't flinch when he goes down the row and gives all three of us a hug.

"I knew I could count on you all," he says.

He looks one more time at the group, but his gaze lingers on me as he steps into the chopper.

"Whatever it takes, Never."

I nod.

"Whatever it takes."

My friends have each risked themselves for me, and I'm more than willing to return the favor.

6

YOU TAKE THE HIGH ROAD

After the kids depart, the rest of us form a circle and start moving outward.

The good news?

It's not too long before we've found a lead.

The bad news?

It's actually *leads*. There's two of them, in opposite directions.

We end up back in the center of the burnt clearing, deep in a debate over the best course of action.

My desire to tear off after the scent Todd and I both noticed northwest of where we found Arthur is strong, but I need to know what the others have planned.

These kids can't afford for you to haul ass into a half-cocked rescue plan, I remind myself.

Instead, they're being taken moon-knows-where for moon-knows-what-purpose while we waste more time squabbling.

"I'm telling you, we found a solid trail that smells just like that jacket and gravestone remnant, going northwest!" Todd's beginning to lose his temper, his voice growing louder as he exposes some very sharp teeth.

"And I'm telling *you*, we're sensing remnants of magic leading southeast. Do you know why you're just an enforcer and we're representatives? Because we're using our brains and you're just shoving your big snout around in the dirt." Occam grins like he's said something wildly clever, his twin mimicking the expression next to him.

Todd is barely holding himself together, but he doesn't want to look like the animal they're accusing him of being. I have no such issues when it comes to uppity warlocks.

"You two pig-headed, loud-mouthed idiots called us in because you couldn't hack it on your own, isn't that right? If you were as smart as you think you are, you'd have found the kids by now, or are you forgetting a failed mission and multiple dead enforcers?"

They're still scowling at me, and Parsim throws his hands out to shove me.

"No!" I hear Nadia yell in the background. She'll have been feeling all the same emotions as me, albeit without the added benefit of everyone's motivations. I can tell the twins are overcompensating because they're more than aware how far short they've already fallen, but I don't care. This won't be good for international magical relations, but they're insulting my friends, and they're jeopardizing the kids with their argumentative attitudes.

I take a step back to gain my balance, then grin at them with lengthened canines and motion the twins forward with one hand, inviting violence.

"Rabid dog," Occam scoffs.

I just keep right on grinning.

I never said I wasn't petty. I've been waiting for an excuse, and pummeling the two of them will help us get back to business a lot quicker than continuing to try to reason with them. That, and a good fight might just make me feel better.

Fog lingers at my feet.

I've got this, I think back toward the dragon.

My eye flashes black at the two warlocks, and my view of them changes as I grow taller. Fur sprouts along my arms and my back. My snout lengthens, and the bones of my face and legs crunch and change.

I let the transformation linger for a few seconds longer than strictly necessary, because I'm enjoying the fear in the brothers' eyes.

Drool hangs off my jowls as I lean in.

"You were saying? Something about, *rabid*?" My voice rumbles with a growl on the last word, which turns into a laugh.

They're both leaning back, withdrawing without even thinking about it. At the sound of my laughter, Occam steps forward with a glare. He raises an accusatory finger at me, and I take a snap at it.

Don't worry, I'm not really going to hurt them. Not much, anyway.

"Beast!" Parsim accuses.

I turn on him next, fangs on full display. With a clawed hand, I grab his shirt and force him toward me. He flinches.

"What was that, *magician*?" They don't like the term any better than we like *dog*. It implies trickery and falsehood, instead of real magic.

"Never. We need everyone to work together for this," Nadia reminds me from my side. I notice she's in her fur as well, and her eyes are locked on the warlocks. She knows who the real troublemakers are, I'm sure of it.

"All right." With a shrug, I let him go, but I'm not gentle. I shove him and send him stumbling back into his brother.

"Actually,"—Hugh runs up to us, placing himself between the warlocks and everyone else—"we don't need to be together. That is to say, we've got enough individuals to travel in groups. We should split up between the trails."

I get dizzy as my intuition is hit with a flip-flop. Part of the group's tension decreases, while in the other half it ratchets higher.

"That didn't work well for us last time. It's how we lost enforcers," Sky reminds everyone.

"Yes, but you didn't have us," Hugh counters.

"And if we find something? What then? How do we notify the other group? Maybe a flare gun from the jet?" Scrub suggests.

Hugh just shakes his head.

"Amateurs," he accuses. "Did you all really think I wouldn't arrive prepared? I packed a few two-way radios. Walkie-talkies, to some. There's no cell service up here, but we should be able to find a usable frequency for these."

He reaches into a satchel he brought along, pulling out a few of the walkie-talkies and beginning to pass them around.

All that's left now is to choose the groups.

Is this what it feels like for humans to be picking sports teams in middle school? I've seen the experience on sitcoms, but I've never dealt with it in person.

Recognizing that it would be a good idea to keep us on opposite sides of this thing, Sky suggested that I choose one group and Occam choose the other.

The warlock gets to go first, because no matter what she says, Sky is still biased and prefers her fellow representatives to unpredictable enforcers.

I'm utterly unsurprised when Occam's first pick is his twin.

"Nahum," I call out for my first choice.

"Scrub." All right, I admit to a bit of shock. I hadn't thought of the lutin as tough, but I have yet to see him in action. Lutins can travel straight through solid objects, and I'm sure that's useful.

"Todd," I state next, well aware from his emotions that they'll drive him over the edge if he ends up with the warlocks.

"Fine. We want the witch." Parsim points to Aggie, whose mouth falls open into that surprised little 'o' she sometimes does.

"Well, you can't have her!" I snap.

Occam rolls his blue eyes, and his brother sneers.

"Forgetting what the rules are already, wolf? It's called taking turns."

"It's called tearing you limb from li—"

"Never, it's all right. I'll go." Aggie places a conciliatory hand on my arm.

She's not happy about it, but she's not frightened, either. I bend down to whisper in her ear.

"If they bother you, strip their magic and leave them under a tree. We'll come get them eventually," I promise her.

"I wouldn't expect anything less from you," she responds with a giggle.

She makes her way over to the twins.

"That's right. Come over to your own kind." Parsim's just saying it to upset me, but it's the witchling he gets a reaction out of. She lifts both hands, flipping each twin the bird.

My training in sassery and badassery is complete.

A few more names are shouted that leave the twins with Sky and Chelone, and me with Feral and Hugh.

"Ji-hwan." I point, and the spotted Were makes his way over to our side, more than happy to be on this team.

"Flare," Occam calls out, pointing to the harpy.

Interesting, interesting. Only Nadia and Jackal left. I know why they don't want Nadia. She's competent enough to make them insecure. They're all representatives, but even at her young age they're well aware she's better at it, and friends with us to boot.

Jackal, though, seems useful enough. Odd that I can feel

they're on edge around him. It's more than not trusting him, although there is that. He makes them nervous.

As far as I know, he's just your run-of-the-mill hyena shifter. Nothing special about him. No genetic variants or odd abilities. Then again, he could always be hiding something.

"Jackal." I make my final choice.

I'll admit to curiosity, but that's not my primary motivation. I feel all my emotions as strongly as I can in Nadia's direction as she shrugs and goes over to the twins.

I need someone with Aggie that I can trust.

She can't hear me, of course. She's not the dragon, but she'll pick up the sentiment.

Aggie squeezes Nadia into a hug, and the two of them flash me a thumbs-up.

"About time. How anyone gets anything done in such an inefficient government is beyond me," Hugh grumps as the groups backtrack to the jet to snag supplies. This trek may take another hour, or it could take weeks. For the children's sake, I hope not.

Aggie tosses a duffel at me.

"Clothes, for when you all shift," she states.

"That's good for the other Weres and Hugh, but I don't need clothes," I remind her.

She points at the bag, insistent.

"You'll want these. Trust me."

I open the zipper gingerly, almost afraid of what I'll find. The others, and Aggie is the primary offender, have taken to giving me a variety of bedazzled and bejeweled and otherwise be-glittered vibrant monstrosities of shirts emblazoned with all sorts of sayings I'd never normally condone.

Let's Hug It Out was a particular favorite of hers.

I reach in and pull out a white, fitted t-shirt covered in rainbow-colored glitter letters.

World's Best Big Sister.

My throat feels a bit tight, and suddenly my eye requires a lot of extra blinking.

I'm not crying. This forest air is full of allergens! Okay?

"Well. I will certainly be wearing this one."

If bright white and rainbow sparkle wasn't the worst possible situation for forest camouflage, I'd throw it on right now. Instead I tuck it back into the bag with care and opt for a muted green shirt instead. This one reads *Hug Collector* in bronze glitter that won't be too noticeable.

Once we're equipped, our groups get ready to move out. Hugh has a couple of bags over his shoulders, in his skin but stronger now that he's a Were. Todd is in his fur, and a few more bags are thrown over his huge neck like saddle bags.

Nadia and Aggie are lingering at the back of their group as we part ways. Aggie gives a small wave, timid for the first time.

I give her a thumbs-up.

"You can always strip them," I mouth at her.

She grins before heading southeast.

7
I'LL TAKE THE LOW ROAD

I did say it would be anyone's guess how long this could take.

For those who are curious, it turns out the answer definitely wasn't an hour or less. We're at least three hours into our trek. In fairness, our group is moving at a glacial pace. We want to examine every scent and potential hiding spot to ensure we don't miss anything.

There could be a kidnapper, or another escaped kid, around every tree.

My snout picks up something, lifting in the air at the same time as Ji-hwan's.

"I've got something!" Todd yells from farther out.

"Me too," I respond.

It's not the same as what we've smelled on the gravestone. Not exactly, at least. But it's definitely magic.

The air a bit in front of our group crackles with intensity, making me want to sneeze.

"I can smell some of the kids!" Todd calls out again. He's right; somewhere near the crackling magic, I scent the same thing.

Careful, Nahum cautions as we make our way into a thicker area of trees, closer to the magic. The foliage overhead makes it darker here, and the temperature a few degrees cooler.

This is the type of weather that has humans donning their extra hiking layers. For me, it's a welcome change after an arduous day of hiking and searching.

"It's somewhere in this part of the grove," Todd insists, his own nose covered in dirt as he shoves it through a pile of spruce needles and some brush.

I agree.

We discard our duffels under one of the trees. Hugh dons his fur, and Feral's eyes gleam as he meanders around the area.

Jackal shakes his head as he sets his own duffel down on the pile.

"I don't like it. All this nothing, and now a huge amount of magic in one spot? Something is wrong."

I get a sense now of what the warlocks saw in him. He thoroughly believes the statement, but he's not afraid.

He's ready.

This shifter is a hunter. I've no idea what kind, but he's no modern-day magical. He's got all the preparedness of our ancestors in the wilderness. A true predator.

"A grove full of nose-crackling magic when we're chasing an enemy we can't identify and kids we have to make sure we don't endanger in a rescue attempt? I'll have to agree with you, Jackal, it reeks and stinks of a trap, but we can't afford to run," I remind him.

He … smiles? But it's laced with menace. It makes *me* nervous. Hyenas are odd that way. Always looking a bit too happy.

"I have no intention of running," he assures me as he dons his fur and my eye goes wide.

He's striped.

I do my best to hide my reaction, but he must see it anyway.

"You were expecting spots, yes?"

"I was," I admit.

When he speaks, his fangs are visible, like he's trying to talk around a badly fitting pair of dentures, but he gets his point across better than many magicals in their fur.

"Just because I have Vitiligo doesn't mean my hyena form is going to change species."

"Right. That was foolish of me. I apologize," I force out.

Don't be so surprised. I can say 'sorry' when I've actually done something wrong. I throw my words around with abandon when I'm pissed off, but Jackal hasn't done anything to me ... yet.

"Thanks," he acknowledges, padding off farther into the crackling magic around us. The fur that goes down his back rises like a mohawk.

There's definitely an area saturated with magic, but I can't pinpoint a source or trail. I'm sniffing and pacing, walking basically in circles. Each time I think I've got a line on the scent it grows fainter, sending me back in the direction I came.

The others' emotions are growing as we search. Desperation, agitation, vexation. It's like nails on a chalkboard, and I clack my teeth together, then shake my head to ward away the feeling.

"You did it! You're responsible for this!"

I spin to see Todd, reared on his hind legs and snarling down at Jackal.

The hyena is backed into a tree, baring his teeth in that creepy, almost smile-like expression.

"You're delusional," Jackal counters as the bear closes in on him.

Without a word, Todd brings his massive paw down, taking a chunk out of the tree bark where Jackal was just standing. The hyena laughs, the sound whooping and echoing as he weaves around the bear shifter.

"Todd! What happened?" I go over to him, but my attention is pulled away by another set of snarls.

Two Weres roll in front of me, tumbling over one another as they slash and kick. The taller and more slender Were has black and white spots, and the other has russet fur and glowing red eyes.

This makes zero sense. My intuition is picking up a dizzying combination of fear and rage, but there's no good reason for either. Hugh is only a fighter when he has to be. Ji-hwan is fine with fighting, but he wasn't trained that way. The Magikai under Amun's rule trained him to seduce, and beguile, because he has an actual, honest-to-moon, gods-given ability for it. Seduction instead of intuition. He started training with me, but he doesn't have a huge amount of experience with physical combat.

He's definitely fighting now, though.

Ji-hwan closes his fangs around one of Hugh's arms, shaking his head. Hugh's eyes flash from red to green and back again. The former vamp gets his back foot up under the other Were and shoves him away. Ji-hwan gasps as he's thrown into the dirt.

"Stop it! What is wrong with you two?" I demand as I stomp my way over and pry them apart. Ji-hwan's already thrown himself back on Hugh, snarling.

"You won't save them."

I freeze, then spin around, ignoring the fighting Weres. I recognize the voice, but the tone is chilling.

"Nahum?"

He's advancing on me, wings spread wide, claws out and scaly jaw open, with fog at the edges.

"When have you ever cared about saving anyone but yourself? They asked for your help, but all you'll do is bring more danger to those kids."

He may as well have slapped me. The growls and yips of the others fade into the background.

"You don't mean that. You can't."

"When you broke free of the Isle? Hmm? You burned it to the ground. You boxed your captor into the sea. *That* was your primary motivation. Destruction. Not helping people. Not selflessness. Everyone else may have bought in to your lies, but I know you better than them. I know the truth. You're selfish."

I can't deny him, but nor can I figure out why he's saying things that are tearing me apart.

My defenses have been down with Nahum. Aside from an accidental nightmare on our first meeting, he's never hurt me. He wouldn't.

"Something is wrong." My voice shakes as I start backing away.

Like prey.

Because I can't face him.

Can't fight back against my mate, the dragon I've agreed to marry.

"You're what's wrong here. Everyone is stressed because of you. Barking orders, picking fights with the warlocks. We'd have rescued those kids by now if you weren't here, screwing everything up. Just like you've screwed up the lives of everyone who's ever befriended you. Including me."

I put my hands over my ears.

"No. I'm not a bad person. I try to help people."

I make a mess of things, sure, but if there's one thing my friends have proved to me, it's that I am a good guy. At least I try to be.

"You're a wrecking ball. You destroy everyone you care about, and everyone foolish enough to care about you. Getting stuck as your mate was the worst thing ever to happen to me. I can't afford to let you slow me down any longer. The rest of us have important work to do, and you're not part of it."

The words slam into my chest like a bullet, but then his emotions follow them.

He doesn't mean it. He's in agony. He's disoriented. He's not angry at me.

This isn't my dragon.

This is magic.

Nahum snarls, fog pouring from his jaws. Before he can send it flying in my direction, Hugh and Ji-hwan go rolling between us. Until I know what I'm up against, I don't have a whole lot of options. While the dragon is distracted, I run.

My furred feet pad the earth as I sprint away from the love of my life. Nahum roars, and I hear the snap of his wings as he launches into the sky. He doesn't go far; he's low enough that his talons could snatch me up if he gets close. The first time he dives, I tuck and roll, coming up ready and running again. The second time, one talon gets so close it takes a bit of my fur with it, but it misses the skin beneath.

I can still feel him. Beneath his actions, Nahum is in misery. What he's doing tells me he hates me. What he's feeling tells me he's suffering. It makes no sense. The dragon feels grief, like he's lost something precious. Like he's lost me. It's how he felt when I first got back from the Underworld and he was telling me what it was like while I was gone.

What could be messing with my dragon, and the others?

I'm distracted, and it costs me. I manage to get myself cornered by a few trees whose branches intermingle, blocking any exit.

Nahum slams into the ground, tucking his wings behind him as he stalks forward.

While I don't know what's happening, I know he can't help it. I know this isn't the real him.

But knowing doesn't help me as he opens his jaws and leaps for my throat.

8
AND WE'LL SEE WHO GOES MAD FIRST

I duck the dragon's fangs, but one of Nahum's talons slices a gash into the ground next to me. I roll again, and a tower of fog billows where I was standing moments before.

My mate just tried to trap me inside a nightmare.

I stare, wide-eyed, as he spins and makes another run for me.

"Would you stop it!"

I know he can't. I can feel as much in his emotions, but I don't know what else to do.

"Never! Back here!"

I spin to see Feral waving frantically. He's way off from the rest of us, tucked under the trees where we set our duffels down. He waves again, beckoning me over.

"Get away from the grove!" he calls.

With one quick glance back at Nahum, whose purple eyes are flickering, I make my decision and sprint for the Founder. With any luck Nahum will follow me out of this mess, whatever it is.

Nahum sends a wall of billowing grey fog after me. I'm almost to Feral when the grey overtakes my vision.

"Nahum, stop! Let me out!" I yell, as if he's going to respond.

For a few torturous moments I'm in a blank fog, just waiting for the nightmare to start.

Then, a setting appears around me.

The last time he did this to me, the nightmare sent me back to the Isle. The person responsible for trapping me there had walked out of the flames to greet me. But I'm not scared of Mizor anymore. I've killed him once, and Nahum's killed him again. There's no coming back for him now. Damien will have tossed him into the worst circle of the Underworld and thrown away the key.

This time, the nightmare takes me to the vampsion. The vampires are milling around while I sit in the dining hall. My favorite satyr-Fae bartender Elios is bringing me a cocktail that glitters blue.

This isn't a nightmare at all.

I take a sip as the doors of the dining room are flung open, banging and echoing against the walls.

It's Aggie.

The witchling stumbles in, clutching her side and bleeding all over the floor.

My drink spills as I drop my glass on the table; my chair squeaks as I shove it back with force.

Running over to the witchling, I scoop her into my arms and lower her down, sitting underneath her.

"Hugh! Chrys! Get some help!" I scream.

"They can't help. No one can help." Aggie coughs.

My blood chills in my veins. My intuition can feel her fear, and the reason. She's dying, and she knows it.

"They found us, Never. All these powerful people we've gone up against. They know what we've done, and they're here for revenge."

I don't want to leave her, but the screaming on my lawn forces my hand. I can hear Nahum's roar, and Nadia cursing at someone in Spanish. The pained sounds of screeching pixies.

Handing Aggie off to one of the vamps, I make my way outside.

The vampsion gardens are a crime scene. Chaos. Everyone unfortunate enough to be standing outside is the victim of a death sentence.

What Aggie said makes sense now. Chrys is sprawled on the grass, clearly dead. Hugh is next to her, on his knees and sobbing. One of his furred ears is torn off and blood drips down his neck.

I look up to see Nadia hiding behind a hedge. When I reach for her, there's an explosion. She's thrown into the air, shrapnel slicing through her until she's so wounded even a Were couldn't heal from the injuries. She lands and shudders, back in her skin.

I'm running, with no destination in mind. I can't even see who's attacking us. The sparks of light, the explosions, they're coming from nowhere.

Nahum is struggling against someone in the sky, but it's an invisible force. Whatever it is rips one of his wings down the center, and he goes spiraling.

I can't save them. I can't save any of them.

The Founders are in a circle on my lawn, with the Sewing Circle members in their center.

The ground swallows them all before I can make it to them.

Thunder claps and two figures appear on the lawn. Damien and Danger. The god of the Underworld and his new mate. Dead, because I couldn't save her life, and now a goddess herself.

"Why are you sending so many supernaturals to me? What have you done, Never?" Damien demands, his grey eyes piercing me.

"You didn't save me. You didn't save them. You're going to be all alone. Everyone you love, gone." Danger is crying as she sweeps her arms out at the carnage. Her judgment gnaws at my intuition.

I spin and run, my hands over my ears.

It's not real. It's not real.

But it feels real. Something is very, very wrong.

I skid to a stop when a familiar wall of black shadows grows in front of me, changing and solidifying until it's the Bone Reader. He's cycling his features, using multiple weaving voices, as he did on the first time we met.

"I tried to warn you, Never. I told you what they could do. You wouldn't listen."

"This is the Riziks? They did this?"

"You said I was cruel. You thought I was doing this to hurt you, but I needed you. They all did. I was doing what I had to, to save everyone. All the people you claimed to care about. But you weren't willing to make the sacrifice, and you let them all die."

The shadows around him are back, growing until they swallow me up. So dark I can't see anything.

"Wait! Wait! I'll help you. I can still help! I can still help! Don't leave!"

The darkness swallows my voice, and I can't hear myself scream.

I JOLT UP, heaving and coughing.

Nahum and Feral are kneeling over me, and Hugh pops his head out from behind the two of them, offering me one of our reusable water bottles.

With a swipe of one furred arm, I wipe something wet off my cheek. Have I been crying? Nahum's nightmares have tired me out, and I let my fur fall away. I sit there in my skin, shivering. I'd almost forgotten how cold the damned things make you feel.

"I think Aggie packed long-sleeves in one of the duffels," Feral volunteers as he goes for the bags.

"You fogged me," I accuse in Nahum's direction, but without any real malice. There's an explanation. There has to be.

He shakes his head, back in his skin, when he reaches a hand out and places his palm on one of my cheeks.

"I didn't. Not you specifically. I fogged a good portion of the grove. I tried to warn you not to go that way. I yelled at you not to, but you ran directly into it."

"You were like a Were possessed," Ji-hwan confirms.

Feral returns with one of the duffels, proffering a sweatshirt that says *Don't Forget To Smile* with a massive yellow smiley face underneath. The sweatshirt itself is a muted grey, though, so I turn it inside out and throw it on. What I wouldn't give for the hot springs on Nahum's island.

"I really ran into the fog?" I ask the Founder after shoving my head through the sweatshirt and shaking out my silver hair. I can feel dried sweat. I need a shower.

Feral nods. Honesty cascades off of him, and concern. He was worried, for all of us.

"You'd better tell me all of it."

Feral glances around at the group, reaching one hand up to fix his black hair, then lowering it again. His green eyes flash once before dimming again.

"You all had spread around the grove where we'd scented the magic. You were sniffing and searching. I thought to myself that it would be a good time to check in with the others and let them know we might have found something. Just so they'd be ready if they needed to meet us here. I was unzipping one of the bags to grab a walkie-talkie when I heard Hugh snarling."

Hugh, who is back in his skin and tugging on a pair of khaki cargos that he would never have chosen on his own, blushes as he shakes out his textured, caramel hair.

"I didn't realize what I was doing."

"I'm sorry for the eye," Ji-hwan offers, and I notice that Hugh does in fact have bruising on one cheekbone, although it's already fading.

I clear my throat, and Nahum shoots the two of them what can only be described as a severe look.

The dragon is hovering nearby but hasn't tried to hold me.

I can feel, that he feels, it may not be welcome.

I know whatever happened isn't his fault, but I still want to hear the truth first.

Feral continues.

"The air in front of me was crackling. We all knew there was magic here; we just didn't realize it was active. I knew everyone had to be spelled somehow. What the two Weres were saying to each other didn't make any sense."

"What were we saying? As I remember it, Ji-hwan ran at me, accusing me of sabotaging the group, and I defended myself." Hugh glances at the other Were.

"You told me you were the kidnapper and then leapt at me," Ji-hwan responds.

Feral shakes his head.

"Not at all. Well, not exactly. Ji-hwan was yelling at Hugh to leave him alone, and that he thought maybe he'd been possessed. He wanted to get Hugh help. Hugh, you were telling Ji-hwan to stop attacking you. You were both on the defensive, but circling one another. You leapt at the same time."

Hugh tilts his head, musing.

"How strange. What we both saw and thought isn't what happened at all."

This is magic unlike anything I've ever seen. I hate it.

"A fake vision, then? The closest thing to that is Nahum's nightmares."

"My nightmares only work face to face," Nahum responds. "And they home in on the victim's fears. I don't control them or use their current settings like what was done here. With what happened to all of us, I was still aware I was in the woods. What about everyone else?"

We all nod.

"Until I was in your fog," I amend.

"You really did run straight into it, Never," Feral says. "When Todd and Jackal started fighting as well, I knew something was seriously wrong. You were alternating between growling at Nahum and whimpering while pulling away. He was stalking you, but he kept tossing his head like he was trying to fight off whatever was happening."

Whimpering. Great. That's what I want to be known for in this group.

I set aside my ego for a moment and put a hand on Nahum's arm.

"You didn't want to hurt me. I could feel it. I was hearing you say all these hurtful things to me, but I could still feel your real emotions."

Nahum puts his hand over mine.

"And I was hearing you say you'd found one of the kids, but you wouldn't let me near them. You looked like you were going to attack them. I didn't want to hurt you, though. Maybe it's all the time I've spent observing people's nightmares, but I knew something was off. Beyond knowing that, of course, you'd never do such a thing."

I nod along.

"Then I heard Feral yelling at me to run."

"That part was real. I'm not sure how I got through to you."

I tilt my head and run a hand through my hair.

"I think … it was once I realized that what I was seeing and hearing didn't match what my intuition was telling me. It was only after that when your voice broke through. Someone mind-manipulated us. That's what I'm going for, unless someone has a better label for the magic that did this. They got in our heads and jumbled things. But Nahum was able to sense it, if not fight it off entirely, because he's used to faux visions. And I couldn't fight it off, but I could still feel your real emotions underneath everything I was seeing in the grove. That's to our advantage if our kidnapper tries this again."

Another tally in the plus column for intuition. Not that I want to repeat this experience.

Jackal has stayed in his fur and is limping around the edge of the group. One of his hind legs is healing from what must have been a pretty nasty break, courtesy of Todd. There's a deep slice in one of his cheeks that's adding to the smiling effect hyenas have. There's also a gash in his side.

I look around for Todd, expecting to see that he's been the victor of this little scuffle, and audibly gasp.

Todd's face is a mess. He's back in his skin, but one eye is swollen shut. His lip is bloodied, and he also has an arm dangling uselessly at his side. He's wrapping one of his legs, and if he's bothering with such actions it's deep enough that it'll take a little while to heal.

Todd, as you may recall my saying a time or ten, is an absolute unit of a bear. A machine. His own personal tank of a shifter.

To have him this seriously injured by one hyena shifter half his size is mind-blowing.

Speaking of minds: what must their minds have been telling them about each other to extract such levels of violence?

Whoever did this is very tricky, I'll hand them that. They had me convinced I was fleeing Nahum's nightmare fog, when in reality I threw myself into the stuff.

Feral is still frowning as he relays the rest of the events.

"The whole thing was incredibly violent. With enough yelling, and chucking things from the bag at people's heads, I was eventually able to lure you all far enough away that the effects wore off. But seeing you all in attack mode against each other reminded me of how I'm viewed when I let my Feral side loose."

I call that side Hyde, for good reason. The Founder's ability is essentially sheer terror on a scale no one wants to feel.

The way the Founder tells it, I'm the only one impacted by the crackling mind magic who didn't try to harm anyone else during this fiasco.

Me, the least violent person in the room?

That's a first.

Jackal clacks his teeth, then takes several reluctant steps closer to the rest of us.

"It's all making sense now. When the rest of us, the enforcers and representatives, came up here before, that has to be what happened. We found those other enforcers in the charred area bloodied and battered. One of them was a firebird, so the scorching makes more sense. The others tried to write it off as the work of the kidnapper, but I knew that version of events didn't match the scene. It looked like they'd tried to kill each other. What if they've used these mind-manipulation zones everywhere they've struck?"

It would explain the trail of dead enforcers, and the limited progress on the case.

If he's right, we've got one hell of a problem.

9

THE JACKAL

As Jackal recalls the scene he and the Magikai members came upon in the woods on their last trip up here, a thought occurs to me.

"Sky said there were four Magikai members attacked, and that three were killed. That means there was one survivor. Maybe they could—"

"Completely incoherent. That's how it's been with any enforcers or representatives who have made it out alive. I went and looked in on the drake who got hurt in these woods. They were strapped down on a hospital bed, thrashing and screaming. Whatever happened or whatever they saw, they're completely mad." Jackal's ears droop.

It's all clicking into place. This has to be the answer. This is how the kidnappers are getting away from experienced Magikai patrols. They're casting these mind-manipulation nets, or zones, or domes, or whatever they are. Then, they're just letting us kill each other.

The other groups hadn't had someone like Feral to pull them out. How long had they been stuck fighting?

Feral looks over at the crackling area behind us, and I can feel he's thinking something similar.

"The magic I'm sensing has lessened. It must fade out eventually. Since the rest of you didn't go mad before, it's likely you found the dead enforcers after it had dissipated. That's why you didn't notice."

Jackal nods, the mohawk hair going down his back shaking with the movement. He lets out a sigh, marked at the end by a yip.

"We didn't know what had happened, but we saw the results. Sky didn't mention this either, but—the third enforcer that died? He was still alive when we found them. He ran at me. I dodged him, and he ran himself right off a ravine."

I scoff.

"A supernatural? We're agile. How would they make that big of a misstep?"

"He was a pukwudgie. They thought maybe he'd expected to be able to disappear and then reappear back on the cliff edge or further down safely, but miscalculated. You know they can only actually transport themselves a very short distance."

I didn't. What I do know about pukwudgies is that their ancestors had attempted friendship with humans prior to the Magikai cracking down, and that it went badly.

"They're not what I'd call combat-ready," I observe.

The creatures are only a few feet tall, small humanoid species with added features like porcupine spikes all over their backs, and noses a bit like a dog's.

"But," Jackal reminds me, "they have venom and use it for their tipped arrows. They're excellent shots. This one was a representative from the east coast. He'd come along to take down the kidnapper personally if we were able to get a clear shot."

But instead, he'd ended up dead alongside two enforcers, and another one was driven mad in the same incident.

And we've probably stumbled upon why.

"So you think that whatever trap we all just fell victim to, the other group stumbled upon something similar." Hugh is taking notes, because of course he is. He's scribbling the information down into a notebook.

"That's exactly what I think," Jackal confirms.

I growl before giving voice to my biggest concern.

"Could they be using this on the children? As a means of control?"

"Arthur didn't say anything about this," Todd reminds me, but it only lowers my anxiety the slightest bit.

"Would he have known, though?"

Nahum shakes his head.

"The kids weren't injured. As fully grown and capable supernaturals, we weren't able to resist whatever this was. It's unlikely the kids could have. I don't think it was used on them."

Feral reaches out with a hesitant hand, then places it on my shoulder.

"Let's focus on what we can use as solid evidence. I know what it's like to lose control of yourself, and I knew I couldn't let Hyde out on you all. I didn't want to risk going in after you. When Nahum's wing got close, I took a chance. I wasn't sure how the magic was getting you, and I just hoped it wasn't by touch. I held my breath, closed my eyes, stuffed some fabric from one of the shirts in my ears, and launched. I got lucky. I snagged the end of his wing and hauled him back. Once he was out, and he was clear-headed, we got to work on getting the attention of the others."

"Everyone except me."

"Because you ran from us, just like Nahum said."

Nahum shoots me a look, and I know I'll have to tell him what I saw in my nightmare sooner or later. I can feel he wasn't aware enough in the moment to know, at least not exactly. Normally he'd see what his victims do, but since everything in our little dome of mind manipulation was full of tricks, I doubt he trusts anything to do with it.

Hugh starts tapping bullet-points on his notes.

"Here's what I have so far. We know there are multiple adults with the kids. Common sense would tell us that's partially due to necessity. This many kids would require more than one person to prevent losing track of them all. We know the kidnappers are aware they're being tracked, and now we have a good idea of how they're avoiding detection. The mind-manipulation zones cause magicals to attack one another, eliminating the need for our enemy to show themselves."

"But that hasn't been the case with everyone," Nahum interjects. "There were two groups searching up here before. The one that ended up with all the dead enforcers, and the one with Sky, Nadia, and Jackal in it."

Ji-hwan nods.

"Anywhere there's been a kidnapping we've sent multiple search groups to scour the area. Are you thinking someone from one of the surviving groups could be helping our kidnappers?"

The group goes quiet as we all consider what he's said. An inside job. It wouldn't be the first time, but ...

"For that theory to hold water, it'd mean multiple double-agents in multiple areas. I'm not saying it couldn't have happened—that's what was going on under Amun. But could we really have missed that many culprits?" I stare at the others, almost daring someone to contradict me. I don't want to think that after all my efforts, this much rot has remained in the organization.

"Or," Todd's voice rumbles, "it's one or two people who have traveled around. The warlocks are here from France, and they're not the only ones who have moved with the investigation."

He fixes his stare on Jackal. The hyena freezes.

"You mean me?"

"How did you end up in this group, anyway? You're not a representative or an enforcer. I get that your niece is missing, but Sky and a lot of the others are all about formality. They wouldn't have thrown just any family member into this case." I eye him suspiciously.

He doesn't so much as flinch. If anything, the hair on his back bristles a bit more.

"I forced my way in. I'd been doing my own investigation into my niece, and following the kidnappers' trail. I'd made it over to the US before several of the Magikai noticed me."

Ji-hwan holds up a hand.

"It's true. From what I hear, he was a bit of a nuisance. Refused to clear the area of active investigations. Insulted and threatened multiple enforcers."

I grin. A hyena after my own heart.

"And you all didn't lock him up?" I can't help asking.

Ji-hwan laughs.

"Lock him up? He was better at following trails than the enforcers and representatives. We'd never have gotten this far without him. His deal was, he would help if he got to stay."

Of all the deals I've made or heard, it's not bad terms. Jackal's emotions wrap around me. He's utterly without malice, at least when we're discussing the kids. For the kidnappers, he feels something different.

It's enough to convince me.

"It's unlikely they've got help from the inside, and if they did, it's no one in our group. Although we could still question the twins. Actually, we'd better radio the others. Let them know what they might be up against." I don't want Aggie and Nadia unprepared for a mind-manipulation zone.

I shove up off my knees and wobble a bit when I stand. Nahum puts an arm around me, and I lean into him—for support, but also to let him know I don't blame him for the nightmare.

Hugh hands me a walkie-talkie, the feedback crackling before I push the button to speak to the others.

"Hello? Anybody there?"

Nothing.

I try not to panic.

"Hey! This is club kickass calling in for the mundane Magikai. Come in, Magikai!"

"Never?" The voice on the other end is staticky, but I can tell it's Nadia.

Relief threatens to steal my words.

"Tell her I say hi!" Aggie's voice chimes in from somewhere nearby.

"Aggie says to tell you—"

"I heard. Nadia, we had an incident. You all need to know—"

There's yelling in the background.

"One second, Never."

"No. Nadia. Don't put down the walkie. Nadia!"

Nothing for a few moments, then …

"Never! I think Nadia and the others found something. It feels really strongly of magic up ahead. It's making my eyes flash, so I'm hanging back until we know what it is, but I'm ready to strip if needed."

"Aggie—"

"Yes, I know. Har-de-har, stripping joke. But it's a good plan. This way, I can have their backs and—"

"Aggie!" It takes me three more attempts at yelling her name before she's got her finger off the button and is listening to me.

"Aggie. Is the air crackling?"

"Yeah. How'd you know?"

The chill lingering from Nahum's nightmares increases again.

They're hours away. I scramble for a solution. I want to tell her to run and not look back, but what about the others?

"Aggie. Strip everyone. All of them. Right now."

If they can't fight, they can't get hurt. She can just wait for the magic to fade.

"But Never, I can't—"

"Right now, Aggie. You need to listen to me. Please."

"Well," I can feel her reluctance through the walkie. "All right. If you say so. I'll try to get them closer. Guys! Come back this way!"

The walkie cuts out. Then, after a good minute of sanity-stealing silence, it crackles back to life.

"Never! Never, something is wrong. Chelone is attacking the twins, and Sky. Flare's gone. He just flew off!"

"Don't get any closer! Just strip them! Now!"

Again, I have to try a few times before it goes through. Aggie's voice is shaky when she answers, and it churns my stomach that I can feel real fear. Since we've gotten to know one another she's grown confident in her abilities, but this is new territory.

"All right. I'll try. I'm doing it n—"

She screams, and the walkie cuts off.

"Aggie! Aggie!"

It's no use.

I toss our walkie on the ground, and Hugh scoops it up.

We go now, I tell Nahum.

The dragon is the only one I warn before I throw on my fur, ignoring how tired and cold I still am.

Then, I run southeast as fast as my legs can carry me.

10

FALSE VISIONS & REAL FEAR

I'm on all fours and moving like my life depends on it. The truth is just as important, because Aggie and Nadia's lives could in fact depend on it.

If anyone's curious how Weres run, given our odd anatomy, on all fours we look like something between a fast and graceful wolf and a gorilla slamming its huge arms down as it moves forward. I stick to two legs when I can help it, but as awkward as this version looks, four legs gives me an advantage when it comes to speed while having to navigate through trees and over downed limbs.

I make the return trip in what has to be a third of the time it took us to go the opposite way, but that's still far longer than I'd hoped.

Nahum's managed to keep up with me by flying overhead, and he swoops down in front of me when I get close enough to spot the others in the distance.

He throws his arm out, making me pause.

We have to stay outside the perimeter.

The area is still crackling, so whatever spell or enchantment we were under is clearly at work here.

It goes against everything my feelings are telling me to do, but I approach with caution. Nahum and I step side-by-side, trying to make sure we don't cross the barrier of whatever kind of spell or ability is causing this.

The other group is a mess. I see one of the twins on the ground, bloody and unmoving, although it's impossible for me to tell whether it's Occam or Parsim.

Chelone isn't moving, either. Her shell is cracked, but it's the fact she's missing her head that tells me we're too late to save her. Not far off is the body of Scrub. The little lutin has been grievously injured, but I can't tell from here whether he's still alive.

"That was my brother!" someone screams overhead.

I look up to see one of the twins floating and flitting through the sky. Levitation. That means Occam, which makes Parsim our quite possibly dead warlock.

Sparring with Occam is Sky. The two supernaturals duck and dive. I don't see Flare anywhere, but both the magicals flying in front of us have blood dripping from their ears, so he's got to be somewhere close. Harpy shrieks aren't as bad as those of a banshee, but they're well capable of rupturing eardrums.

Frustratingly, and terrifyingly, I don't see Nadia or the witchling.

Occam throws his arms out, and for a moment Sky sways, no longer in control of her own flight pattern in the face of the warlock's ability.

"Can you get them apart?" I ask Nahum. The dragon is already transformed and ready to take off.

"Wait!" Hugh yells, huffing a bit as he comes up behind us. "You need to protect your eyes and ears. If Feral's right, it's what helped him get you out. This thing preys on our physical senses."

I spot the rest of the group not far behind Hugh. Todd and

Jackal are bringing up the rear, each one still moving as though injured.

Time is of the essence, but no one wants to endure a repeat of the mind games we suffered before. I can feel that much.

"We'll cover ourselves, then," I agree. "Nahum can fly for Sky or Occam, and I'll go in and feel for the girls. I'll be blind, but I'll use intuition to try and identify their emotions, then follow that."

Hugh rips up one of the shirts in our duffels and we stuff fabric in our ears. He pulls longer strips off and insists on providing everyone a blindfold.

"I'll be able to smell them," Nahum assures me as he clocks where the two flying magicals are. He shoots into the air.

Frantic, I keep scanning for the girls, but they're nowhere to be seen.

I take a page out of Nahum's book and tie the strip of fabric over my eyes. Relying on my nose and intuition, I wander into the crackling area. The heavy scent of blood obscures things a fair bit.

There's plenty of rage and confusion.

Concern. Concern for someone else, not for themselves.

Pure selflessness.

That's got to be one of the girls.

Scrambling along the ground, I make my way toward the emotion. When my furred hand hits something wet that makes a squelching noise, I shake it and jump back. I've got to be near either Parsim or Chelone. My focus is on the girls, but I keep my intuition open for everything else. We still haven't seen Flare, and I don't relish the idea of getting hauled off into the sky and thrown over a ledge.

Recognition, relief, and apprehension hit me square in the snout like a punch.

I'm getting close. I throw my arms out, feeling my way until, apparently, I reach the other end of this blasted mind-manipulation net and the crackling ends.

A hand closes around my furred wrist and I use my other to throw off the blindfold and pull the fabric out of my ears.

Aggie, with an unconscious Nadia cradled in her lap. The witchling is crying.

"I tried to do what you said, Never. Flare came back and was going after Nadia, so I tried to strip him. I hit one of his wings, and he went down somewhere that way." She points even further away from the mind-manipulation area.

"Have you seen him since?" I give the perimeter around us a good look, just in case.

She sniffles and shakes her head.

"No. But after he left, Nadia turned and looked at me. I followed your advice and didn't get any closer to the area. Instead, I ran around the edge of where everything was crackling. Nadia tracked me. She was hunting me. I didn't want to hurt her. Honest, I really didn't."

I reach down and put a hand on her shoulder.

"I know, witchling. I can feel it. You had to strip her too, huh?"

Aggie nods her head up and down swiftly, snorting and sniffling again. I offer her the fabric that I used for a blindfold as a tissue.

"Thanks." She takes it and blows. I grimace. I *hate* snot. But for the witch, I'll sacrifice.

"You did what you had to do. She will understand," I reassure her as I bend down to scoop up the unconscious Nadia. I could lift her either way, but it helps that she's in her skin. Glancing up, I see Nahum has wrestled Occam to the ground and hauled him close enough to the perimeter for Todd and Jackal to each grab one of the warlock's arms. Feral guides Nahum out as well.

Sky is nowhere to be seen.

Their group had worse luck than us. We only had Nahum to worry about in the skies. They had three supernaturals capable of attacking by land or air.

I lead Aggie back around the perimeter. We're maybe two-thirds of the way when I spot a dark dot in the sky, plummeting and getting closer.

"Shit."

Sky didn't go out of the perimeter. She just went up. And what goes up must come down. And what goes down ... well, it goes right back through the mind-manipulation area.

The growl in my chest rumbles against Nadia, and she groans but doesn't wake up.

"I've got you. You're okay." Maybe she can still hear me. She relaxes a bit in my arms.

Aggie throws her arms out, ready to strip the wind elf as she barrels toward us.

"I've got her, I can—"

Sky twists in the air, avoiding Aggie's stripping. She's picking up speed as she gets closer.

"What's going on? I was—" Nadia struggles in my arms, waking to what has to be the memory of whatever awful sights the mind manipulation showed her before.

I try to soothe her, but she jumps and stumbles out of my arms before I can, bumping into Aggie and throwing the witchling's next shot wide as well. Aggie yelps as she's thrown to the dirt.

Sky is smiling, arms out and preparing to snatch the girls.

Oh hell no.

Not today.

It's not that I don't consider our fun, crackling barrier. I just don't care.

I run straight into the danger zone, leaping at the speeding wind elf. We slam into each other, and I do my best to roll us toward the edge of the barrier as the crackling echoes in my ears.

Sky is struggling and kicking.

At least I think she is.

"Stop it! I don't want to have to put you down!" I warn her as she socks me in the jaw.

Her hand reaches for something, and she pulls out a dagger. Darned elves and their magically enhanced weaponry.

If the dagger is real. If any of this is real. It's impossible to tell inside the zone.

I can hear the girls screaming behind me.

I can feel them too.

Worry. Anxiety. Fear.

That's real. I know that part is real. My mind may be playing tricks, but my emotions don't lie.

Fending off the elf's blows, if they're really happening, I keep her close and scooch backward. I literally feel my way to the girls.

"Your Were friend likes me better than she ever did you. I should have picked you up and thrown you from a height so high your bones shattered. You ruined the Magikai, you vicious bitch," Sky shrieks.

Yep. Delusion is definitely at play. I saved that sad government agency. No doubt. And while she and I may not be the best of friends, she's respected me enough to include me in this mission. I doubt anything I'm hearing is coming out of her mouth.

Sky twists and jabs at me again, and the blade glances off my arm, if my physical sensations are to be believed. The edges of the wound burn. Unless I'm very much mistaken, whatever's on that blade is eating away at my skin.

An acidic dagger, perhaps?

Lovely.

I manage to grab hold of her by the neck. I could crush her

throat if I wanted. After all, she's attacking me, and she's attacked two people I care for.

I can't deny being somewhat tempted.

But no matter how much Sky has annoyed me, no matter what she's done wrong, she's never done it out of a motivation to harm. She's done it out of a motivation to defend. A somson orb, her fellow Great Plains supernaturals, and in this case whatever she's seeing in her mind.

I can feel her desperation and her worry for something. She's attacking because she's convinced we're going to destroy something she loves.

I throw her away from me, leaving nothing more than a scratch mark on her neck.

When we've reached the perimeter of the crackling barrier, she dives and tries for another stab, but I grab hold of her wrist with one hand. With the other I reach for her neck again, then I shove my feet up under her sternum and kick. Hard.

It's more force than is strictly necessary. The elf did try to kill Nadia once, and I'll be the first to admit I hold a grudge when it comes to my loved ones.

Sky flips and goes sailing over me. I pull myself the rest of the way out of the circle, out of breath.

"You got her out." Nadia is surprised as she stares at the elf's slumped form.

I tap my heart.

"Intuition. We've all just been the victims of some very powerful, magical mind games. But no matter what you see or hear, people's emotions are still real. Tap into those."

Aggie runs over to help the injured wind elf.

"I think you might have broken her sternum," the witch informs me.

I shrug.

"She'll live."

Nadia is still shaky, but with me supporting her and Aggie helping Sky, we make it the rest of the way to the others.

What's left of them, anyway.

Feral, Jackal, and Todd are each pulling one of the bodies from the mind-manipulation zone's perimeter.

I can see now I was wrong to hold out any hope for Parsim or the lutin. They're no better off than Chelone.

Three more dead.

And we're all going to have to face the consequences.

11

MISTAKES WERE MADE

Everyone recovers not long after we get them out of the dome of madness, or whatever we're going to call these mental booby traps being set for us.

After my last adventure through Fae and a murderous CoED castle, I suppose I should count myself lucky we're not dealing with zombies, compelled shifters, or duplicitous Fae royals. Having said that, it's hard to feel lucky when you've got three dead bodies, a missing harpy, a devastated warlock twin, and a guilt-ridden wind elf.

"I have no intention of harming Nadia or Aggie. I want you to know that," Sky assures me.

I'm standing off to the side of the others, who have split themselves in two. This time we're not divided by the teams we've picked. Everyone is divided up by emotions. One group is sad, and the other is angry. We'll rally together soon enough. One thing I've learned from Chrys, Nadia, and the witchling, is that you've got to take a moment to process big emotions. If you don't, you end up like me, isolating yourself and becoming a one-woman hit squad for people who might be using you to their advantage. At least that's my experience.

I grunt at Sky in acknowledgement as I pace the edge of the still-crackling perimeter.

"You could have killed me, but you didn't. Why?" Sky asks. She tilts her head at me, blue eyes blinking. She has interesting features. If she hadn't pissed me off from the get-go, maybe we'd be friends. She was against Amun, just like me. We even look somewhat alike. Kind of. She's got silver hair, albeit shades lighter than mine. Her eyes are paler blue, and her skin is near-impossibly pale, where mine is just fair. And of course she still has both eyes and an arguably better attitude, depending on whom you ask.

She's a more sophisticated and less rugged me, at least by looks.

And she's still waiting for a response.

I sigh.

"I could feel you. Nadia and I don't appear to be impacted by these little mind traps the same way as the rest of you. Our intuition can still feel real reactions, so we have something to grab onto and pull ourselves out of the visions we're seeing. I could tell you were worried. You were seeing someone or something of great value to you under threat of harm."

Sky nods.

"That's true. But I know I was trying to attack Nadia and Aggie, and I know you don't care for me. You had an excuse to take me out, if that's what you wanted. You didn't take it. Thank you."

She offers me a hand, but I just stare down at it.

"Despite what some representatives and other enforcers have heard or believe, I'm more than just some rabid dog the Magikai were keeping controlled on a leash. When I take people out, it's because they deserve it, not just because I don't personally care for them. I'm certainly capable of making rational decisions."

We're all aware there are plenty of times my decisions were

less than rational, but Sky doesn't need to know that. I'm trying to make a point here.

"I dislike you because you almost killed Aggie. I distrusted you because, while you didn't support Amun, it took my meddling for anything of substance to get done in the Magikai. You and the other representatives could have done more, acted sooner. You didn't. Yes, I judge you for it, but I also appreciate what you're doing now to rectify things. Keep working to put your desire to protect supernaturals into action, and we won't have any problems."

Only once she nods do I reach down and shake her hand, letting my fur fall away.

No matter how you slice it, we've wasted a full day of searching. The moon rises, and we're plunged into a darkness broken only by its light, and that of the stars.

My group didn't enjoy our little trip through the mind field, but Aggie and Nadia's group has been wrecked. Occam is inconsolable about his brother, and while no one can remember for certain, he's also convinced he's responsible for a dead Chelone.

"The warlock won't be any good to us moving forward. We need to get him back," Jackal suggests when some of us who are a bit more level-headed huddle off to the side.

Cold. Callous. Practical.

It's been hours, and the crackling perimeter has long since faded, but Occam hasn't calmed down even an iota.

Nadia sighs, reluctant to agree with splitting up again.

I shake like a wet dog until my hair falls in my face. This instant read on not only emotions, but also their motivations, is still new. Sometimes it clutters my already hectic mind, and it's not the most pleasant sensation.

I look at the younger Were.

"The hyena is right. At the very least, someone should transport the bodies back and give them the respect of a proper funeral. Occam would want to go with his brother, I'm sure."

The others are staring at me, and Todd says what they must be thinking.

"They'll need escorts. We've got the jet pilot waiting, of course, and he's a capable gnome, but he can't fight off Occam if the warlock decides to make the plane fall out of the sky. He's not emotionally stable right now."

The rest of us seem all right. But it's true, we don't know the long-lasting effects of the mind manipulation zone. The warlock might not be trustworthy.

"I'll take them back." Sky raises an arm. "We have no head representative anymore, but I'm looked to as a lead on the committees. As a leader, I take responsibility. I'm going to trust the rest of you to see this through. After all, you want these people caught as badly as I do."

She locks her eyes with mine, and I don't blink. We won't quit on her.

"We are of course being paid enforcer wages for all this time, right?" I can't help asking.

I'd do it for free, but as long as we're renegotiating how this mission is going to go, it can't hurt. I grin, and Sky actually breaks into a half-smile, relenting.

"Yes. Of course. Well, that's settled then."

Nadia and Ji-hwan walk off together and start muttering. After a few moments they head back over, emotions set and decided.

"We're not done. Someone else needs to go. Sky, you're powerful, but so is Occam. If it comes down to a one-on-one fight, there's still a chance he could crash the plane. You'll need someone else for backup. Ji-hwan and I are both part of the Magikai, and Weres. Our skills on this trip are redundant. One of us should go."

I frown at Nadia. I just got both of them back.

But this isn't about me.

These kidnappers are pissing me off more than they already had, I complain to the dragon.

We'll stop them. Whoever they are. And when we find them you can tell them how upset you are that they ruined your family reunion, the dragon teases.

Hard to do that if I rip off their heads first, but I'm sure I can fit in a complaint or three.

Ji-hwan steps forward.

"I should go with Sky. Nadia and Never are the only ones who can feel their way around this mind manipulation. If you encounter it again, the two of you are the most useful people in the group. I'll help Sky sort everything else out, and call the herds and packs with missing children to let them know what we've found so far."

While the others help create a couple of travoises to haul Chelone, Scrub, and Parsim, I pull Sky to the side.

"What about Flare? Are you sending anyone back to look for the harpy?"

She shakes her head.

"We can't risk it. Now that we know what we're up against, anyone sent up here is likely to face the same fate. Keep your eyes open, and once you all solve this, we'll send a search party. I'm counting on you all."

I'm sure the harpy knew the risks, but it drives home that we are officially on our own.

Once they're out of sight, Hugh claps his hands, drawing the rest of us to attention.

"That's settled, then. Everyone else, we need rest. We'll be no good to these kids if we go scrambling through the woods exhausted and with our judgment impaired."

Jackal puts his skin back on, and most of his wounds from Todd have finally healed. He scowls at my historian.

"We shouldn't all sleep. Someone should keep watch. I volunteer."

The hyena isn't fooling me. He may be mostly healed, but he's still nearly dead on his feet.

"We should take shifts. Nahum and I will go first," I state, shooting a glance at the dragon.

I wait until I can feel the others drift into unconsciousness, and then I start walking about the perimeter of our little group with the dragon.

"Are you feeling okay?" Nahum asks.

"Other than a nagging sense that a mind-bending crackling could descend at any moment, the fact that we've still got a lost harpy out in the woods, and a heavy responsibility to save these kids as soon as possible, I'm doing great. Why?"

He switches to our minds.

You haven't made any deals since we left your house. After fighting off Sky and the mind magic, shouldn't you be lagging a bit?

I hadn't even thought of it, but he's right.

When I returned from the Underworld, the Bone Reader pronounced me a Rizik. I never wanted to be one of his kind of magical creatures, but I was given no choice in the matter after B.R. shoved a dagger into me and sent me to the land of dead supernaturals and on a journey back through Fae.

He's given me precious little to go on in terms of learning my new abilities, but having to make deals is a pretty important part. I'm meant to barter my skills—in my case, enhanced intuition—and in exchange I get a power boost and whatever price I charge people. A win-win, with the Rizik reaping all the rewards.

B.R. didn't exactly provide a timeline, but it was heavily indicated that as a brand-new baby Rizik I'd need to make deals more often if I didn't want to feel like a hollowed-out husk of a person.

And yet, I really do feel fine. Physically, at least.

"Maybe I'm a natural?"

Nahum nods along, but his worry eats at me.

"I suppose it's possible that with your intuition being constantly on anyway somehow supplements the power? After all, the Bone Reader primarily reads bones, and it's not like he's doing that all day as a hobby."

I wouldn't be so sure. I wouldn't put anything past B.R.

Lately, though, he's done a lot more than bone reading. According to him, all the other powerful stuff he's done has come out of a stockpile of magic he's amassed with over ten thousand years of deal-making.

I'm only four hundred and change, though, and have been a Rizik for less than a month. My savings account of power shouldn't be very high at all.

"Maybe you should make a few deals with the others before we move on, just to be safe."

I frown. The deals mean I have to demand a price from people. A magical price. I hate taking advantage of my friends. If I was going to need deals, I should have made them with Sky and the others before they left. I'd have felt less guilty about that.

We're in the situation we're in, though.

"Just one or two," I allow.

Now I just have to decide whom to ask.

There's always the hyena. I've got no idea what I could ask him to pay, but I'm not close enough to him to feel bad. Aggie's off the table entirely. She has very little in the way of spare cash or possessions, aside from what she's collected since our friendship. Other than that, I'd have to ask her to use magic, and I'm not draining the stripper. My ego hates to admit it, but she's the most powerful member of the team, with the exception of the dragon. We can't afford to have her weakened just before trekking after a mind-bending villain.

We've made our way in a loop and are getting closer to the

others again as I continue to puzzle through everything. Nadia is off the table, same as Aggie. Limited resources to pay me with, and a skill we desperately need if we run into more mind-manipulation fields. My friends would all readily volunteer, but I've already made deals with them and taken from them.

"I'll ask the hyena," I decide.

"Ask me what?"

Jackal rolls and stands, back in his fur and on all fours. He shakes out his mane before making his way over to us.

"Couldn't stay asleep. Ask me what?"

I mentally give Nahum permission to divulge my Rizik status. The way B.R. guarded it, you'd think it was the world's biggest secret, but I don't mind if my allies know it.

Once Jackal's been given the bare-bones rundown of how my abilities work, he just stares. To anyone else he'd look entirely disinterested, but I'm not just anyone. He's very intrigued.

"All right. What've I got to lose? I'll do it. But you can't ask me to give up my hyena, right?"

I actually don't know if a stronger Rizik would be able to pull something like that off, but I would never ask it even if it were possible. I shake my head.

"No. I ask for usage of abilities, tasks that your magic lets you perform, objects or items you've acquired. That sort of stuff. And I name the price after we've made the deal."

Which will be tricky, now that I think of it. I've no idea what he has. The Bone Reader just tosses out seemingly random demands. Potion ingredients, a ride. Now that I'm thinking of it, some of the crap he's asked me for really doesn't qualify as magical at all, but given he's old and powerful he can probably afford to make some weak deals. I can't.

All I know about Jackal is that he's British, or at least has spent some time there, and he's a hyena with a missing niece. Also, from what I've seen, he can fight. And I suppose feign sleep very convincingly. And he makes the representatives nervous.

Guess I have more to go on than I thought.

A wicked idea pops into my head, and I can't help grinning.

Jackal laughs.

"Whatever you just thought of, that is a hyena-worthy smirk. What do we do, then? I just ask you to read my emotions? I'll be honest, I don't really want you digging around. Can I ask for something obvious?"

I shrug. I don't see why not.

My guess is he'll ask me how he feels about his missing niece. That's as obvious as it could get.

He doesn't, though.

"Tell me how I feel about working with the Magikai."

I focus as he lets the feelings wash over him, and then bark out a laugh.

"You, sir, are more likable than I thought. You feel uneasy and on edge, because you don't trust authority. You are a bit contemptuous of them, and feel they already bungled the running of the organization badly enough that you're not sure they deserve another chance. You're suspicious and think they could be untrustworthy or inept, or worse, both. But you've been impressed enough with a couple of the members and quite frankly desperate enough to find your niece that you're willing to team up with them, if that's what it takes."

Beside me, Nahum laughs, the sound deep and soothing.

"So you're saying he's basically you?"

I smack him on the arm—not hard, mind you. The dragon is a tease.

"Yes, yes. Never the Were, with her distaste for being told what to do. I'd like to remind everyone that when I don't trust someone I'm typically right."

"Unfortunately, I tend to be good at guessing people's characters as well, but I'm no intuitive. What you can do is impressive. You're right on the money," Jackal allows.

I slap my hands together.

"Now then. The price. I want you,"—I see him flinch for just a moment—"to steal me something."

"What?"

"What?" Nahum echoes.

"I know you're a skilled fighter, and an experienced traveler, and you've clearly got some sneaking skills to have followed the Magikai's trail for so long without them noticing. I recently had a bartender friend of mine break into a Magikai castle in the UK and leave with a particularly powerful trident. That kind of heist sounds like fun. Pick any Magikai-owned property you like, and steal me something magical. Anything interesting."

The way I see it, I've done the Magikai several large favors. Not just Amun. Taking out the murderous elf who was after me no doubt helped them, since he'd been killing and spelling all sorts of magicals. And did I get paid? I did not. I'm owed. In that sense, this is really me just collecting a paycheck. If I'm stealing, I'm only stealing from myself.

At least that's how I choose to see it.

Nahum just rolls his eyes and shakes his head.

Jackal grins.

"That, I can do. It would be a pleasure. Now then, you two grab some sleep. I can take it from here. I'll wake up Todd to watch with me."

I raise one eyebrow, giving the hyena a pointed look.

"What? He beat the stuffing out of me. He's a good fighter. That's who I'd want watching my back in a moment like this."

Practical. He's not holding a grudge. Less like me than I thought.

I'm not going to refuse, but I have no intention of sleeping. Instead I grab the dragon's hand and drag him deeper into the woods.

12

ONLY ONE

Whether it's my lack of ability to rest on a case, or a magical boost from making a deal, I'm too hyped to go to sleep.

The others need time to recharge, and from what I felt with Jackal, he'll do everything he can to keep them safe.

Holding Nahum's hand, I pull him just far enough away that I judge we won't be easily overheard. I have my own mission for the evening. I'm going to make sure the dragon knows that no matter what happened in that fog, our relationship is not impacted.

"We're alone in the woods. You have me all to yourself out here. What *are* you going to do with me?"

His voice rumbles low in his throat.

"I can think of several things."

Before I can plan a smartass comeback, Nahum scoops me into his arms, puts his wings on and flies us even farther into the woods. I listen for any telltale crackling, but there's only silence. I can't smell any magic, either. Only the scent of the dragon—the saltwater scent of the ocean and the air just before it rains. Greedily, I breathe it in.

"I would never hurt you. In fact, I'll do everything in my power to protect you and anyone you care about. I know you can feel it, but I still wanted to say it out loud."

"I know, and I appreciate hearing it out loud. As far as I'm concerned, it's whoever's behind these mind fields who's responsible. They should watch their back, but we can't do anything more about it now. Everyone needs to recharge if we're going to be of any use to the kids."

He tilts his head down to look at me.

"Then should we be sleeping?"

I shake my head vehemently.

"Absolutely not."

Pleased at my response, happiness and a fair amount of lust spread through the dragon and wrap my intuition in a warm embrace.

"What do you think?" He swoops into a clearing. "Will this work for my mate and fiancée?"

It's the first time he's mentioned the engagement since we left for this mission. Maybe I should comment on it, but I'm not spoiling the only romantic moment we had or are likely to get for who knows how long.

"This pile of dirt and grass? Splendid." I reach out and tap him on the nose, with a wicked grin. His eyes cross as he stares down at where I booped him, and while he's distracted I hop out of his arms, sliding my body down the front of his.

He smirks at me.

"You need to make deals more often."

I laugh, then sober up a bit.

"It's not the deal. That's the thing; I don't really feel all that different. When I first got back from the Underworld and made deals with all of you, I felt better. But was that the deals, or just getting back to a realm where people are alive? It has to be the deals, though, since I'm a Rizik, right?"

Nahum frowns, puzzling it over.

"That's what the Bone Reader told you. He indicated you'd feel a difference in power, though. I don't like it, Never. Do you think you should make some more, and see if that helps?"

It might be the prudent thing to do, but I honestly don't feel like I need them. Even after a long day and getting dumped into one of Nahum's nightmares, my Were abilities have healed me up just fine.

"No, I'm not making more deals right now, but the Bone Reader may have to answer some questions for me once we finish this."

I'm not eager for another visit, but if I'm living as a Rizik, he'll have to give me more to go on than a few faint clues. I need things answered. Like, for instance, why I'm a brand-new Rizik toddling about with seemingly very little need of deals in the first place. It could be there's something to Nahum's theory that using intuition constantly keeps me boosted, or it could be the Bone Reader is a sneaking, lying little two-timer who is once again keeping things from me.

I give my head another shake. B.R. is not what I want to think about right now. It's been a busy few months; really, it's been busy for the last year plus. The rest of this case is only going to get worse, the way I see things. For one night, I want to focus on Nahum, and Nahum only.

He wraps his wings around my back and pulls me in closer to him.

"I wish it could be just the two of us, alone," he murmurs.

"It is just the two of us."

"Perhaps somewhere a bit more romantic than in the middle of the woods, hunting down a criminal."

I just smile at him.

"Why? That's when I feel most alive."

Inside, I agree with him. I'm all for action, but if things ever settle down enough that I can risk it, I'm taking the dragon and disappearing on a months-long getaway. No murderers, no kidnappers, and no fighting. Well, maybe a little fighting, for fun. I'm sure we can spot a stray ne'er-do-well on our vacation. But no Magikai cases!

I wrap my arms around the dragon's neck and pull him close until our mouths meet. After a quick nip at his bottom lip, our tongues are tangling together.

Nahum has one arm braced against the tree behind us, and another holding me close to him as I wrap my legs around his middle.

I couldn't even tell you how we go from standing against a tree to splayed out on the forest floor. I'm not even sure how long we spend moving together, with the dragon's eyes locked on mine.

I just know that when we're both still and I'm laying my head on his chest, all my emotions crash into me.

I love Nahum. I love his steady support, his deadly protectiveness, his compassion, and even his obsession with books. It's not lost on me how much he loves me, having left said hoard of books unguarded by anyone except his pixies while he accompanies me on these adventures. It's a good thing he can't die unless I kill him. I'd never survive it. And that's saying an awful lot, given all the things I have managed to live through.

While I may have said earlier I wasn't tired, I do manage to sleep, wrapped in the dragon's arms.

He gives me a soft shake to wake me up, and I blink my eyes and notice light creeping through the trees.

"Did I tire you out?" he asks, pleased with himself.

"Yes, but I'd be more than happy for another round." I lick my lips as I look at the dragon and laugh when I feel his pride, affection, and a hint of worry slap back at me.

"Don't be concerned. You didn't drain my Rizik powers. I'm not sure that's how it works."

Although hell if I know how it does work. What actions are supposed to be draining me?

I roll off the dragon just before the others tromp into view. Aggie is blushing, and Hugh smirks at me as I wipe some stray leaves off myself.

"Lady Never. Perfect timing. We've just had a quick breakfast and discussed our options. I've been up for hours, looking over that piece of stone. I'm more certain than ever it's a gravestone, and I now think I know what kind."

Hugh pulls the thing from his duffle. I'm glad we kept it when we sent the others back.

"Now, the letters on the portion we have appear to be 'Lyet,' which I think comes from the phrase 'Here Lyeth,' and if you'll look above that, you'll see a portion of what may be a circle, and these markings I believe are meant to be claw marks."

He holds it out and I stare down at the piece of gravestone. The letters are faded, but his interpretation is accurate, as far as I can see. The arc over them could very well be a circle. The jagged lines he thinks are claw marks?

"Maybe. Why claw marks, though?"

Hugh is practically vibrating with the excitement he only gets from knowledge. He waves the thing in front of my nose, but just before he can speak, Nahum butts in.

"You think it's from a supernatural graveyard. One just for magicals."

Instead of getting upset, Hugh becomes even happier, so eager he is to have someone else swept up in his discovery.

"Precisely! A magical graveyard. I think that this gravestone signifies either a clue to the location our kidnappers are headed, or perhaps a key to get in there."

I hate to burst the Were's bubble, so I'm glad when Todd does it for me.

"That seems like a stretch, Hugh. What makes you think that? Why would they be taking the children to a graveyard?"

Hugh just scoffs in the face of the bear's doubt.

"Magical graveyards have been a thing for centuries. Much like family plots on historical estates and farms, they're kept separate from your general resting places. For supernaturals, they were placed in very hard to reach spots, and often magically warded, and—"

"And there are atlases pinpointing locations of their known or suspected whereabouts, which frequently include mountain ranges unreachable by the majority of humans," Nahum finishes for him.

Hugh holds the piece of stone in the air in triumph.

"Precisely! We're in just such a location, and possibly at the end of our kidnappers' trail. You said yourself that they've been practically everywhere around the world except here. As for the reason ..."

He becomes more subdued, and I don't think I'm going to like what comes next.

Aggie clears her throat as she places a hand on his shoulder.

"Witches sometimes use places like graveyards as settings for powerful spells and conjurings. Not light-magic witches like myself, but others. If they've got something big planned for the children, something that requires an intense spell, it would be an ideal spot."

"It's not perfect, but it gives us a starting point," Hugh finishes.

"Which way, then?" Jackal asks, throwing on his fur and ready to go.

"Back northwest," Todd growls, putting his fur on as well. "When our group was searching yesterday, we scented the actual children."

"And our group got nothing but a crackling forcefield and no scent," Aggie adds.

"Plus, going the way Todd suggests would send us further

up into the mountains, which would be the most likely location for a supernatural graveyard." Hugh is staring at the piece of stone like it holds the answer to this mystery.

It could be a trap, just another way to trip us up, but I don't think so. They worked hard to put multiple mind fields around this place, but only one matches what we found. We've got nothing better to work from.

"All right. Let's retrace our steps. Back into the woods we go."

It's suggested that we keep an intuitive at each end of the group to guard against potential magical interference. Nadia volunteers for the first lead, and I'm more than happy to bring up the rear.

Hell's bells.

After all we've been through, it makes sense that I'd be watching my ass.

Duffels are swung over shoulders of those not in their fur, and everyone begins trudging off. I can feel how relieved they all are to be leaving this place.

We can only hope whatever comes next isn't worse.

13

HASTE & HURRY

Nearly a full day of hiking later, we have long since passed the mind-manipulation field where I was thrown into a nightmare yesterday. There's been no sign of the missing representative harpy, but we've caught the faintest scent of the kids a few times. It fades just as quickly as it appears each time. Our kidnappers have to be covering their tracks somehow, and not just with the mind fields.

I'm only partially invested in Hugh's theory that our destination is a cemetery, but either way it appears we're headed in the right direction. The vampsion historian is at the back of the group just in front of Nadia, while I take my turn at the front. He's spent a good portion of the last several hours with Nahum, discussing graveyards and how they were chosen for supernaturals. Feral's throwing out the occasional comment. If Hugh is right, between the three of them we're likely to find the location.

Part of me thinks Hugh is just hyper-focusing to take his mind off Chrys. The two have been joined at the hip for quite a while now, and she's alone at the vampsion. At least the place is in capable, if expensive, hands.

Aggie and Todd are trading the odd comment here and there about the importance of magical sites to witch magic, and Lynx's kids, and kids in general.

It's a comment about the kids that makes me realize what's bothering me about this whole theory.

"But why the kids? We suspect we're chasing someone who's going to the cemetery for its secure location and the way it helps certain magics, but what role do the kids play?"

Jackal huffs from behind me.

"That's been the question all along, hasn't it? What kind of sick people take kids? They've killed some of us adults, sure, but only when we interfered. It's part of why I think we're on the right trail. If we're running into traps, they've got to be protecting something."

The logic is sound enough. I have Chrys spell the vampsion, and CoED has its own magical defenses as well. You don't protect a pile of nothing. You protect things of value.

"Whoever is behind this, they're an absolute kebab," Jackal states.

I bark out a laugh.

"I thought Brits liked kebabs."

He shrugs.

"In England, you can make any noun an insult if you use the right tone."

My face splits into a grin, and Aggie groans.

"Why? Why would you tell her that? I already know it's going to come back to bite us in the butt."

I give her a good-natured shove.

"Oh, don't be such a soggy potato! I promise not to abuse this knowledge."

It only takes five minutes for me to attempt everything from 'you great big shoe,' to 'you stupid zebra.'

"Enough! I'm going to tear my ears off. Honestly. This is worse than the mind manipulation," Todd whines.

"Fine. Back to the case. Our villain is powerful enough to control minds and end enforcers, but they're focused on kids. Why?" I puzzle out loud.

The others focus on me as I ramble.

"These people can't be trying to form an army like Ekaitz. Kids wouldn't be of any use in a fight."

The rest of the group will get the reference, but I give Jackal a bare-bones rundown of the Jeweled Claw.

"They could be recruiting kids? Training up soldiers who won't question things because they got to them when they were young? The Magikai spend years training most of their enforcers. Maybe whoever this is wants their own version."

Supernaturals are long-lived and patient, but I can't imagine anyone wanting to be responsible for hundreds of children just for the sake of maybe, eventually, being able to brainwash them all for a goal you can't achieve until years later. There are simpler ways than that. Compelling, spells, and the like. We've seen this before. After all, that's what Mizor did. Then we had a mess trying to separate who was compelled and who was responsible for their actions. In a way, it was simpler when the elf was just going around murdering people to use them or their powerful attributes in a spell to restore himself to power.

"Oh no."

"Oh no, what?" Jackal prompts after I go silent for a few seconds.

I don't want to say it. Don't even want to think it. I'd like to scrub out my mind with soap, rinse it, and wring out the idea. Let it drift away in the breeze. But it sticks in my head instead.

Rather than answering Jackal directly, I pull the group to a stop and face Aggie. I hate that I'm about to ask what I'm about to ask. I know her so well I can already predict the way her face is going to fall.

"Aggie, if you weren't a light-magic witch, you'd have to use living things for your spells, right?"

She screws up her face, lips and brows scrunching.

"Well, yeah, but I don't do that."

"But you would? That's how Chrys's magic works? And the Sewing Circle witches? What do they do? Drain things like plants, and small animals, and things like that?"

Her already fair skin pales a bit, but her emotions smack of denial.

"Yeah. Things like that. Any living thing will work, but blood is best. A squirrel is going to get more magic than a flower petal."

"And what about kids?"

She visibly recoils as the full weight of my suspicion hits her. Her eyes go wide, and her hand flies to her mouth. Todd has his lips raised like he's going to snap someone's hand off with his fangs. Nadia must be overwhelmed by the emotions, because her whole body goes tense. Within seconds I have the full group looking at me with disgust.

But I know it's not really directed at me.

"Never." Aggie visibly relaxes. "No. That's not how it works. They wouldn't be taking magical kids if that were the case. Other witches may have a different source, but the principle is the same to light magic. We have to sacrifice something to *get* the magic. It's a balance. You can't just take magic *from* magic."

"Mizor did."

She scowls, her anger rising at the mention of the elf.

"That's different. He was, and I hate to say this, very intelligent as well as ruthless. He used spells and killed or tricked witches or necromancers to get some of those things. I'm sure he couldn't have done it on his own. Even then, he was targeting very specific people for very specific needs. This person is just targeting any kid with magic. Even if you are suspecting a witch or warlock, witches don't take magic from other supernatural beings. Well, I mean, not unless they're a stripper like me."

She gestures to herself, head to toe and back again. When her hand reaches her chest she freezes.

"A stripper, like me." She echoes her own words, now a whisper. That same horrified chill is back, and it stabs at my intuition like freezing rain.

"Would it be possible?" I'm asking Aggie, or Hugh, or Feral, or Nahum. Anyone who might have knowledge of this topic.

Hugh is shaking his head, but it's not a denial.

"What Aggie does," he starts, "is she just wipes the magical abilities away. I'm not sure where the power goes, but it's not as if she gets to keep it. She dampens a shifter's second soul, for instance, but they always get the ability back."

Nahum is tapping a finger tipped in a claw against his chin, worried but trying to reassure me.

"Strippers are rare. From what I recall reading about them, some pull magic, and some physical strength, but I can't remember that I've ever seen one benefiting directly from the magic. The move is hated and feared for a reason, but it doesn't add to the stripper's personal power. It just doesn't drain them if stripping is their key."

Feral nods along, and his sparkling green eyes dull a bit as he fights back Hyde.

"They're right. That's been my experience as well. Strippers take, but they don't keep."

The others are becoming more and more relieved with the statements, but my blood is ice.

"I know one stripper who could. Well, I knew one. One warlock. He could strip magical beings on the brink of death, and when he did he could use their magic to fuel his own. It was a temporary boost, and it wore off eventually, but ..."

I let my voice fade out. I've told Nahum, in the few moments alone we've had together, about my life before being Never.

About how I lost my family, and my packs. But none of the others know, and now isn't the time. The important thing is, what they're discussing is possible. I've seen it with my own eyes.

"What if whoever is leading this is a stripper? One who can use the kids' magic? It would make sense then, wouldn't it? Going after physically weaker magical beings?"

The sheer panic is catching. Now that the idea is out there, they're grasping at it.

"Nadia. Run through the list of kidnapped magicals again," Aggie demands.

The rest of us stand silent as Nadia does just that. We listen to the names, species, and any known abilities of dozens and dozens of supernatural children from around the globe.

What Aggie says at the end echoes my own thoughts and confirms my worst fears.

"Whoever did this took mainly shifters, and other beings that come into their power early or have it from birth. Your list only has a few witches or warlocks on it, and they're all old enough to have some control of a key. These people haven't taken anyone too young to have magic they can control. It's like Never said. Physically weak and easier to take on than adults, but magically just as valuable."

We could be wrong. This could all be a spiral. One bad theory based on another.

But we could be right.

"We need to move faster," I insist.

14

DON'T SLEEP ON THE JOB

Everyone is fully invested in the new theory, and for that reason we don't even stop to eat. We've walked the rest of the day and into the night without rest. Hugh passed out snacks from the duffels on the go. My stomach would kill for a latte, or some of Todd's homemade pancakes, or one of Elios's cocktails, but instead I'm subsisting on lackluster granola bars.

Moon save me.

Most of us still have usable vision in the dark, and with the exception of the witch we're all built to endure a lack of sleep when necessary.

"Why don't we take just a few hours to nap? Then we can begin fresh at sunrise," I suggest. It's for the sake of the witchling, though I don't draw attention to her by pointing that out.

I have no intention of sleeping. I'll keep watch. Maybe I should have spent more time napping and less time rolling around in the pine needles with Nahum when we stopped before.

Nah. I regret nothing.

"This spot looks as good as any," Todd says when we get to

an area that's clear enough on the ground to sleep on but still has some tree cover overhead.

Most of us can just sleep in our fur. Even Feral is rugged enough to be fine sleeping outdoors. It's Aggie who will be the least comfortable. I go over to her and help arrange some of the duffels as a makeshift mattress.

"I'll keep watch," I announce.

Hugh rolls his eyes, and he and Feral share a look.

"You'll do no such thing. We will keep watch, and you will go to sleep. After all, Hugh and I got plenty of rest last night. It makes the most sense," Feral reasons.

Maybe he can sense my reluctance, because he turns around and starts patrolling the perimeter before I can disagree.

I don't put up nearly the fight I typically would. I stand by the fact that I feel much better with only one deal under my belt than the Bone Reader led me to believe I would, but as soon as I put on my fur and lie down on the dirt I feel how tired I am. I'm so close to sleep, a single step away from dreamland, when several thuds hit the earth around me.

Feral snarls, and I crack my one eye open to see that his are a shining green. An aura of menace is coming off him in waves. Hugh's eyes are flashing red, and he's got his fur on and his claws out.

My eye adjusts to the dark quickly, and I can just make out the silhouettes of several uninvited guests. The glowing red eyes of most of them tell me we're dealing with vampires, and the crackling sparks over the hand of another individual tells me we've got at least one warlock.

He launches a ball of moon-knows-what at my head, and I yank Aggie from her pile of duffels before pulling us out of the line of fire.

"For fuck's sake!" I snarl as I throw on my fur.

When I get home I'm going to have a chat with my own

vampires about their habits. I've always thought of the beings as relatively safe. Gluttonous? Yes. Hedonistic? Sure. But they're generally too busy imbibing alcohol, shopping, sex, or blood to be out causing trouble. At least that's what I thought. In recent months, I feel I've seen more than my fair share of vamps.

Either I've got them all wrong in my head, or the ones here are being paid handsomely. Or both. I'm not ruling out both.

One thing that's quickly apparent is their odd fighting style. The times I *have* faced vampires in a fight, they've been aggressive. These are taking full advantage of their speed. They're charging us, but pulling back and running away before we can get a hand on them. It's maddening.

I snap my jaws shut, just sure I'm going to hear the satisfying crack and crunch of vampire bones breaking, only to find that once again I've come up short. Nahum's wing shoots out in front of me, and he roars as something sizzling makes contact with it. It's coming from the warlock I first spotted, although I notice there are at least a few more.

Thanks, I got distracted by the vamps, I admit.

He's in pain, but he swallows it down.

For you, I would do that again and again.

I don't doubt it, but I shake my head and get it back in the game regardless. Vampire behavior is not something I can afford to think about right now. I just need to catch the slimy little suckers.

There's a bear roar, and a lot of yipping to my left. I turn in time to see Jackal bite into the arm of one of the vampires. Even regular hyena jaws are stronger than that of a lion. As a shifter? Jackal's got half the vamp's arm removed in less than a second. Todd goes for the head.

The bear and hyena turn their attention to another couple of sprinting vampires. As soon as the two are out of range, a couple more vampires sneak in and take the body of their fallen friend. I waste several precious seconds staring, trying to figure out what's going on as the remains of the vampire are taken away and the two vamps carrying the pieces disappear into the woods.

"Never!" Aggie jumps in front of me and throws her hand out, stripping another vampire who's sprinting toward us.

Stripped vampires are undeniably ugly things. I'd call it a cross between a classic zombie and a raisin. All dried out and sad. The vamp's eyes are the only thing that still look alive, flaring vibrant red with thirst. I leap to finish it off, but another vamp hauls it away from my jaws at the last second, and into the woods.

"What in the hell is going on here!" I demand, spinning so my back is up against Aggie's.

We turn in a circle, waiting to be attacked again.

Farther in the woods, through the branches of a large tree, I spy a flash of light and then see vines growing out of the ground. They wrap themselves around Feral's legs.

"Follow me!" I scream at the witchling.

I run toward Feral, with Aggie trailing behind. I don't even get halfway before the Founder has ripped the vines off himself and put an end to the warlock responsible.

He must hear us coming. He whips around, and fear suffocates me. Months of friendship with the Founders, and even an explanation from Feral, and I still can't put into words exactly how his abilities work. The other Founders are straightforward enough. Eon can compel other vampires and supernatural beings; Ayuna controls the blood in their bodies to bend them to her will; Midas touched things and turned them into treasure.

Feral? He just *is* terror. He freezes you, without visions like the dragon's but with a choking, all-consuming certainty that your own fear is going to eat you alive. A scream works its way up my throat, but the Founder drops his hold when he sees who we are.

I'm relieved. Sometimes when he gets into Hyde mode, he has trouble differentiating. I know he's been working on it.

"Sorry about that."

I shrug it off.

"Don't worry. Aggie would have stripped you dry and we'd have been good to go."

Behind me, the witchling in question gives a small squeak and a timid laugh.

"Oh yeah, sure. I totally had it under control. You know me, head witch."

She's shaking as I pull her into a side hug. Feral feels miserably guilty, but he doesn't have time to dwell on it as more vamps leap from the trees.

"We should have traveled at night! If we were resting during the day, we'd have the advantage," I yell as I kick one and send her sailing into a tree trunk.

"But we didn't know there were vampires!" Feral reasons before turning his fearsome gaze on one that's incoming.

They're moving too quickly for me to aim at them. I can douse the whole area and put them in a nightmare, but you'd all have to get out of range, Nahum informs me.

Could you get back in the sky and try to give us an overhead view? Then you could warn us if—

"Ouch! Son of a—" I clutch my side, where one of the little bloodsuckers who had just darted out from a tree bit me. Aggie's eyes are wide as saucers, and she's too focused on me to notice the blurred form of another leech coming right for her. I tackle the witchling, shielding her as the vampire breezes by. I get a chunk of my forearm chomped on for my trouble.

I'm all right! I yell up at the dragon before he can panic.

Feral roars, the sound sending shivers down my spine. He goes to his knees, shot in the back by whatever shocking magic one of the warlocks is wielding.

With all three of us down, we look like easy prey. We aren't, but I know that's how we appear, so the warlock and vamps ought to close in.

They don't, though.

Why?

I risk raising my neck up to look around, doing my best not to leave Aggie too exposed.

Nadia is shaking her arm to dislodge a vampire, but it's gone and running into the trees before she can attack it. Todd snarls, and a purple ball of magic slams into his muzzle. Another hits Jackal in the ear.

They're trying to pick us apart, piece by piece. They're not pulling their punches, so it's clear they don't want us alive. I take a deep breath and focus.

Malice. Aggression. Annoyance.

It's like our presence here has derailed whatever their plan is, and more than anything, they're upset about that. They want to kill us, but their main objective is not being caught. They're too hesitant and careful for anything else.

Another vamp goes down, and two others haul it off immediately. My intuition picks up on it now: fear.

This is the only time they're really fearful, when they've got a body to get rid of.

Because they cannot afford to let the body fall into our hands.

I don't have to know why, but I know I'm getting a piece of that vamp.

Watch Aggie! I yell to the dragon in my mind.

As soon as I feel Nahum's confirmation, I'm on my feet and running.

A vamp could outrun me, if we were sprinting on open ground. But we're in the woods, and I was raised in the woods. It also helps that I'm not hauling a dead body.

When I catch up to vamps, I throw myself on the dead one, pulling him out of the arms of his fellows.

"Why the hurry?" I ask, fangs dripping as the other two turn to me with a hiss.

As one, they launch themselves at me.

It's no skin off my back, because I'm confident I can absolutely take out two vampires.

Actually, I spoke a bit too soon. There *is* some skin off my back, because one of the vamps gets his pesky little claws into my shoulder and slices down my spine.

I finish the other vampire first and then reach behind me and grab hold of the annoying little back-climber, slamming him into the dirt.

My teeth have just left his throat when a glint of red catches my eyes. Another vamp.

Then, more dots of red. Quite a few more. Vampires materializing from the tree in droves.

I do the only thing I can do—stand over the fallen vamps in a defensive position as I snarl up at the others. One way or another, I am leaving here with a piece of vampire.

The red dots appear to fly as scores of vampires leap from the trees and throw themselves at me in a wave.

I might need some help here, I manage to shout to the dragon as the first few vampires make contact.

One of the few benefits of being tossed into the Underworld recently is that somehow, during the journey, part of my connection with Nahum was broken. Not the mate bond, but the bit that forced him to feel my pain. He already has to suffer whatever physical pain he inflicts. I'll admit I might have a bit of a habit of starting fights, and knowing he won't feel dozens of pairs of vampire fangs sinking into his skin is at least a small comfort to me as I'm buried under a pile of the bloodsuckers.

I'm not going down without a fight. I kick, claw, bite, snap, and howl. I manage to roll, taking several vampires with me who are clinging to my fur. My momentum is stopped by a tree trunk when I slam into it. Not my most stunningly graceful move, but I do manage to knock another vampire unconscious. I'd call that a win. Also, if anyone else asks, the move was totally intentional, definitely not accidental. I certainly didn't crack one of my ribs.

And if you believe that, I've got some oceanfront property in Arizona I'd love to sell you.

I hear Nahum roar and, while I might be imagining it, I think I can feel the trees shaking from their tops to their roots.

Jackal, Todd, and even Nadia beat my mate to the fight. Nadia sends a vampire sailing into three more, knocking them all over. She may not enjoy these skirmishes like the rest of us, but she took my lessons to heart.

Todd savages the throats of a few vamps, and Jackal, well, hyenas rip things apart piece by piece. Enough said.

When Feral arrives, Aggie behind his shoulder, I can feel the tide turning.

Nahum has swooped down, hauled multiple vampires up in his claws, and has dropped them from up high.

It's raining leeches.

The rest of them release me and run, hauling their injured and dead with them.

"Oh, no, you don't," I snarl, clamping my teeth onto the claw-tipped hand of one of the vampires. He's in such a hurry to leave that he goes without a few of his fingers that I rip off.

We start after them, but the warlocks toss several spherical objects.

When they hit the ground, multicolored smoke erupts.

15

IF WE MUST

"Stay back! The smoke could be poisoned!" Nahum yells at everyone.

If it is, we don't have Chrys here to help us. She'd be able to call in a family favor.

We watch the colored smoke dissipate. By the time it's gone, the area we're standing in is quiet again. Not a single vampire. Not a single body.

"Did anyone else notice?" Todd asks, now that they're gone.

"Notice what?" Hugh asks.

"They stopped to take their injured and dead," Jackal supplies.

Todd slams his front paws into the earth, turning our attention back in his direction.

"That was odd, but it's not what I meant. Some of them had the faint smell of young supernaturals lingering on them. They've been near the kids."

"He's right. I smelled it," Nadia adds.

I could hit myself. I was too focused on their actions and feelings to pay attention to my nose.

I lift my snout in the air, sniffing.

It would help us if we could just follow their scent, but now we won't be able to do that.

"Whatever they threw contained magic- and scent-masking perfume," Feral guesses as he scrunches up his face, green eyes fading to their normal shade.

It's exactly what my nose has just told me.

Todd growls, slamming his paws into the earth again. This time, he rips up chunks of grass and dirt. He's so upset, I think he'd be happy to destroy the whole forest.

"Now what do we do? We almost had them!" He slams his paws a few more times, then huffs.

I clear my throat.

The bear and the others look at me.

"What? Spit it out, Never," Todd demands, still frustrated.

I flash my teeth and do just that.

Three vampire fingers fall into my waiting palm.

Emotions hit my intuition like a strong wind. Awe, elation, and more than a little bit of disgust.

"You just left those in your mouth while we were figuring out what to do?" Nadia asks, and she doesn't bother keeping the judgment out of her voice. She knows I can feel it, but I can also tell she's impressed, even if she thinks it's gross.

"How are those going to help us?" Jackal is the only one who's confused.

"He only reads bones in his cave," Todd says before I can answer, hopeful but still determined to be grumpy.

"Now, now. Let's see if we can turn that frown upside down," I respond with a wink.

After everything he's put me through, I'd say the Bone Reader owes me a house call.

It's not my first choice. It's not even my fourteenth choice, but we've got to be close. Otherwise, why send all those supernaturals after us? We can't afford to lose them now. Not if I want those kids, and not if I'm right.

And when it comes to bad luck and negative predictions, I'm always right.

I let out a deep sigh and throw my head back as I reach up with the hand not holding the fingers and tap twice.

For several seconds nothing happens. Not long by normal standards, but for the Bone Reader? An eternity.

When I'm beginning to get antsy, dark shadows swirl on the ground and pull together until the solid form of the Bone Reader is in front of me. At least, as solid as he gets. He's doing his cycling-features thing and weaving his voices.

Jackal jumps back with a yip, and the mohawk of hair down his back raises like a dog's hackles in the presence of the powerful being.

"You called?" B.R. drawls, half-amused and half-annoyed.

His feelings actually comfort me a bit. They're much closer to how he used to view me before he plotted to turn me into a Rizik.

My stomach sours.

That's just how I remember it. He was always plotting. I only caught on later.

"I need you to read a bone." I unclench my other hand, and the fingers roll in my open palm. My hands were gritty and bloody, so the appendages now have a good layer of grime.

"Blech, Never. The things you're willing to put in your mouth for a good cause."

I sputter and turn to the witchling, who is all cunning smiles. She points at herself.

"The student becomes the master."

"In your dreams, witch. But yes, good one." I wink at her.

The Bone Reader clears his throat.

"I do not intend to be summoned and then ignored. You expect me to read the bones here? Now?"

Typically, B.R. uses an ice-formed goblet inside his ice cave, and who knows what other fancy tricks. But I've seen him perform plenty of even more impressive magic far away from his home. Surely he can pull something like that off.

"Yes. Here. Now." I don't bother tacking on a *please*. He's not intuitive, but he'd know I don't mean it.

At my back, all the others except for Nahum have a small thread of nervousness running through them at my irreverent tone.

I used to feel the same around B.R., but I can't manage it now. That's what happens when you risk someone's life in the hope they'll unwillingly turn into a Rizik for you to help end a sibling spat involving several-thousand-year-old powerful supernaturals who may as well be deities in the making. Not that I think there's a lot of people in my situation. Maybe I should form a support group and find out?

Victims of Bad Rizik Deals Club?

Doesn't have the same ring as CoED.

If B.R. had asked me for help, like any of my other friends, this whole thing could have gone differently. I can feel how badly he needs whatever he's looking for from me. All he had to do was ask.

But he didn't.

He couldn't trust me to do what he needed, so he took the choice from me instead.

I don't know if I'll ever get over that.

I'm scowling at him, and for an extra moment or two his features freeze in one expression.

Regret.

My intuition picks up on it, and I wish I could ignore it.

"Very well, hand over the bone," he orders, before I'm forced to acknowledge an emotion I've never felt from him like this before. Not in such an all-consuming way.

"You know, Bone Reader," I try as I hand the fingers over, "you could do more than just read this. We're after maniacs who have captured magical children. Over two hundred kids are in peril.

It's going to be tricky getting rid of the perpetrators while keeping all those kids safe. As long as you're here, we could use the help."

If there was ever a time to play the guilt-trip card, it's now. He should consider the opportunity an olive branch.

B.R. doesn't answer beyond a grunt. He closes his eyes while the rest of his features cycle and he holds the fingers. He closes his fingers around the ones I've handed him, and when he opens his palm again there's only a pile of gleaming white bones.

Even as he works, I can feel him considering the answer to my request, and I can pick up that he's motivated by a desire to get back on my good side. There's also something further. He wants to convince me to ...?

His attention shifts, and with it his emotions. I lose the trail of his feelings.

Instead, shock slams into me, so hard I take a couple of steps back. Nahum catches me under the arms as I stumble. Nadia has dropped to one knee and is clutching her head. When the Bone Reader feels, he feels big.

"What was that for?" I snap as he opens his shifting hand to reveal the bones disintegrating to ash in his hand.

Funny, I always thought he kept those.

"I'm sorry. I can't help you."

He lets his features slide into his Visitor facade, staring at me with a beseeching look.

"Can't or won't?" Jackal demands, back in his skin and shoving past Hugh to get at the Bone Reader. "Listen here. I don't care who you are or how tough you are. We've all got a responsibility here. Those kids need us, and if you can aid us, you're going to do it. Got it?"

Jackal moves to jab the Bone Reader in the chest.

He's got guts, I'll give him that, but even I could tell him it's a stupid thing to do.

The others freeze with apprehension as B.R. reaches up and grabs Jackal by the wrist.

The hyena yowls, and I'm well aware he's feeling the dry-ice burning sensation that the Bone Reader's touch can cause. I wouldn't recommend it, having been the recipient multiple times myself.

Jackal goes to his knees, but his emotions are all defiance and rage as he glares up at the Bone Reader.

Since he's got Visitor's face on, his expression is solid and chilling as he glares down at the hyena.

"A fighter. That's good; you'll need that confrontational attitude to get you through what you're facing."

B.R. lets go of the shifter, shoving him back a bit.

The others are relieved, but I'm intrigued. The Bone Reader could have turned Jackal to ash. I've seen it. But he didn't, and he doesn't want to. He wants us to succeed. He's even more invested in it now, since he's read the bone.

He's on our side, for whatever reason.

So why not help us?

Why not tell us whatever the bones have told him?

I gasp as I remember a pesky little detail the Bone Reader provided when he wasn't able to help me kill a certain elf back at CoED.

"Riziks can't interfere with other Riziks' deals," I whisper to myself. Then louder, so the others can hear. "Riziks can't sabotage the deals of other Riziks. One of your kin is involved in this travesty!"

He smiles when I get it right. I can feel the assurance down to my own bones.

"I'm glad you're intelligent," is all he says after several moments of silence.

"Never." Hugh's voice catches me off-guard. He steps forward in his fur and puts a hand on my shoulder. He's basically eye level. I've gone and thrown my fur back on and started growling to boot.

Hell's bells.

How I've survived under the human radar this long is anyone's guess. Being a loner has helped in my self-preservation, I would assume. Maybe I was just better at keeping my fur contained when I kept myself busy with regular enforcer assignments and didn't care about anyone else.

"What would one or multiple of your siblings want with supernatural children?" I ask.

"That I don't know, but I'd like to find out."

"Then help us. Do the decent thing, for once."

He starts pacing, features shifting again and a trail of shadow in his wake. He's muttering in a low voice, but I catch snippets of it, including "consequences," "why not," "never did anything for me." He looks as discombobulated as I feel in the middle of these investigations.

In contradiction to my desires, I wave the others back when they try to approach.

"He's lost his mind," Jackal whispers to me, his teeth lengthening and that eerie smile making an appearance.

"Not sure he had much of one to lose." Nadia looks at the shapeshifter. "*Usted es que está caído del zarzo.*" He may have helped us find her, and he's saved her before, but she's also seen how he operates. Even so, I'm not sure insulting him is going to work in the Wereling's favor.

Everyone goes silent when B.R. does. The shapeshifter strides back over to us, putting Visitor's face back on. His emotions are decided, and deadly serious.

"I can't go with you, and I can't intervene directly. What I can do is give you a location. I can tell you where the warlocks and vampires were heading, and if you make it there I think you'll find what you're looking for."

It's not that I'm not grateful; I just don't know how to keep my big mouth shut.

"Isn't that interfering?"

"I'm just telling you to go somewhere. What you find and what you do when you find it is outside my control."

"I doubt that very much," I counter.

He just raises a brow and gives me a half-smile.

"Still. Thank you. I suppose," I force out.

"Oh I just knew you'd change your mind and help!" Aggie dashes past me, arms out and ready to hug. She freezes inches from Visitor, and my intuition picks up on her hesitation as she remembers his dry-ice abilities. Visitor, for his part, is wide-eyed.

His flabber is completely gasted. He's tensed, arms up and pulling away, then he relents.

"Well, what's the harm, really? Just this once."

He drops his arms and holds them open, and Aggie flings herself forward and wraps what might be the world's most frightening and meddlesome magical being into a hug.

"She didn't burn," Hugh observes as Aggie releases the Bone Reader and takes a step back.

Visitor dusts off his sleeves.

"No. I turned it off for the moment."

"It's optional?" I yell at him.

"It takes effort to suppress it, and when I'm dealing with you my focus is always elsewhere. Like on your shouting."

My head is shaking, ready to explode as I clamp down on a snappy comeback. He more than deserves it, but now's not a great time.

He feels ... happy. As close as B.R. has ever come to it, anyway. He's included. Part of something. Even with his twisted sense of friendship toward me, it's the closest I've ever felt to him considering himself a member of this group. And he likes it, against all his better judgment.

I'm not going to be the one to ruin it.

My personal feelings aside, we are going to have to work with B.R. to fix this, just like he intimated. And if a witch hug can put him in a helpful mood? All the better.

Visitor clears his throat. The moment dissipates, and he's back to business.

"You're on the right track going this way. The group you're after is headed to a private supernatural cemetery up this path. You won't find it on any maps, but when I looked at the bone I saw a twisted metal gate, in complete disrepair but still marking the entrance to the graveyard. The stones are worn and old from time. I suggest you go there, and when you arrive, don't let your senses fool you."

"Are the kids all alive?" Todd blurts.

"Is the cemetery magically protected?" Hugh asks.

"Are there traps?" Jackal demands.

Visitor just holds up his hands.

"The cemetery. Trust your instincts, not just what you see. If you want what you're after, that's where you should start." He stares pointedly at me.

My intuition gets hold of his emphasis.

The kids are alive. At least for now.

"Oh thank goodness," Nadia breathes out as she feels my own relief.

Visitor just holds a finger up in front of his mouth. He's said all he's going to say on the matter.

"You've proven most helpful," I allow.

"I live to serve," he snarks, more like me than himself, "but Never? Don't forget our remaining deal. Your bones, dear. I'd wager it won't be long now."

I owe him. I'd help him anyway, if it meant preventing whatever cataclysmic event his sibling has planned, but even if I wanted to sit that adventure out, I am in debt up to my very bones.

Even with his little Underworld stunt, as I weigh things B.R. has done, there's more good than bad. At least when it comes to being able to help people I care about.

"The price?" I remember to ask.

"When I do call in our deal for your bones, bring your friends for backup."

The price is steep, but if I'm being honest, they would have come anyway. Whatever the Bone Reader is going to have me do with the promise I made of my bones, I have no doubt they would have tagged along regardless.

Even now, he's given us more information than I hoped for.

Not that I should have had to make a deal for it.

Come to think of it, I should ask him why, even with limited deals, I still feel fine.

And while we're on that train of thought—

"Bone Reader!"

"I must take my leave." He starts turning to shadow, but he's staring at me.

"If Riziks can't interfere, what am I supposed to do? Why am I able to work on this case? Something is very fishy here!"

His movement freezes. He's mostly shadow, but those blue Visitor eyes have me in a hold.

"Everything isn't what you think it is."

Then, he disappears entirely.

Hell's moon.

"Oh, no, he doesn't!" I snarl, tapping furiously at my silver eyepatch.

By the fifteenth attempt, Nadia grabs my hand.

"Never. He's not coming back."

No. He's not.

I'm pretty certain I'm not what I thought I was at all.

16

PLAY IT AGAIN

We're not up far enough into the peaks for it to be solid snow, although that could be the warmer than normal temps. It's definitely not a straight shot into the mountains. We're spanning back and forth so we don't miss any clues.

The Bone Reader may have provided our heading, but this is a large swath of wilderness. It'll be easy to miss our target if we're not careful.

"Anything?" I call back to where the others are fanned out behind me.

"Nothing yet," Todd calls back.

"Same here," Feral echoes.

The rest of them confirm the same. We're not straying from B.R.'s direction, but as of now his help hasn't amounted to much.

I trudge onward. The only hint I get that we're in trouble is a faint crackle. It's windy up here, and at first I think the sound is a leaf crunching under someone's foot. I take another step, and the crackling intensifies.

"Magic!" I manage to shout before the illusion closes in on me.

I jump back when Nahum slams onto the ground in front of me, tucking his wings behind him and stalking toward me.

"Get down," he warns, fog billowing out of his jaws.

My instincts are urging me not to do what he's asked. If I'm on the ground I'll be in a more vulnerable position. Is he even real? If he is, is he really doing what my mind tells me?

"Never!" he yells, mouth opening and fog billowing.

He feels concerned for me. I'll have to trust that. I tuck and roll out of his path as a cyclone of fog shoots over where I was standing.

Instead of hitting me, it hits Feral, whose green eyes are glinting. He's in Hyde mode, claws raised above where I was standing. He brings them down in the empty air, slicing into nothing just before the nightmares hit.

"Wait. No. That's not right. Feral wouldn't do that."

Or would he?

The emotions, Never. Focus on the emotions, I remind myself.

Whatever maniac is causing this can't alter those. I'd like to tear whoever it is apart. They're not the only one I'm upset with, though.

More than anything, I'm furious at myself for wandering into another one of these mind-manipulation zones. The only thing I can do is try to fight my way out, or feel my way out, in this case.

I take a few deep breaths in and out, trying to keep them slow as I watch Nahum slice his claws across Feral's chest.

Beyond them, Todd's eyes are glazed, and he's charging full speed at Aggie. Her back is turned; she's focused on Hugh. She's not going to see him in time!

The bear slams into her and her hands flash with light as she screams.

"Aggie!"

No. It's not real.

I focus on their emotions.

Aggie.

The little sister; the family I needed.

She's worried, and she's confused, but she's not agonized.

Her mind must be playing tricks on her as well, but she's not hurt.

With a sigh of relief I spin back to the fighting Founder and my mate, but my view is blocked by a russet-furred Were, his fangs dripping and his eyes deep red.

"Lady Vicious." He runs his tongue over his fangs.

I try to read him, and I can feel Hugh is truly close to me, and he's frenzied.

"Did I ever tell you about how my transition from human to vampire went?" This has to be one of the mind tricks. Hugh, the real Hugh, is well aware that I know his story.

When I reach for the Were's emotions, I can sense them. He's really in front of me. He's conflicted, and frightened. Maybe I can reach him somehow. If emotions are triggering for me, maybe I can say something to target his and get him back.

"Hugh. You worked in a museum. You studied dead and dying languages. All languages, really. You're like a dragon that way, hoarding knowledge." The Were blinks at me, his eyes flashing green, and for a moment I think I'm in the clear. Then, the red snaps back in place.

He snarls.

"It wasn't even that painful, you know. When the vampires turned me. But when *you* turned me ..."

He needn't say more. I can feel the emotions, and I know that no matter what his mind is showing him, he's reliving the memories. Me slicing and kicking and biting into his skin before shoving poison down his throat.

It still doesn't sit right with me, which is probably why my voice shakes.

"You chose to be a Were, Hugh. Remember? You wanted to be able to go out in the sun. You wanted a say in what you are."

He nods, saliva hanging off his fangs.

"True. It might have been nice if I'd become an intuitive as well, but you didn't share that particular gift, did you? You kept that for yourself."

I can feel real resentment, and it's impossible to tell whether it's about my intuition, how much he suffered to become a Were, or something else entirely.

For all I know, Hugh is seeing a totally different scene than what I am right now. I don't know enough about how this magic works.

The desperation is real, though, when Hugh swipes out with his claws and clocks me in the jaw.

"Moon's hells! That hurt, Hugh!"

His red eyes roll, and around us I can hear snapping and snarling. This won't do. I'm not going to get out of this by fighting. That will just escalate the negative emotions, and I suspect add fuel to the illusions.

I need to go back to targeting his emotions. That's what will get us out of this mess. I have an idea of what might jar him enough to break free of the mind manipulation, but it's risky.

"Aggie, lend me your positivity on this one," I mutter.

When Hugh throws himself at me again, I step to the side. As he launches past, I wrap my arms around him. At first, it's a bit like wrestling, but I manage to twist us until we're both standing and I have the other Were wrapped in a hug.

"You are my friend, Hugh. My family. One of the few people I trust. I know you're scared, and I'm sure you're seeing something awful, but I'm right here. You're not alone. I've got you, and I'm not letting go."

He thrashes in my arms for several seconds as the words sink in. Then, he goes still.

He twists enough to face me, and his eyes fade to green again.

"Never?"

He's confused, but less fearful and less angry. After just a few moments, his legs start to twitch again, and I can feel the negative emotion building.

"I'm going to get us out. Try to stay still," I instruct as I throw us both to the ground and roll us.

My head clears and the crackling fades once we reach the invisible perimeter of the zone. Hugh stops fighting me and lies in the dirt when I get up and brush myself off.

His breathing is fast and ragged, but he only clawed me one more time. All in all, I'd call it a win.

Nadia rushes over to us. Since I was in the lead on this leg, that put her in the back of the group.

"You managed to shout a warning before you were sucked into whatever you were seeing," Nadia informs me as she bends down to check on Hugh.

"What about everyone else?" I twist to look. I know I saw Feral, Nahum, and Aggie in there with me.

"Aggie was just barely inside the perimeter. I was able to reach in and grab her. Todd kept hold of my legs and hauled us both back out," Nadia states, gesturing to the two of them.

Aggie doesn't appear injured, although I can feel she's working to hold herself together. She's huddled up against a tree trunk. Todd is standing with his massive, furry head placed over her.

Nahum stumbles toward us from somewhere deeper in the woods. He's rubbing his head as he lets his scales fall off and puts his skin on.

"What happened to you?"

"I heard the crackling and your warning, so I made a split-second decision to shut my eyes, plug my ears, and dive in after you. I may have made a slight miscalculation, though, and I ended up flying myself into a tree."

I make my way over to him and throw my arms around him, then plant a kiss on his temple.

"It's the thought that counts."

"Really? I thought you were more of a 'results' type person."

"Maybe I'm a hopeless romantic."

He laughs at that, the pain in his head forgotten.

Jackal and Feral are the last to be accounted for. Jackal has managed to blindfold himself and stuff fabric into his ears. He's dragging Feral out by the ankle. As they reach the edge of the mind-manipulation zone, we help haul the Founder out.

Jackal puts his skin back on. He sits on the ground with his arms behind him. His breaths come in deep heaves.

"That damned vampire is heavy!" he complains.

Feral thrashes once or twice; then his eyes clear.

"I didn't kill anyone, did I?" The first words out of his mouth are to check on everyone but himself.

Hugh is smart enough to pass out snacks, even though he's got to be as rattled as the rest of us. I didn't even think to pack any.

"I don't know about everyone else, but these mind fields make me shaky. Everyone eat up!" He shoves a cranberry oat bar into my hand, and I stick my tongue out at it.

"Veggie jerky?" he asks, holding a packet out to me as a second option. I glare at the offensive food, and Hugh sighs. "I keep it on hand for Chrys."

The witch is a vegetarian. In her mind, it helps balance out her magical karma.

I, a lifelong fan of bacon and all things tasty, am thrilled when Nadia digs around in the bag and pulls out real beef jerky.

Once we're done with food, Nadia helps Hugh check the

packs. The crackling has faded to nothing, and we're ready to move again.

Jackal is standing, staring at the area where the mind-manipulation barrier was previously. He's got an intensity to the look, and his feelings.

"Your niece?"

"My work keeps me occupied, but I make it a point to see my sister at least a couple times a month. I watch Charlotte while she cooks us dinner. Or, if I'm cooking, I balance the process with making sure Charlotte doesn't get burned. She's only six, but she's fearless."

His emotions shift from longing, to nostalgia, to grief, and back to determination. He worries about what we might find, but he refuses to linger on it. If any of us stopped to let thoughts of what might have happened consume us, we'd never be able to keep going.

In most situations, I make it my policy to assume the worst. In this case? I have to hope for the best, because the alternative is unthinkable.

"What do hyena cubs like to eat, anyway?"

It's just a distraction. Most shifter kids eat just like humans unless in their fur.

"Spaghetti, with meatballs. I will say, though, she prefers the meatballs served rare." He chuckles to himself. "When we find whoever took her—" His fists clench at his side, and he doesn't bother finishing.

"All packed up here! Now, who's going to help me carry all of this?" Hugh distributes the duffels. Todd gets three, being back in his fur.

Nadia rotates to the front of the group, and we get moving again.

Our latest foray into a mind field has left me discombobulated—a word that's almost as fun as *flabbergasted*. At least it's a sign that Bone Reader is right. If they're still attacking us, we've got to be on the correct trail.

We're headed toward a Rizik. A Rizik I shouldn't be able to interfere with. On top of that, I'm climbing mountainous terrain immediately after another mind net mix-up full of energy. I've only made one deal this entire time, and I'm pretty sure that means my energy should be in the basement.

I like to think I'm not an idiot, so it's becoming clearer and clearer to me that the likelihood of my actually being a Rizik is low.

I relay my theory to Nahum, and he has his own thoughts.

This is good, though, right? It means you don't need deals. Plus, it means you're an intuitive Were and nothing else. That's what you wanted, right?

Yes. But I'm not just a Were. You stopped feeling when I'm in pain, and I can now see the motivations and trains of thought connected to people's feelings. Something definitely changed.

Nahum more readily accepts good news than I do. He gives a mental shrug.

I'm not going to say I miss the pain, but I do wish I could know if you're in trouble. At least you can still speak into my mind and tell me. I know all the extra emotions make your brain buzz, but they're proving helpful on investigations. I'd call it an overall win.

Yes, a win.

But that's the problem, isn't it? When the Bone Reader was busy hedging and avoiding my questions, I was reading him.

He wasn't devastated. He wasn't upset. He was just ... secretive. And I know B.R.

He's spent years manipulating our way into this situation. He used a lot of power and free deals to get me to the Underworld. If things hadn't gone his way, he'd be morose, or more likely livid. That means there has to be more to it.

There has to be more to *me*.

I may not be a Rizik, but I'm something.

And whatever that something is, it's either powerful enough or useful enough to still fit within the Bone Reader's plans.

The idea should terrify me, but instead it energizes me.

I just hope I can figure out what I am and how to use it to my advantage before we meet whoever has the kids.

17

LET'S PLAY WITH LIGHTNING

We spend the rest of the day, all night, and now well into the following day traipsing around the trail. We've managed to avoid five more mind fields, and this morning we scented the kids.
Lots of kids.
We're catching up.
We crest another hill, and I let out a whoop.
Tucked between the hills is exactly what we're looking for. Hugh actually gasps in delight, pulling the stone out of his pocket and holding it up for comparison.
We've reached the graveyard. The headstones, at least from what I can see at first glance, are all old. They're weathered and worn. Some are tilted sideways or missing chunks. Several have lichen or vines obscuring bits of the writing, and a few are so old the weather has worn the writing down to where it's not legible at all.
There are several chunks of rock or granite that are so old it's impossible to tell whether they're gravestones or just boulders dropped by the mountain itself.

Jackal growls, the mohawk of hair down his back puffing up even further, as we approach the twisted gates.

"I don't like it."

"What do you mean you don't like it? We've been wandering around the terrain for days!" Hugh grumps, offended that his excitement is being forcibly dampened.

Feral scans the whole scene.

"The hyena's right. It's too easy. Based on what we've seen, there should be a solid wall of that crackling magic surrounding this place. At the very least, we should have run into a bunch of vamps and warlocks. If this is our destination, why isn't anyone guarding it?"

Hell's damned bells. He's right.

I hate that he's right.

Todd is snuffling the air.

"I can smell the kids. The scent is strong, and recent. They've got to be here somewhere. If they aren't, they're nearby." The bear is one sniff away from barreling in, no matter what traps might await us.

Whether I hear crackling or not, we need to be cautious. No sense in mucking everything up now.

"Let Nadia and me check the perimeter. If it's clear, we can enter the graveyard. How about that?"

Todd blinks.

"It's surprisingly reasonable, coming from you."

"Sure you wouldn't prefer to just set the place on fire and see what happens?" Feral teases.

I roll my eye and shake my head.

"You burn a few things to the ground and no one ever lets you forget it. Come on, Nadia, we can get to work while everyone else sits on their duffs." I wave her over, and she smirks at a ruffled Feral and Hugh as we stride past them and toward the graveyard.

At the front of the whole thing stands a set of warped, black metal gates. It's just like B.R. said. One is leaning to the side, part of the bottom edge freed from the ground and covered in dirt. The other is twisted in on itself. They're anchored into brick pillars. It's clear there used to be an entire brick wall surrounding the cemetery, but it's in shambles.

"No need to knock, I suppose," Nadia states, voice barely above a whisper as we approach.

"We won't be going in. First, let's do a thorough sweep of the surroundings, and make sure our minds aren't at risk."

I have no desire to repeat the fun-filled hallucinations of my first two trips into the magic.

As we get closer to the entrance, white lines of light snap between the twisted gates and all along the brick wall. They're like lightning, patching in the pieces of broken perimeter.

There is a border to the cemetery after all.

"At least it's not mind magic," I grumble as I lean forward and sniff.

It's just run-of-the-mill lightning. I have no doubt it would send any supernatural creature flying backward, possibly burnt to a crisp, but it's not going to induce any visions.

I lead Nadia left. We take our time, meandering up the hillsides and then down a steep slope that boxes in the western portion of the graveyard. Not a single crackle.

It should cheer me, but it just convinces me there's something worse waiting for us.

As we continue our journey around the perimeter, it becomes clearer and clearer that the scent of the children is centered inside the graveyard. The scents are so varied and complex that I doubt it's a trick.

We finish up and end in front of the gates. Nadia waves the others over after I declare the graveyard a mind-manipulation-free zone.

Even without that particular issue, we've still got the lightning fence to contend with.

"Anyone want to volunteer to try and jump over? Hope we don't get fried?"

I could fly over top; it doesn't look as if the protection spans that high, Nahum volunteers.

Excellent idea. I hate it.

I'm far too suspicious to like the idea of his going first.

He just grins at me, but I can feel there's no humor in him.

He's right, but I don't like it when he's the one risking himself. I flatten my lips into a thin line, my jaw tense as I bite back a plea for him to remain on the ground.

No one else urges him to stay put, although Todd has the decency to feel uncertain about the whole thing.

But, it's for the kids.

Nahum shoots into the sky, wings already prepared even though he's in his skin. He throws his scales on as he arcs at a certain height, angling himself for the graveyard. The moment he reaches the border, one of the white beams of light shoots upward and slams into his scaled foot.

"Nahum!" I scream at the same time he starts to. The lightning illuminates him, searing his scales.

I don't stop screaming as he jerks in the air and then drops like a stone, directly into the cemetery. A few of the grave markers are shattered when he slams into them. He lies motionless.

"Are you insane!"

I barely register Todd's statement, but I feel his arms wrapping around me in his bear form. I begin shifting, determined to break free and reach my mate, when a voice hits my mind.

I'm okay. Can't die, remember?

I sag in Todd's arms. When he realizes I'm no longer a threat to myself he lets me go, but I lean up against him for support.

Nahum's in the middle of the graveyard, and he sits up and coughs black smoke.

"I wouldn't recommend that method to anyone else," he warns in a hoarse voice.

"Maybe you can let us in from your side?" Jackal calls in, taking the dragon's singed scales in stride.

I'm turning to snarl at Jackal's careless comment, but then the motivation for his emotions hits me in the snout.

The hyena has seen worse, and he needs this mission to be successful. Wants it more than anything in the world. He'd throw us all under a bus and use our bodies as stepping stones if that's what it took to get to his niece.

Can't say I blame him, but he'd better not become a liability. Not this late in the game.

Hugh clears his throat.

"Whatever we're going to do, we should act fast. Who knows if that triggered some sort of alarm."

Dammit.

I've bungled it big-time, folks. I was so focused on the mind manipulation that the lightning fence seemed a minor inconvenience in comparison.

More fool me.

Nahum makes his way toward the back of the gates, limping a bit. I can see crispy, seared holes in his wings, but they're already healing up. When he reaches for the gate the lightning flares, and he snatches a claw back.

"Guess I'm not supposed to bring guests," he observes from his side of things.

"We should run the perimeter again; see if there's a weak point. This place is old, and the magic doesn't feel new. Magic can fail, just like human walls. There's got to be a way around it," Jackal insists.

"Good idea. We'll go in pairs," Todd adds.

We already gave the whole perimeter a good looking over, but Nadia and I weren't looking for holes in lightning; we were listening for crackling magic.

"Nadia, can you guide me around the edge?" Todd asks the young Were. The two of them trudge off together in the downhill direction.

Ah, the good old buddy system. An excellent way to have added protection, or just a fantastic way to run off alone with a killer and get stabbed in the back? You decide.

"I'll wait up by the gates with Nahum. I can try to see if it's possible to strip the magic out of the fence," Aggie decides.

"We'll search further out. There could be a hidden entrance somewhere we're not considering." Feral beckons Hugh away from the cemetery and back into the trees.

That leaves me with the newbie.

The cemetery isn't all that big, but we start climbing the hill that the cemetery backs into, just in case there's an angle there.

"So," I start before Jackal can get a word in, "you've kept yourself to yourself successfully this trip. When you're not rescuing your niece, what do you like to do?"

He tilts his head at me, one of his hands reaching for a rock.

"Is this your idea of a conversation? We're risking getting ourselves shot off a pile of loose rocks by lightning, and you want to hear my life story?"

He shakes his head and gets back to it.

"Aha!" I point at him, and one of the rocks under me goes skittering. I'm forced to wheel my arms and manage to get my footing back, but I'm still pleased. "You're annoyed, but you're also impressed. You like my nosy attitude, or at least you respect it. You're just as curious about the rest of us."

"True, but you all are much more open books than I am. A few of you talk more in the span of an hour than I might in a week."

He's thoughtful, and I force myself to focus on looking for cracks in the lightning fence. After all the yammering-on he's accused us of, silence turns out to be just what he needs.

"I was a watcher for our cackle."

He must read my look of confusion.

"A cackle is what you call a pack of hyenas, and a watcher is a position within the cackle. I'm charged with monitoring any potential threats to us. It's gotten a lot harder, now that members of the cackle are integrated into human society. It's not like hyenas are traditionally found roaming around the Lake District, you know."

I huff as the claws extending from my padded feet grip onto the side of the hill. Loose rocks shift under me, and a few smaller ones tumble into the fence. The lightning snaps and fries even those inanimate objects.

"That's where your cackle resides? The Lake District?"

He shakes his head.

"All over England. There's only one cackle there, and we're spread across the country. The Lake District is where we're the most concentrated. My sister and niece are there, but ..."

"You don't live there."

"No. But I consider my residence in England less of a home, and more of a home base."

I don't bother saying it's the same thing. I know better.

"When you're not watching, what do you do?" I press, thinking that someone trusted to safeguard an entire cackle across a whole country would make a very useful enforcer indeed. Not that I'm in the business of Magikai recruitment.

In fact, I find myself thinking *I'd* like to recruit him. But what is my motley crew exactly? Nothing official, that's for sure.

Maybe that should change.

"Never!" Aggie's voice reaches us. Strained, hoarse, and tired, but triumphant.

Jackal and I rush back down the side of the hill and around the cemetery's perimeter.

Aggie is swaying on her feet, but she's smiling.

"I figured it out. I've been working on it ever since we helped take down the Magikai's previous head representative.

When the Bone Reader enhanced our abilities, you remember?"

Of course I do. It's the closest I'd ever gotten to what I can do after my trip to the Underworld. And what his little boost did to Aggie's powers? Forget about it.

"Chrys helped me. I used the same concept she does when she weaves elements like water into her defensive shields. I use my stripping, but I also throw in some other nullifying magic, and it gets the job done."

She throws her arms out and gestures to the perimeter of the graveyard. A good portion of the lightning is still up, but the gate is blasted wide, and there's no lightning in that area.

"This is like what you did when I first saw your powers, when you pulled the magic out of my wound," I observe, recalling how she saved me from a poisoned weapon.

She blushes.

"Yes. At that time, I hadn't been very successful in trying to strip magic from objects, just people. I was surprised I didn't actually strip you then."

I shrug. She's feeling guilty, but all I remember is that I didn't die in a field like an idiot because I failed to see a weapon. If it weren't for my friends, I'd have died a dozen times over the past year or so.

"You did good, witchling." I clap her on the back, and she grins.

We call the others back over.

Hugh snags a water bottle for Aggie, and Nadia hands her a pack of dried fruit and nuts. I also see a pack of Canadian gummy snacks in Nadia's hand. The witch beams.

Nahum walks through the back of the gate.

"Shock-free!" he announces, throwing his wings wide.

The mood lightens significantly.

We're one step closer.

18

CURSES & COMPLICATIONS

Turns out I'm full of crap. We're no closer at all.

After wandering around every stone and grave marker in the place, everyone's negative energy is back. We haven't been able to find any sort of magical entrance or hidden hideout, let alone the actual kids. Hugh guessed the chunk of gravestone we've got might be some sort of key. He's taken it around to each and every headstone and tried to get it to fit.

So far, no dice.

I'm ready to claw my fur out. The despair, the frustration, the agitation, the need to vent that energy that crawls along people's skin like ants.

And, lucky, lucky me, all the rest of it. The despair, because a dear friend's child, or a niece, may be suffering and we're just standing here sniffing graves. The frustration, because we came this far and it appears to be a dead end. The agitation with each other, and the fact that none of us has a better answer.

Thanks a lot, intuition, as if I really needed the reminder.

"Hell's bells and hell's moon and moon's hell! Could you all *please* stop feeling so damned loudly?" I demand, stomping a foot in the grass and tugging at the fur on my arms. It's itching with all this negativity.

Nadia sighs, clutching at her head when all my outburst does is send the pessimism up multiple degrees.

"We're all doing our best here, Never," Todd reminds me. He's trying to keep his voice in check, but of course I know he's annoyed.

"Are we sure that shape-shifting being can be trusted? Maybe he's in league with whoever has the kids. This could be a fake trail. In fact, we may need to get out of here, or risk being trapped in this graveyard." Jackal is baring his teeth at the cemetery gate like he expects it to close us in at any second.

I bark out a laugh.

"B.R. is far from trustworthy, but,"—I hold up a finger in the face of his protest—"he most certainly is not in league with whoever is doing this. If this kidnapping involves a Rizik, B.R. won't be helping them. He's gone to great lengths to place himself firmly against them."

Stabbing me in the gut, drawing me into a murder investigation, sending me to the Underworld.

But also manipulating someone who is sympathetic to me into a position of god of said Underworld, feeding me tidbits of needed information, being at my beck and call via a magical eyepatch.

"If the Bone Reader sent us here, there is a reason. We're just missing something." Feral has been quiet until now. He paces the interior perimeter of the graveyard as he makes this observation.

"*Usted si que es menso, pues claro que los niños no están aquí!*"

Nadia is right. The kids are nowhere to be seen.

"But it smells like they are. Like they were," Nahum argues back, even as the scent continues to fade.

I give the air a good sniff, and another.

"Todd." I wave him over to test a theory. "Where is it strongest?"

Todd lumbers around the graves and goes back and forth between a few spots several times. Eventually, he plops himself down in front of one of the hills that makes up the back edge of the cemetery. It butts up to the larger mountains above us.

"Here."

Something is very fishy about this area. The moment I get close, I have the urge to turn and check the rest of the cemetery again. I'm thinking about this interesting turn of events when I notice Todd walking the other direction.

"Hey! What are you doing?"

He blinks, surprised.

"Oh. I ... I don't know. I just, I was thinking I should check somewhere else."

This spot is fishy as hell. I don't smell magic, but something witchy is definitely at work. And if that's the case—

They wouldn't bother defending something that wasn't important, Nahum speaks in my mind, echoing my own thoughts.

"B.R. told us to trust our instincts, not our senses," I think aloud. "Hugh! Bring that bit of rock over here."

"Technically, it's not just rock. It's—" He snaps his mouth shut and brings it over when he sees my expression.

"Now what?" he questions. "There's nothing here."

I'm not so sure.

"Do you remember what the Bone Reader told us? We all feel like we're in the right spot, but we can't find a way in. Just. Don't leave this area. Focus. Don't let yourself be deterred. Think of wanting to find the kids, and ... stop that!" I snap.

He's hefting the bit of gravestone like he's about to throw it away. When I yell at him, he stares down, perplexed.

"I didn't even realize I was doing that."

"Magic. In the mind fields, we can't trust our senses. I think this is the same thing. There's magic to keep us away from this area, which means it's exactly where we need to be."

Hugh refocuses and sweeps the stone in the air in front of the hill. He starts low, at the level of the other gravestones, and then rises. He's on the tip of his Were toes and waving the stone above his head when something happens.

The air in front of us ripples, and for a moment, I see something in the side of the hill. A door.

"Hugh! Put it back to that spot!" Feral yells, coming back over.

Hugh does what the Founder instructs, and the rippling comes back. Soon, the vision clears and we're all left staring at two huge stone doors built directly into the hill. Hugh's bit of gravestone would fit on one side.

Feral reads what he can of the worn text.

"Here lyeth the remains of those magicals most renowned, and highest esteemed. Protected in death from the monsters who have hunted us in life. Their bones kept safe from those who would use them with nefarious intent. Their souls free from this world."

I let out a low whistle, and Todd does as well.

"Were they trying to keep out humans, or other magicals who would use the bodies for parts?" Aggie asks, reaching a hand toward the doors.

"Both. Being powerful is not always all it's cracked up to be," Feral responds, nonchalant as he insinuates his own level of strength.

I think back to when Damien killed Ekaitz but I got the credit for the dragon's death. I can't lie. Our vampire coven used and sold the teeth and scales. They were valuable, and Ekaitz was an ass. But if it had been a magical I respected? I'd have put him somewhere like this if it meant protecting the remains.

"Hugh," Nahum starts, his voice hardly more than a whisper, "add your piece. Everyone else, be prepared. We don't know what will happen if those doors open."

We all nod, prepping our claws and fangs.

Hugh lets out a deep sigh, and then shoves the bit of gravestone into the doors. It clicks into place, and with an echoing groan, the doors slowly open.

We take a few hesitant steps into the dark.

"We're in a mausoleum," Hugh breathes, awestruck as he takes in the grave markers lining the walls to our left and right.

Todd growls, the rumbling sound echoing.

"More like catacombs." He points to the end opposite the doors, a black, yawning opening that leads further into the side of the mountain.

"Who in their right mind would bring children down here?" I snarl as I stare at the dust-covered gravestones and spot a bone poking out of one that's cracked down the front.

"These people aren't in their right mind. That's the whole point. We're dealing with psychopaths," Feral responds, that aura of terror lingering on his skin.

I'd worried joining our little group might undo the control he has, but maybe we've given him focus. I've never seen him use the ability while keeping it this contained before.

"Nice job, Hyde," I whisper after stepping closer to him.

"We brought flashlights, right?" Aggie asks, nervous. Nadia hesitates before handing her one. The rest of us see well enough in the dark.

Hugh snatches the thing from her hands.

"How about, you hold onto me while we search? That way we keep the lights off and the evidence of our presence to a minimum?"

Aggie gives a shaky nod, and Hugh sheds his skin to put on his Were form. Aggie digs her fingers into some of the plush, russet fur.

"Well," Jackal snaps, "what are we waiting for?"

Todd sniffs again.

"I don't like it. They've had all sorts of traps this whole time. There's no way this entrance wasn't booby-trapped or rigged somehow. Surely they've got to know we're coming. At the very least we'll encounter more mind-manipulation nets or vampires down this tunnel, and how are we going to fight our way out when we're boxed in?"

Jackal shows that eerie smile, but the meaning is aggressive.

"Sit in here with the dead bodies if you want. I'm going after my niece."

In spite of his words, he just stands at the yawning entrance to the dark beyond, fur bristling and fanged smile plastered on his face.

I can feel everyone's hesitation, and certainty. This is it. Whatever we're looking for, the search ends here.

If we're too late, the best I'll be able to do is try and reach Damien. I don't want to contact him again so soon, or perhaps at all, but if what we find is bad …

The least I can do is ensure things go better on his end than they did on ours. No lost souls or suffering in the Underworld on my watch.

"We should still have an intuitive go first, just in case we run into a mind field," Nadia insists, breaking the awkward silence.

"And if we do? How do we get around it in this space?" Jackal demands, glowering at her like she should have the answer.

I step between them.

"If that happens, we'll shove on blindfolds and stuff fabric in our ears and run through it. We'll just have to hope no vampires or warlocks take us out before we get to the other side."

"Peachy," Jackal grumbles, but he's still eager to go.

"I'll take the lead," I volunteer.

I step in front of Todd and into the dark. I scent the air,

begging and pleading to all the gods I've ever ignored that I only smell old death.

My relief over smelling just that is marred by the competing smells of the children, alongside what I judge to be their vampire and warlock kidnappers.

I turn to wave the others in after me, and feel the hair on my arms rise as the sound of crackling magic booms outside the mausoleum. A figure steps in front of the entrance, raising their arms as they begin to shift. The sun behind them makes it impossible to see the figure at first in any great detail.

I guess we won't have to worry about running into a mind field. Someone's brought one right to us.

"Ears! Eyes!" Hugh shouts at everyone. The others slam their eyes shut, plugging their ears with their fingers or fabric they've been carrying from one of the ripped shirts in the duffels.

We can't save the kids if the person controlling the mind manipulation follows us. We have to be able to get away.

Well, *they* have to be able to get away.

I'm not volunteering myself because of my lack of self-control, my big ego, or the simple fact that launching myself into danger has just been a habit for over four hundred years.

Only an intuitive could fight this battle and win, and I'm not going to ask Nadia to sacrifice herself.

It's time to test a theory.

Grab the bit of gravestone we used to get in. Find the kids. Keep everyone safe.

I run through the others, shoving a snarling Jackal and a shocked Aggie out of the way. Nahum's right behind me.

Please, please, please.

Those words are just for me. I can feel how conflicted he is. He knows what I know. We need an intuitive. He's also only recently gotten me back from the Underworld, and the very last thing he wants to do is risk my making a return trip.

His feelings are fighting each other, and as we reach the doors of the mausoleum I have no idea whether he's going to grab me or the bit of gravestone, like I asked. Nahum leaps, his wings giving him some lift. His talons close around the stone and yank as I launch myself through the doors.

They slam shut behind me.

19

EVIL IS AS EVIL DOES

The figure in front of me drops their arms, and the crackling ceases.

I'm safe from any mind-manipulation for now, although I can't imagine why they're not using their most valuable weapon.

The being in front of me is radiating curiosity, and I'd wager that's the only thing saving me.

I'm staring into the eyes of a bear shifter, standing on its hind legs.

"Hello." Her voice rumbles like Todd's in this form.

A bear shifter? That's who's been messing with our minds? I've never heard of such an ability. Her fur is the same color as those toffee chews grandmas insist on carrying around in their purses. I know, because Gladys and Rose from the Sewing Circle keep some on hand.

The bear drops to all fours, lumbering toward me. As she gets closer, she bares her teeth. For a brief moment, the expression morphs into a smile. The fur drops away, and I expect to see a shifter in their skin.

Instead, the bear transforms into a nagi. She has a twisting snake's tail with emerald scales, and some scales of a similar shade dust her cheeks and arms.

"Not possible." My voice is barely a whisper.

There's no way she can be both things at once. My brain buzzes; my body is ready to fight as she slithers a slow circle around me.

What could have magic like her mind manipulation? A witch, maybe a hag? A dragon, but surely Nahum would have recognized a dragon power? Or a Founder, perhaps, but Feral never made any mention of a Founder of Minds.

The only other being I know who can access magic of so many kinds, and change his appearance is …

"You're the Rizik."

I'd expected B.R.'s siblings to stay behind the scenes, like he does. Clearly, I was sorely mistaken.

The tail trailing around my side disappears as she makes her way back to my front. Instead of a nagi, I'm staring into the fiery eyes of a fox, with several bushy tails trailing behind her.

"And you must be my brother's plaything." She moves her features until they sit somewhere between fox shifter and elf, human enough to sneer.

"I'd rather play with your brother. He's much better at these games than you are."

She shifts her head to that of a wolverine and snaps at me with a lengthening neck.

"Not a fan? Your brother appreciates my sense of humor," I taunt as I sidestep the attack. Not that I'm fool enough to assume I can dodge her forever.

If B.R. is anything to go by, Riziks are serious opponents. After all, I can't even touch him without getting burned. I find myself wishing I really was a Rizik. Instead, I'm a who-knows-what stuck fighting one off, or my friends and a bunch of innocent children will be in jeopardy.

Speaking of the kids.

"What do you intend to do with all those supernatural children?"

Her face morphs back into that odd elf-fox cross.

"No manners, I see. You haven't even introduced yourself."

I bite back a response that includes the words 'up yours' and think of the children.

"I'm Never, and from the sound of it, your brother may have mentioned me. I'm an intuitive Were, and an occasional pain in his ass. I'm also the being who's about to kick yours."

I pride myself on professionalism.

She's livid at my response, but she just laughs, the sound trilling.

"My brother and I are not on speaking terms. I learn through spying and observation. He's not the only shifty being out there."

"And yet your 'shifting' doesn't look the same as his," I observe. If I can keep her talking, maybe I can learn something that can help us. Barring that, I can at least give the others time.

"Of course not. Riziks are unique in a way you common shifters are not. My brother shifts between boring human features. I shift species."

I yawn, not bothering to mention I've seen her brother transform himself into a bird.

"That's all fine and dandy, but I noticed you haven't introduced yourself, either. I must admit, I'm a very big fan of names. I showed you mine; now it's your turn. After all, wasn't someone here just prattling on about manners?"

It's the first time her anger and superiority have been laced with any real amusement. She may not like me, but my sass is amusing her, at least. She's more like her brother than she wants to admit, and less like her brother than I want. If she'd turn her chaotic, manipulative tendencies toward the side of good, that would be swell. Not that I'm holding my breath.

She's already crossed the line by taking the kids. All that's left is to figure out how to get rid of her. That, and to shelve how thankful this makes me for the Bone Reader until later. No need to open that can of worms at the moment.

"What have your group been calling me?" She tilts her head and morphs into a dragon twice my size.

I just manage to keep myself from taking a step back, suddenly faced with a green-scaled face full of teeth the size of my forearm.

"We've been calling those little traps you left for us mind fields. Is that your title? Mind Manipulator?" It would be fitting, since B.R. goes by the Bone Reader. Maybe they all title themselves based on their skills.

She just scoffs at me.

"Hardly. They call me Shiftress."

She's really proud of this name, and she waits for my reaction.

"Not very original, if you ask me. It's just as obvious as Bone Reader," I snark as she turns herself into a harpy.

She kicks out and snaps her talons a few inches from my face.

"What would you know? You're nothing more than a pet project to him, and you're just as much a contrarian as he is. You can laugh now, but you've aligned yourself with the losing side. No matter what you think of my brother, he is the weakest of us. Even my shifting is better. What does he do? Change his hair? His eyes? I manipulate every body part. What I do is a more advanced and skilled variation of what he does."

That's her opinion, anyway. She's angry, and arrogant. I can use that. Strong emotions mean strong reactions.

"Advanced, you say, and yet your brother never needed a bunch of kids to get his work done. He's able to use magic like nothing I've ever seen, with only his deals."

Her expression sours, and I know I've struck gold.

"You are less intelligent than my brother gives you credit for. Those children aren't for me. Not directly. They're for the warlocks I've recruited. Why align myself with mere shifters or regular supernaturals when I could create something more?"

My intuition follows her triumphant train of emotions straight down the path to their source.

"You *do* have a stripper."

Her eyes gleam as she transforms into a hellhound, fire glowing down her muzzle and four eyes sparking in my direction.

"Perhaps not so dumb after all. Yes, a stripper. But tell me, Were, do you have any idea what we plan to use them for?"

Give them time, Never. Give them time.

I'm almost afraid to go down this path, but if she's rambling on to me, she can't hurt my friends.

"My best guess? Your stripper is even better than mine. They can use the power they drain from others. That's why you needed a lot of supernaturals. You want to have a long-lasting power source for the stripper, and you've realized it would be a lot simpler to corral hundreds of kids than dozens of fully grown magicals who could fight you off."

The hellhound in front of me laughs, deep and low, and smoke comes out of her jaws. I swear I can see coal burning in the back of her throat.

"Is that what you think? All those kids to power one warlock? Oh no. Do give me more credit than that. One stripper is fine, but I'm sure you've seen limitations with your own. Why would I settle for one, when I could use his abilities not only to take the power but distribute it to others? And why pull power that will be used up, when I've found a way to make sure the warlocks keep it permanently?"

Aggie mentioned the importance that location could have

to a spell. Could she really do that? Take the children's magic and pass it out to a chosen few?

She continues to cackle, then shifts into a lioness. She prowls in front of me, her tail flicking my snout.

"Cat got your tongue? Nothing clever to say, hmm?"

Nothing. If she really can do what she suggests, she'll be draining these kids and giving their abilities to a whole slew of warlocks. She'd be creating a warlock-shifter cross. Beings housing the keys of warlocks, and the physical power and endurance of shifters. And who knows what else, based on the species she took.

One piece still isn't making sense.

"Why recruit the vampires? What good will it do you to give them powers?" Is she trying to create her own version of the Founders? I don't dare say it out loud, in case that's something she isn't familiar with.

The feline in front of me sits back and licks one of her front paws.

"The vampires are merely a cleanup crew."

"A cleanup crew?"

"What use would I have for a bunch of essentially human children? Once their powers are gone, they're of no value."

Her cold and calculating feelings as she talks through her plan hit my intuition like a punch to the gut. I don't want to accept what she means. My stomach churns, sickened. I gulp down air to settle it, and she purrs.

"You didn't think I'd return them, did you? You can't really be that naive."

She shakes her head at me, laughing.

Vampires. Bloodsuckers. Leeches. Draining all the blood out of …

My own blood thunders in my veins; a pounding pulse hammers in my ears.

I've thrown myself onto the Rizik before my mind has even caught up to my instincts. I'm scratching and snarling, doing my damnedest to puncture all four eyes as she morphs back into a hellhound and snaps fiery fangs at my throat.

All around us, the air begins to crackle.

20

TURN UP THE HEAT

The crackling grows louder as Shiftress activates a damned mind-manipulation net. Field. Dome.

Damn. Should've made her tell me what she calls them before pissing her off.

I'm staring into a throat full of smoking coal as she snaps at my face again and flames lick the fur on my cheeks.

I don't let it show on my face just how close she's gotten. If she's really even there. Now that she's using her mind manipulation, everything is on the table. For all I know, she could be barreling into the mountain after the others.

No.

Wait.

She couldn't.

Use your intuition, Never! Focus, dammit!

Shiftress's emotions are real enough. This Rizik hates me. To be more specific, since I can be, she hates my connection with her brother. Boy oh boy, does she hate his guts. If I were a therapeutic Were, I'd try to sit her down on a couch and ask her why that is.

Instead, I'd like to pummel her into the dirt until she can't shift anymore.

She turns herself into a lightning bird and soars above me, forcing me to dodge lightning strikes as she rains them down.

At least I think that's what she's doing. For all I know, she's standing in front of me, laughing at my confusion.

Nope. No humor.

I just keep reminding myself to follow the emotions. That's what will tell me the truth of her actions, and where she's at.

I wish I knew what she looked like when she wasn't shifting. That would be something else to watch for as well, if her appearance changed to something I could know was fake. It might help if I knew what the Bone Reader looked like in default mode, but he's never thought to share that.

I jump as Shiftress turns back into a nagi and flicks her massive snake tail at me. She starts to laugh, her voice hoarse like she's spent the last few centuries with a chronic smoker's cough. I watch her snap her tail at me, but when I twist away, fangs sink into my arm.

I'm woozy before I hit the ground. Snake venom. Based on her feelings of triumph and elation, I'd say the injury is real.

This won't do at all. I need to be able to see her. The real her. Otherwise, how do I get close enough to strike? This isn't like before, when I could drag the others out of the net and wait for things to return to normal. The magic is wherever she is; there's no running away. I need to beat her here, at her own game.

I spend the next several minutes trying to fight something that is half real and half illusion. After a few more shifts, I notice a pattern. She always turns into something with fangs or claws when I'm getting close, and then the actual attack comes from the opposite side of where I'm watching.

I follow the feeling of superiority oozing off of her, and she transforms into a griffin. I duck like I'm dodging her beak, but instead throw myself to the side as talons slice through the ground where I was standing.

Her shriek, and the accompanying feelings of anger and disappointment, confirm my theory. While she's still distracted, I fling myself back toward the griffin talons, and my claws close around feathers and fur.

I'm not waiting for a second chance.

Her shock lets me know I've made a real hit, so I sink my claws into her. I have no idea whether I've got her by an actual leg, or her neck, but I don't care. I clamp down and squeeze, digging my claws in as deep as they'll go.

She recovers from her shock, and when she does my skin begins to burn.

"All hells!" I leap back, waving my arm in front of me. Her skin burns like fire. Someone could tell me I'd just dunked my hand in molten lava and I'd believe them. There's a sickening smell of burnt flesh and singed fur, and with my expedited healing it's already blistering. If my eyes are to be believed.

Her emotions seal the deal for me: triumphant, and with that sick and twisted joy some people get from inflicting pain. It's got a specific feel to it, like sleet so sharp it slices into your skin.

I'm seriously injured, but I can't ruin this opportunity. Before she can twist away, I sink my claws back into her. She shifts forms, but I keep myself attached. If I lose her now, it'll be hard to find her again. Particularly with melting paw pads on my hands. I wrench feathers out of the wings she's now wearing.

"Think you're so clever, don't you?" she spits at me, now in harpy form. She's beginning to worry. Not enough for me to feel confident I can win, but enough to tell me I really got her.

"As a matter of fact, I do find myself rather clever. I've got good on-your-toes thinking skills. I also happen to think you're an arrogant piece of work and an absolute bucket."

Going to have to thank Jackal if I make it through this. He was right. Any noun can be an insult. This leaves so many possibilities open to me.

My smarm doesn't have quite the same zing without Jackal's accent, but I'll get the hang of it with practice. I always do when it comes to insults and finding a way under people's skin.

Shiftress morphs into some sort of bird shifter I've never seen in real life, but she's like a great owl. As massive as Todd's bear form. I scramble up her leg, always leaving at least one claw on her, even as she screeches and tries to shake me off. My blisters are burst and oozing as my skin is burned over and over, but I keep going.

Under my claws, she morphs again.

She's a drake, and I roll until her belly is exposed and start to sink my teeth in. She's a vampire, and I try to jab out one of her red eyes. She's a tiger, and I yank at her ears.

Shiftress rolls through another half-dozen forms, and I manage to hold on.

The Bone Reader's skin is like dry ice, but hers is like a wildfire I can't escape. Staying attached to her is costing me dearly. I'm yowling, no longer capable of putting together a snappy comeback. I'm pretty sure I can see bone in a few of my fingers, and I swallow down some sick and resolve not to look again.

I snap at her, snagging onto what might be an ear as she turns back into a fox.

My head is pounding; my brain trying desperately to alert me to the emergency that is my body. The pain is immense. Her touch is burning me alive, slowly. I get in a few more hits, but it's not going to matter. I'll be dead before I land any sort of killing blow. If it's even possible. I've never killed a Rizik.

She shoves me, and I lose my grip and go rolling in the dirt.

Come on, Never. You can't quit. You do, and all your friends die like this. And those kids. Remember what's waiting for them? She's not going to send them home with a lollipop. You need to get it together. Right. Now.

I allow myself one more self-pitying whimper, then push up from where I've fallen on the ground. Thank the moon I've kept my tail wrapped around hers, so our connection isn't broken. My padded palms protest. They're so burnt that bits of grass are embedding themselves into the wounds.

I ignore it.

For my family. For the kids.

Another blow hits my side, and fur is singed away. Boy, will some of the others get a kick out of this if I survive. Feral and Calder have both made fun of me for burning things down. Bet they didn't think I'd end up on the receiving end.

She lands a blow in my stomach, and I can't breathe. I nearly go down again.

For my family. For the kids.

I land a few more hits, and I'm satisfied when I feel pain. Hers. The fact that she's not immune to it is the only thing keeping me going.

There's got to be a way to beat her.

The Bone Reader let me come here, and he needs me. Desperately. Enough to risk our friendship over it. Enough to spend years and years manipulating it. He wouldn't have given us that information about the warlock if he thought I was just coming to die.

And then he reminded me of that whole "Riziks can't interfere with other Rizik deals" thing. That has to mean something. I've already figured out I don't need the deals to survive, and I'm certainly interfering.

I'm not a Rizik. I guessed it before, but now I'm certain.

That just leaves one question.

What am I?

Shiftress and I continue to go round and round. I'm just

lucky she's someone who likes to play with her food. Otherwise I'd be toast.

Well, in fairness, I am getting toasted.

Yeah, I know, it's not a great joke. I'm doing my best here.

B.R. was so certain you were a Rizik when you came back from the Underworld. You felt it. That means he had to change his mind at some point. When was it? What made him think his plan had failed? And why isn't he more disappointed, after how much he's risked?

He'd be devastated. Unless.

Unless whatever I am now is just as strong as a Rizik.

And if I'm as strong as a Rizik, I can beat a Rizik.

I growl, launching myself at Shiftress again and ignoring the pain that would be blinding otherwise. She rolls us, and my claws scramble to hang on as she morphs into a bear.

She growls and shoves me so hard I go flying off of her and land with a thud against one of the gravestones.

I stand, waving my ruined hands as I try to find her again.

"Do you know, I think I'll let you stumble about for a bit. It's like blinding someone and watching them walk themselves right off a cliff. Actually, that sounds fun. Maybe I should do that."

I spot her lounging against a headstone, as a mermaid. She taps one finger against a cheek as she considers. Her emotions are coming from that direction, so I'm at least looking in the correct spot.

"What do you say? Should I blind you and see what happens then? Or maybe ... maybe I could pay your mate a visit. I know what he is, of course. I told you I have my own ways of gaining information. He's an empath. Very, very interesting. A challenge worthy of my talent. I'm certain I could find a way to kill him, but I might have to give it many, many tries."

The rage I feel burns hotter than any of her wounds.

"You won't lay a finger on him, you *bitch*. You'll never get within striking distance of any of them again."

With all my cursing, I really do reserve that particular word for only the most dire of occasions. This happens to be one.

She cackles in that same hoarse voice. She sounds less like she's laughing and more like she's dying.

Dying!

That's it!

The Bone Reader showed up after I tried to save Danger's life, after her zombie bites. I attempted to use my fledgling Rizik powers and a deal to prevent her death, but it didn't work. She died anyway.

Well, technically she became a goddess, but that's really the same thi—

A goddess.

The Bone Reader was alarmed when it happened. And why should he be? He'd explained it away as them being mates. If he knew the reason, what made it frightening? Just the fact that there was another new god? That can't be right, because he had a hand in Damien's fate in the first place. He's tight friends with the Fates themselves.

His reaction was for me. Thinking back, I'm certain of it.

It's too huge to be believed, but that has to be it. When I play back through the Bone Reader's actions and emotions from my Underworld exit until now, that's definitely the moment things changed. Plus, the Fates had said they'd be visiting to see which of them had won their bet with B.R. on what I became. They never showed. Which would make sense if they both lost. If I'm something totally different and they already had their answer.

Shiftress turns herself into a banshee and screams. I clutch at my ears.

She'll kill Nahum and every one of my friends for fun. This has to work.

By all the moons and gods out there, if I'm supposed to kill her, you'd all better help me.

I have no idea how to do what I'm attempting, but I've got to try.

When I was trying to save Danger I was desperate, and focused. I channeled all my energy into the one goal of trying to help her.

I do the same thing now in reverse.

All my energy, all my focus, all my desire, goes into wanting Shiftress dead. Needing her gone. Knowing I have to find a way to end her.

She has to die.

The silence is deafening.

The banshee scream stops.

And the crackling does, too. It's just ... gone.

I spot movement to my left and spin as the illusions fall.

Sadly, I really am burnt crispier than bacon. And even sadder, she can still shift. She makes herself into a hag, with long, darkened nails and a gap-toothed grin. Her hair is blue and white, twisted and tangled all the way to her knees.

"However you did that, it won't matter. You're still no match for me."

Lying. She's lying. She's terrified. She's never had anyone break her mind field before. I can do this.

She needs to be dead. She needs to be gone. She can't continue to threaten everyone.

All my thoughts and emotions are centered on my goal.

I run at her again, even though my burnt feet are begging me not to. She lifts her hands, ready to burn my face right off.

I need a way to beat her.

I'm mere steps away, focusing and chanting in my mind, when I hear something pop overhead, and then the sound of something whistling through the sky as it falls. Instinct tells me to put a hand out and catch it. My ruined fist wraps around something slender and wooden.

Her eyes go wide, and she puts her hands up to shield her face.

"No. You can't be a—"

Her fear is enough for me.

I swing whatever in my hands without thinking—and slice her clean in half.

Her body has disintegrated before it hits the ground. Not even dust. Just nothing. Emptiness where a powerful Rizik once stood.

As soon as she's gone, the headache eases and my burns begin to heal.

I stare down at my hands to see what object I've managed to summon to save myself. It will be the clue to unlocking what the Bone Reader has made me into.

When I look, I see a scythe.

21

WATCH YOUR BUTT

I slam the bottom of the scythe into the ground, and lean against it for support. My breath comes in huffs as my blistered and melted skin puts itself back together. Once fur covers my arms again, I'm able to take deep breaths.

I think I might even have enough energy for a victory dance.

I let out a whoop, pumping one fist in the air.

"Yeah, baby! Did you see that? I smoked her ass! I'm amazing. I'm a badass. I'm invincible. I'm ... going to pass out."

Maybe not as much energy as I thought.

The scythe slides from my hands and I tilt dangerously to the side, my fur evaporating as I shift back to skin.

Blackness dances at the edge of my vision, and when I feel strong but gentle arms catch me instead of a hard and unforgiving ground, I begin to wonder if I'm hallucinating again.

Nahum stares down at me. I'm trying hard to keep my eye open, but it's not cooperating.

"Very impressive. A badass indeed. Although I think you might have overdone it," he warns me. "Stay still for a moment."

"You heard all that?"

He quirks his head to the side and snorts at me.

"You seriously thought we'd run down into that mausoleum and not even have someone wait to see what happened to you? There are several paths inside the mountain. The others are exploring the options and reporting back. I stayed at the entrance to defend it, in case anyone else followed us in. And, of course, to make sure my mate was okay. You had me worried. I was just about to step in, no matter what you said, when you killed her. How did you manage it? I cracked the door open and saw her disintegrating, but that's all I could see. I rushed over as soon as I saw you tilting."

Anxiety washes over me, a dose of adrenaline giving me enough energy to scramble for my new weapon.

"The. Scythe."

He leans down to grab it, and his hand passes straight through.

"More mind games?" He leans over my neck protectively, snarling at an unseen threat.

I place a hand on his scales, attempting to calm him.

"No. The scythe is real. The mind manipulator is gone. I'm thinking, maybe only I can hold it?"

He maneuvers so I can reach the handle. I pull it toward myself and lay it across my chest. As I do, it disappears.

"Did you see that?"

Maybe my mind is playing tricks on both of us after all.

He nods, but he's not happy.

"I saw it. Never, what are you?"

His emotions are telling me he might already know, and he's not sure he likes it.

"Nahum, wha—"

"We did it! We found the path to the kids!"

Hugh and Feral skid to a stop next to us. Looking behind

them, I can see Jackal guarding the mausoleum doors. There are no kids, no Nadia, no Todd, and no witchling.

"Aggie and Nadia?"

Hugh helps Nahum get me to my feet, and Feral rushes to reassure me.

"Todd is with them. The mind manipulator must have done something to the mausoleum. We kept going in circles, but then something broke and we realized there were only two actual tunnels. We figured that meant either you'd won, or something terrible had happened that took the attention away from us. Aggie, Todd, and Nadia headed down one of the tunnels."

"Hell's bells! And the rest of you thought it took this many people to carry my sorry butt inside? We need to help!"

Hugh scowls.

"We started going down the other, then we heard Nahum's roar and the door scraping back open. We thought you might need us."

I struggle to my feet, limping my way to the doors as my body tries to finish repairing itself. I shove off help, and as the three males follow me, Nahum whispers to them. I hit the doors, but instead of greeting me, Jackal dodges around me to go chat with the others.

I whip around when I feel the quick change in emotions.

They're all four looking at me like I've grown a second, or even a third, head. Hugh is oozing awe and reverence in my direction that make me want to squirm or disappear. I've never been the recipient of this emotion. The closest I've gotten was when I freed the Isle and the villagers named me *Vabastaja*, a Liberator. But my friends have always kept me grounded.

Feral is in utter disbelief. His flabber is fully gasted. His shock higher than someone struck by lightning. His surprise ...

Well, you get the idea.

"Lady Vicious." Uh-oh. Hugh hasn't called me recently. "Do you know what a Reaper is?"

If not, I can tell he's dying to tell me, but since our friends could be *actually* dying ...

"Can someone provide the explanation on the move?"

He nods.

The five of us walk into the dark. I breathe a sigh of relief when the doors don't slam shut in our wake. My eye adjusts, and I can see they were right. Two tunnels. Only two. And unless there's an exit at the end of them, only one way out.

I didn't come this far to muck things up now.

"Which one did the others take?"

Feral steps forward.

"They went down the right tunnel. Nadia planned to use her intuition to watch for any other mind fields. Aggie planned to strip everything in the vicinity if she felt one."

"Hugh. Follow them down the right tunnel and make sure they're okay. We shouldn't have to worry about any more mind fields."

But we still have to worry about a stripping warlock, the others waiting to receive powers, a bunch of scared children, and a vampire cleanup crew.

Hugh heads down the right tunnel after the others.

"Nahum, can you stay at the entrance and make sure no one tries to follow us in? Those vamps surprised us in the woods before. Some could still be hiding out. If any of them try to follow us in, throw them in a nightmare."

My heart wants the dragon with me, but the doors to the mausoleum might be the only way out, and he stands the best chance at protecting them.

The Founder offers me an arm. I hook my hand through his elbow. Jackal takes my other side as we head down the left tunnel.

Hugh sped down his side, but our group is moving slower,

between my exhaustion and Jackal's insistence that we check every square inch.

"You never know. Even without the mind fields, there could still be obstacles."

When he trips something on the wall behind us that sends a barbed and glowing net falling from the ceiling, I'm forced to admit he's right. We just manage to dodge it.

Feral is itching for action at my side, but I can tell it has nothing to do with the kids.

"You know what a Reaper is too, don't you?"

"I do. Hugh wants to be the one to tell you, but—"

"You think I should know now?" I guess, not that it takes much guessing with intuition.

Feral sighs. I stumble over a rock, of all things, and he adjusts his grip. My strength is returning little by little. It doesn't matter. When we reach the kids I'll throw myself into a fight by sheer willpower if necessary. No way I'm letting the others handle the warlocks and vamps alone. Except the stripper. Aggie can have him if she wants him. I feel like she'll take his crimes personally.

"You know, I'm as much a fan of knowledge as Hugh," Feral reminds me.

"You do both like to surround yourself with old and magical things." I think of Hugh's many books, and Nahum's. Feral's somson orbs, which I can't fault him for, since I have my own set.

"In this case it's not just knowledge I've collected secondhand. You'll recall all of us Founders are ... aged. I can remember when the last Reapers were around in person. There haven't been any for thousands of years. No one knows exactly what happened, but I have my guesses. When the Bone Reader ran CoED with me, we discussed it at some length, and he told me the gods had grown jealous and killed them all off. I'm inclined to believe him."

"The gods ... killed?"

I can't manage much more than that. Put me up against a flesh-and-blood opponent any day. Even a Rizik, which I wouldn't have said until recently.

But a god?

Damien's the only one I can picture mustering up the courage to fight, and it's with all the reluctance in the world that I admit I can't beat him. Not now.

Shit. Am I going to have to kill a god to avoid my own murder? Because I've got to say I'm getting really sick of people holding a personal grudge against me.

"They killed them because they were threatened," Feral continues at my side. Behind us, Jackal yips as he steps on a rock that sinks into the ground and releases spears from the right side of the tunnel. We clamber out of the way. One slices Jackal's front paw, but it's just a glancing wound. He licks at it and limps after us while it heals.

"If the gods were threatened by Reapers, does that mean that, as a Reaper, I have the ability to kill them?"

Feral, frustratingly, shrugs.

"And the scythe?"

He shrugs again.

"I know they carry them, but not much more than that. I can't tell you how to make it reappear. I'd assumed Reapers just carried them around at all times. I've only seen a Reaper in action a couple times. All I took away from those instances was that the scythe should be avoided at all costs by your opponents. The ones I saw were graceful death personified. They always hit their target."

That could certainly come in handy, if I still had the scythe.

I squeeze my eyes shut and clench my fists, trying to bring it back.

"What *are* you doing? You look constipated." Jackal laughs.

That's just fabulous. I've got a finicky scythe.

Maybe when we get home, Gladys could help me. The Sewing Circle witch is a conjurer. She stores all sorts of stuff in a pocket universe. My scythe could stay somewhere like that?

At the moment, though, I've got no idea where it's gone or how to bring it back.

I've never been a weapons gal. I was always more into fangs and claws than swords and shields. But after witnessing the scythe take down a Rizik that could burn flesh and melt minds?

I'm a believer, baby. Hand me the pointy piece of metal on a stick and step back.

I stop for a moment, concentrating again. All my muscles tense, and my head starts shaking as I contract and flex, trying to force the scythe back into existence.

"Are you sure you're okay? Now you look like you're about to explode." Feral grabs onto my arms, giving me a gentle shake.

"No. I'm good. Just trying to lay my hands on that scythe again."

"You got it while you were trying to defeat the Rizik. Maybe it comes to you in battle?" Feral guesses, and I take a few tentative steps forward on my own.

Everything going well? Nahum calls into my mind.

Nothing so far. I'm healing up. What about your end?

No one so far, but I promise nothing is getting through me.

I'm still feeling wiped out, but it's more like I've just finished an especially grueling workout and less like I've been run over by a train and then tossed down a hill into a garbage heap.

One of us sets off another trap, and blue smoke shoots from the ceiling of the tunnel.

"Drop and crawl!" Jackal yells.

He tucks down to the ground as much as he can and we follow suit. By the time we've army-crawled past the smoke, we've managed to miss the worst of it.

"Well, that went better than expected!" I stand, wiping my arms off.

"Just don't look at your butt," Jackal warns. "It's not pretty."

I round on him.

"Excuse me? How dare you insult my—"

Feral clears his throat and I twist.

Ah.

My backside is covered in angry red welts. I hadn't even noticed. After my fight with the Rizik, these smaller injuries aren't even registering.

"Good looking out," I say to the hyena.

He lowers his chin.

"No problem. I want all of us in fighting shape when we reach the kids. I'm not letting them hurt Charlotte, and I know I'm going to need help."

He's learned that "how to work as a team" lesson a lot quicker than I did.

A scream echoes down the tunnel from up ahead.

"Is that Aggie?" I lunge forward.

More screams follow, including a chorus of thin, high voices.

"The kids!"

The three of us forget the traps and begin to run.

22

NIGHT AT THE THEATER

The damned scythe refuses to make an appearance as we rush down the passageway. There must be hundreds of supernaturals entombed here. Living out their lives in the mountain, hiding away from pesky humans, and remaining hidden even in death. I can only imagine what their spirits would think of thru-hikers and extreme adventure enthusiasts disturbing the area, let alone our intrusion.

"No!" Aggie is yelling again. The end of this section of dead people curves, and ahead of us a light flares. The three of us spill out of the tunnel and into a dome of some sort under the hills. Not a mind-manipulation one, thank the moon. I've had all of that I care to ever have. It's a relief to see actual horror and not some illusion.

As we enter at floor level, or the dirt which passes for a floor here, I see stone benches rising on every side, encircling us. The circle that makes up this base level where we're standing has a few stone workbenches or tables, and in the center a stone slab that is sized to fit at least an adult shifter.

"It's an operating theater."

I jump a foot in the air as Feral identifies where we're standing.

I'd like to ask more, but the scene in front of us demands our attention. All around the stone seats of the theater are children. Dozens and dozens of them, and dozens more. They're crammed into the space. Some are sitting obediently, and some are running in the aisles and headed in our direction via a series of stone steps. There are warlocks chasing after the loose kids.

On that large table in the center of the room are two children. Jackal rips a strap off the table that held one of their hands to the blasted thing. Behind the slab is Aggie, although I've got no idea how she got down here if she took the other tunnel. Based on the insults she's hurling at the warlock across from her, I'm guessing we've found the other stripper.

He's hurling the insults right back, and the two of them are tossing barbs and shots, each ducking the other.

A stray vampire gets hit by Shiftress's stripper and goes down.

"Dammit Greg, watch your aim!" yells one of the other warlocks.

Greg? Seriously? That's got to be the lamest name for a super-villain I've seen in a while.

"Let him have it, Aggie!" I scream at her.

I leap backward when Nadia rushes up to me, ushering a few small kids toward the exit.

"*Apúrese, vamos*! Hurry kids, hurry!"

"I thought you all were in the other tunnel!" I yell at her as she whizzes past.

She stops briefly, turning to me and grabbing my arms. Horror and revulsion roll off her, making me nauseated. The motive follows soon after.

"It's worse than we thought." Her words echo what my intuition has already picked up. "They've got more kids than we realized. This is one of two theaters. Each of the main passages leads to one, and the two theaters connect to each other. When we got to the other theater, the stripper ran and Aggie chased him down. Hugh and I heard Aggie yelling, we ran over here. She'll need help, but—"

I swallow down the expletives I'd like to yell.

Calm, Never. For the kids. Calm.

"But we have to get the kids out first and make sure no one can follow them out. We're on it. You take this group back down the tunnel we came through. I think we've cleared it of any traps. When you get to the doors, swap places with Nahum. He's been guarding our backs. Send him down here to help out with this mess, but you wait with the kids outside."

"The Rizik?"

"I took her out, but we can't be certain there's not something else lurking in the woods."

They've already surprised us with the vampires and the extra warlocks. I'm not letting them get the jump on us again.

Her defensiveness rises up, and she circles her arms around the kids in a protective gesture, shuffling them to the tunnel.

Todd roars, and I turn to see him coldcock a vampire who's just torn out a chunk of his shoulder. He hasn't put on his fur yet. He's trying to talk to some of the kids.

"We need help in the other theater! There were too many vampires blocking the exit to get out that way!" he yells.

"They brought the vampires into the theater," Feral whispers.

A stripper to drain the powers. Warlocks to wield them. And greedy, gluttonous vampires to take care of the powerless, human children that would have been left behind. This room is the end game. It was going to be their last stop.

I speak through clenched teeth that are growing pointed once more as fur climbs up my back.

I tip my head back up with a howl, and once I have my

crew's attention, I yell loud enough for them and our enemies to hear.

"Every child gets out. No one else leaves alive."

When I feel their agreement wash over my intuition, it's like a soothing balm.

The Magikai can do what they want when they're the ones who catch the bad guys, but today, we're the ones here. We'll do this our way.

"We'll take the other operating theater," Hugh volunteers, grabbing Feral by the arm.

"Hugh. Kids out first, then let the Founder do his thing," I instruct.

"Yes, Lady *Vicious*." He emphasizes the last word, saying it more like agreement on how we're going to handle these villains than the name they've given me. Feral's eyes are already glowing.

"Don't worry. I'll keep Hyde in check until the kids are clear. That's a promise," he reassures me as the two go through a smaller tunnel that must connect the two theaters.

The whole round of conversations has taken under a minute, but it's all the delay I can handle.

"Stay still, you brats!" A warlock in the stands throws his arms out, and the kids nearest him slam into an invisible barrier as they try to run in our direction.

My fur is on fully now, and I leap for the lowest row of stone seats, encased behind a metal banister. It creaks as my claws close over it, pulling a rusty edge out of the stone. The warlock who's been yelling at the children turns to look at me and throws out one of his arms in my direction, but he's too slow and I'm too infuriated.

I yank him away from the kids and fling him down onto the theater floor.

"Make sure he doesn't come back up," I call over my shoulder.

Jackal is only too happy to comply.

"Lottie! Do you see Lottie?" he yells when he's done. His niece Charlotte. Right.

"Is anyone here a hyena?" I ask the children.

A few of the kids shrink back. I know I must be a sight. A massive, silver-furred Were with one eye staring down at them, saliva dripping from my fangs and presenting nothing but claws to them. I'm no expert on looking less threatening in this form. I save that for my skin, and I'm not willing to put it on right now.

All the better to protect you, and all that.

None of them answer, but a few of the braver kids inch toward me. A bear cub stumbles up to me, snuffling and grunting. I reach a hand down tentatively and give his head a pat. He snuggles up to my leg. I wonder if he's one of Rex's. Following his lead, several of the other kids crowd around me. Soon I've got a cluster of tinier than normal green and gold pixies squeaking and flitting around one of my arms. A gnome is crawling up my left arm, and some supernatural I can't even identify with vines sprouting from her arms toddles forward, holding a tiny leopard shifter. One of Lynx's triplets.

My heart hammers in my chest as Little Miss Vines for Hands passes off the infant feline, and I hold him gently in the crook of my right arm.

"It's all right now. You're with me. Auntie Never's got you."

When Lynx had jokingly suggested the title to me, I'd laughed myself out of my chair.

Now, though?

I shuffle a good fifteen kids, counting the whole cluster of pixies as one since they're moving too fast to grab a head count, to the theater floor and toward the entrance of the theater.

"Follow this hall to—"

A scream echoes from farther down the tunnel.

Nadia!

I charge forward, moving as fast as the kids shuffling around my feet will allow. A dragon swoops into the crowd, the kids scattering as Nahum lands.

Let me. It's harder for me to fight in here anyway. Too tight to fly comfortably. I'll handle whatever is threatening Nadia and the kids outside.

You can throw them into nightmares if you need. We'll come take care of them later.

The dragon just flashes his teeth.

I see no need for nightmares. No reason to give these individuals any more time on this side of the Underworld.

Remind me later, when we've saved all these kids from mortal peril, how attractive I found you in this moment.

He just flashes his teeth again, more of a smile this time, and sheds his scales. I hand Lynx's child to him.

I'll protect the children with my life.

Given he can't die, that's an awfully good thing.

"Follow the dragon out, kids. He and another Were will keep you safe. We'll get you all back to your families and sleuths and packs and whatever you may have."

Some are still hesitant, but the bear who ran up to me, along with a few of the others, lead the way. One by one, all the kids follow my mate.

I head back into the fray, checking in after taking out a couple more vamps.

All good?

I've got it handled, Nahum assures me from his end. He's feeling accomplished, and violent. I'll leave him to it.

Todd rushes past me, ushering another group out, including a few of the missing bear cubs.

"Have you seen Lynx's daughter?" I ask.

"Nothing yet. Hopefully Feral and Hugh have her."

Todd's holding back, refusing to say what we both know. We're counting on this being all the kids. But what if we missed something? What if all the kids didn't make it? What if we got here too late?

I take all my fear at the idea and channel it at a line of vamps who are chasing Todd and the kids down. I've grown fond of my own little bloodsuckers, but these leeches aren't from my coven.

I let out a roar worthy of a dragon.

One by one, I remove their heads.

Something searing and burning slams into my side. I look down to see a gaping hole that's quickly filling with crimson, and then back up to a grinning warlock preparing to lob another projectile at me. Whatever is floating over his hand looks more like a small meteorite than a regular fireball. It's got substance, and I can vouch for it packing a punch.

He's so satisfied already, convinced I'm going down.

I force my mouth into a snarl against the pain, revealing all my bright, shiny teeth.

"Wrong move," I warn him as I leap down from my side of the seats, rush across the theater floor and make my way to him.

I ignore the dust and debris sticking to the open wound in my side. I duck and dodge the rain of meteors until I grab onto the banister on his side and one grazes my hand. There goes that side of my palm. I swing myself over the banister and kick the warlock square in the chest. I'll admit to being fully satisfied when I hear his sternum crack.

"It's a shame warlocks are so fragile," I taunt as I stalk toward where he's fallen. "This will go too quick for it to be any fun." He throws a few more of the meteors, and one singes some fur on my ear.

It's not enough to save him.

"Never!" Jackal yells. He's sprinting toward some small hole that's opened in the back of the room. "He's chasing Aggie, and he's got my niece!"

I throw my head back with a groan.

"Shit! Why is there always a hidden exit?"

Todd gets the last of the kids out of this theater and to the hall. He turns, blocking vampires from going after the children. With one paw, he lifts three of them off their feet and sends them sailing across the room. The determined little fiends are back on their feet in moments.

When it comes to vampires, you really need to go the route of burning them to ash, or lopping off heads. Just trust me on this one.

After a hurried glance around the theater, I count two more warlocks left, not counting Greg the stripper.

I take out the vampires Todd threw across the theater, which leaves only three more, plus the warlocks. Todd and I can easily handle five supernaturals.

Four for me, and one for Todd.

Kidding. Kidding. I know the bear can fight.

He takes the head off one of the remaining vamps before I even reach him.

Four to go.

One of the warlocks starts waving his hands around. At first nothing happens; then one of the stone benches where the kids were sitting rips and comes sailing in our direction.

"Duck, Todd!" He barely rolls out of the way before it slams into the side of the tunnel entrance and cracks down the middle. The tombs shake, and debris rains down from the ceiling.

"Are you trying to bury us all alive, you idiot!" I snarl, throwing myself on top of the warlock, slamming his head into one of the benches.

The warlock brings his hands up, each holding a chunk of stone, and tries to hit me on either side of my head. I twist, but one of them connects. It's enough to make me dizzy. I'd bet dollars to donuts I was just given a concussion.

"Enough," I slur as the room spins. My aim isn't pretty, but I slam one claw through his chest.

Another pro tip: rip out someone's beating heart, and that takes care of the problem. At least for beings like warlocks.

Todd's finished off another one of the vampires, and he's fighting a warlock who is sending jets of green light shooting at him. I couldn't even begin to guess what they do. When they hit him or the air around him, small green clouds float in the air for a few moments.

"Don't breathe it!" Todd warns through clenched teeth. He's swaying on his feet.

The remaining vampire is creeping around behind him. But one threat at a time. I dive onto my stomach as the warlock turns around and throws what must be poisoned air at me. Chrys's family would have a field day with this. Poison for a warlock or witch on the go! Shame we can't keep this one for study. When Todd roars and slashes at the warlock, he turns his attention back to the bear. It gives me the perfect opportunity to slice my claws across his back. The warlock falls to his knees, and within moments, we've gone from one warlock to zero.

Todd snarls, slamming his back against the fallen stone bench at the entryway. An injured vampire hisses and crawls away from the angered bear. Todd's bleeding, but he'll make it.

I dispatch the last vampire as more rocks fall from the ceiling, blocking off our original exit plan.

Todd starts toward the second theater, but I haul him back the other way.

"Aggie and Jackal need us. That stupid stripper Greg still has at least one kid."

Todd snorts, following me to the smaller door.

There's another exit. We're going after the stripper, I inform Nahum.

We've got it handled out here. Hugh says their last group of kids is out, and Feral is finishing off any remaining threats in the second theater.

And Lynx's daughter?

We have her. Hugh and Feral found her.

Relief floods through me, and the bear, when I inform him of the news. I knew my confidence in my family wasn't misplaced.

I'm thinking we'll come out in the hills somewhere. At least that's where I would put the exit for a secret escape tunnel, I tell him as Todd and I run through the dark.

As soon as the kids are calmed down I'll fly over and try to spot you, the dragon promises.

Assured that Nahum's not about to come rushing through a collapsing tunnel for me, I turn my attention to our escape route.

It leads down another passage, so narrow that we both have to put our skin on to fit through it.

As anticipated, it leads directly to the outside. We're on a flat bit of open land with just a smattering of trees. High enough that some snow is clinging to the grass.

We both throw our fur on as soon as we see what's waiting.

Jackal is snarling, guarding the witchling, who has collapsed under one of the few trees. Cowering behind the fallen witch is a tiny hyena.

Greg, whose lackluster name I still can't believe, takes aim at Jackal.

Todd is almost shifted when Greg twists and throws his arm in our direction. The bear's fur falls away and he collapses onto the dirt, unconscious.

23

ANYTHING FOR A FRIEND

"Todd!" I run for the bear before the stripper can reach him and inflict any more damage.

When Greg gets close, he raises his arm again. I throw myself over Todd's injured body and snarl, mentally reaching for my scythe. I can just feel the edges of it when a striped blur hits the warlock.

With my attention distracted, the scythe disappears. Jackal sinks his teeth into the warlock's arm, and the stripper screams. Having your arm savaged by a hyena can't be any fun at all.

For Greg, anyway.

As for me? I'm truly enjoying this moment.

"Todd, wake up!" I shake the shifter by the shoulders, and when that doesn't work, I slap him across the cheek. He groans.

Thank the moon.

It's probably not the best thing for a shifter who's taking only shallow breaths, but I hug him close to me.

"My bear." He shudders, not finishing the statement.

Gone. Gone, and I don't know if there's any way to get it back. Not unless Aggie wakes up and can pull it back out? The witchling has pulled magic from things before, but she's never directed them anywhere. She's certainly never returned magic.

I'm not familiar enough with Greg to know how his key works. It's possible that if I slice the warlock in half, any stolen magic is gone for good. This whole mission with the kids has involved me utilizing a lot more caution than normal. I'll have to continue that trend if I want a chance at retrieving Todd's second soul.

"I'll be right back," I promise the shifter as I lay him gently in the dirt and move to the witchling. The tiny hyena, Charlotte, starts yipping at me and baring her teeth.

"It's okay! I'm a friend. I promise. I'm here with your uncle."

She yips a few more times. I'm guessing she hasn't mastered speaking in her fur. She does back down, though, so that's one good thing. The small hyena is terrified, but she was trying to defend Aggie. I like her already.

I get Aggie leaned up against the tree. She opens her eyes, and her head moves sluggishly back and forth, following the fight between Jackal and the warlock.

"Aggie!" I snap my fingers in front of her face. It takes her a few beats to meet my eye. "Focus up, witchling! We need you. That shithead took Todd's other soul. Look, I know you're hurting. I know you're tired and you're worried you can't win, but I believe in you. I think you can do this, and more than that, I *need* you to do this. Please, Aggie."

She mumbles something incoherent as her head lolls forward. All I catch is "Never" and "better than me."

I scoff.

"Horseshit. And I know you can hear me. Horse. Stomping. Shit. You listen up, witch. That two-bit, back-alley magician couldn't beat you in his wildest dreams."

She focuses on me but starts to cry. Behind us, Jackal is whooping and yipping as he dodges the warlock. A stray bolt of power comes our way and I dive, shoving Aggie and Charlotte under me before repositioning us on the other side of the tree and out of the line of fire.

Aggie's hand curls in my fur and she tugs me closer.

"Greg took all those kids. He was working with a Rizik. A being that powerful thought he was a worthy ally. You're the only other person a Rizik has cared about like that. Greg convinced those other warlocks and vampires to listen to him. I've never done that. I don't command armies. No one listens to me." A tear trails down her cheek.

My heart squeezes painfully as I'm torn on what to do. With a deep sigh, knowing what this could do to the relationship with the sister I never had, I go for tough love.

"Agatha ... you know what, I actually don't know your last name, but you can borrow mine since we're related anyway ... Agatha Vicious!" And *I'll* borrow a name the vamps gave me. When I became Never I kept it a one-word title. "Agatha Vicious, you listen to me and you listen good. If you want to have an emotional breakdown when we get home, you are more than welcome to it. Moon knows, you're entitled. You've already sacrificed so much for us, and I know you've been hurt more than you ever should have been. As soon as this is done, you can hole up in one of the vampsion rooms or my Sacramento house and cry and eat chocolate all you want. I'll even ship in your favorite candies from Canada. And I'll tell you all the ways you *do* matter and why we all *do* listen and care about what you have to say."

She sniffles and reaches up like she's going to hug me.

"But,"—I hold out an arm—"not right now. Right now, Todd is suffering. He's still alive, but he's feeling all the pain of being ripped in half. Now I believe, because I have to, that his bear is still being held by that stripper. If he uses it, though, if he sucks up Todd's power and uses it himself, then it's gone. I need you to get it back. I can't do that. I could try and kill Greg, but we'd be risking Todd's second soul. You have to pull yourself together and get out there, because right now *you* are the hero. The only one we've got."

Aggie sniffles a few more times, wiping her nose on her sleeve. Behind us, Jackal starts laughing, but then there's a booming growl. The warlock is going to shift. He's done fighting without claws.

Charlotte cowers.

"Now, Aggie," I practically plead.

I could collapse in relief when I feel the determination settle deep in her bones. She looks around the tree at Todd, and the feeling deepens.

She stares back at me, sea-green eyes flickering and lips set in a straight line.

"I can do it, Never. Let's go."

I nod.

"I'll distract him so you can get close. If he strips me ... well, I'm trusting you."

Aggie gulps, but her determination doesn't waver.

The two of us step out from behind the tree as the warlock starts to shift.

He's got none of Todd's grace; none of his panache. He's shifting a body part at a time, which gives us a window into where his movements are awkward and unbalanced. Jackal must think the same. The hyena is full of malice as he rushes the warlock.

Greg whips out a hand that grows into a massive paw, backhanding the hyena and sending him flying into a tree. Jackal yelps, sliding down the bark. He might have been all right if not for the tree limb that has impaled one of his legs. He's yanking at it, unable to free himself, as Greg sends a jet of magic crashing into his chest.

Jackal bellows as his fur falls away, and Charlotte starts yowling.

Greg wraps up his shift.

It's sickening having to see Todd's bear worn by this hack and knowing what I'm about to do. At this point, I'm not even sure it'll work. I don't know what we can do, now that Greg is using this form, but we still have to try.

Please, Aggie. Please.

I release the loudest howl I can as I chase the thieving warlock down and leap onto his back. He lets out a sound that's still far too human for a bear shifter, yelling as he rears up on two legs. The movement throws him off-kilter, and he tumbles to the side. I manage to reposition so he misses crushing me entirely, but one of my back legs is still under him when he slams into the ground. A bone cracks.

"Excellent," I hiss as I pull my leg out from underneath the bear.

Off to the side, Aggie is muttering to herself, weaving her hands in a pattern I don't recognize at all. If she's taking her time, it's because she's determined to do this thing right. And I'd do anything for Todd. That bear threw the witchling, Lynx, and his own friendship into my life when I had nothing on my agenda but counting down the days on my contract with Damien. My only life goal had been to get revenge, or die trying.

A fun time, but not fulfilling. I didn't even realize what I was missing until I let them all in. I'd shut out any emotions that deep, afraid of losing what I loved most again.

I'm not making that mistake this time. If they go down, so do I.

I sink my front claws into Greg as he rights himself on all fours, tugging myself up onto his back and flinging my injured leg up as well. It'll heal soon enough. The faux-shifter makes his way to Jackal again. The branch that went through Jackal's leg has broken, and he's hauling himself across the ground.

Greg opens his mouth, and I lean down to see bright magic in his jaws.

"That's new."

Behind us I can feel concern rising from Aggie. And looking back down, I see Greg's eyes flickering.

Hell's bells.

"Jackal, it's the stripping power! Get away from his mouth!"

I have no idea what a second hit would do to him. He's only got one soul left.

I scramble to the back of Greg's head and slam my claws down, trying to reach his eyes. From experience, I can say it would definitely distract him. Unfortunately, my claws just glint of bone, but it's enough to throw off his aim. The tree behind Jackal splinters.

Gregory roars, rearing onto his hind legs again. I start tumbling but manage to dig my claws into his shoulders. The warlock snarls and twists his head, trying to get at me.

"That's right, you useless shower loofah! Up here!" Not sure Jackal would be proud of that one. With my one good leg I kick him, slicing a gash down his side with my back claws. He bucks, and I flail. My injured leg slams into his side, and I wince and suck in a breath at the pain. Supernatural healing is great, if you give things a chance to heal. Slamming an injured limb into the side of a polar-sized grizzly isn't the best way to go about that.

"Never!" Aggie yells, voice tense. "Now!"

Greg tries to spin toward the witch, but I'm not having it. I kick off with my back legs, even though the broken one hates me for it, and launch myself back toward his head. My front claws sink into his cheeks, and as I tumble over him I use all my weight to try to flip him.

It's less than successful, but it accomplishes our goal anyway. His neck is twisted and his head slams into me as I hit the ground.

"That smarts," I wheeze. At least a couple of my ribs are

most likely broken. I keep my hold on him as he flings his head, dragging my back across the dirt.

He tenses as something slams into his back end—I'm guessing a stripper. The magic makes its way up his limbs, and when it gets to his neck, it hits me like a gale-force wind. I let my claws loose, and I'm thrown away from him, sliding on my back across the grass until I slam into a tree trunk.

I blink, staring out my one good eye to see the bear pretender shrinking and his fur falling away.

He's not the only one. This isn't my first time getting caught in the crosswinds when it comes to Aggie's stripping, but it's awful timing. Being naked and furless in the middle of a magical battle isn't on the top of my favorite-things list by any means.

Normally, when Aggie strips, the magic is just gone. I have no idea where it goes. I think she snuffs it out. This time, though, there's two shimmering lights above the warlock as he turns human. One is a shining light blue, and it's shaped like a storm cloud. The other is a burning orange sphere, majestic like the sun setting. Aggie's got one hand focused on the colored lights and the other on the warlock. He's glaring at her, lifting a hand to throw something back. She flings an arm out, and his shot at her is tossed away. Aggie raises both arms, with her fists clenched like she's holding onto something. Then, she pulls her arms apart, like she's ripping something in two.

With one last scream, she flings the blue cloud in Todd's direction, and the orange sphere in Jackal's. For a moment, the shimmering blue lingers over Todd; then it sinks into his skin. His complexion goes from sunken and ashen to a healthy deep brown again. His chest rises as he takes a deep breath, and his amber eyes blink open.

"Duck!" I yell at Charlotte. She's hovering over her uncle, who has passed out at some point. She jumps back, and the orange sphere sinks into Jackal's skin. He groans, his eyes blinking open. Charlotte squeaks and throws herself at him.

Todd manages to sit up. He lifts one arm, and claws grow from the ends of his fingers. He smiles, then drops to the ground again.

A twig snapping pulls my attention away from the healing shifters. Greg is up and stumbling toward the bear. I hear yipping and see little Charlotte running for Greg from Todd's other side.

Greg holds his hands up, one aimed at each of them.

"Oh, no, you don't!"

My limbs are shaking like a leaf in the breeze, but I may be the best shot we've got. Aggie is still standing, but she's got one hand on the side of her head, and if the hurt and agony I'm getting mean anything, she's also got a pounding headache. Stripping comes easy for the witchling, but I'm guessing redirecting a soul has wiped her out.

I pull for my fur, but it refuses to come. When I pull for the scythe, I can almost feel it. Just before I can wrap my hands around the handle, a searing pain hits me in my chest.

Greg is huffing, but he's smiling as he approaches. He's got both hands directed at me.

"The hyena's power would have been fun to play with. You, though? I've never pulled from a shifter who's already been stripped by someone else. What will happen? Do you know what I think? I think you'll die. Magic crushed into oblivion and damaged beyond repair. I wonder what that feels like."

My mouth is clamped shut so tight that my jaw aches. I won't give him the satisfaction.

More than happy to share the experience with everyone else, though. It's excruciating. Worse than being stabbed by the Bone Reader. Worse than losing my eye to the Fates. Every nerve ending is on fire as I bite back a scream.

"Do let me know what death feels like. I've always been curious."

He smirks as he closes his fist, pulling any remaining magic away from me. It feels like he's skinning me alive.

I fully intend to respond with something quippy like "I've already died once and it's not as bad as I thought," but when I open my mouth, all that comes out is a scream.

Once it starts, I can't hold it back.

Greg's laughing now. I have no idea what state Jackal is in, or Todd. I don't know where Charlotte's gone. I can't tear my eye away from the warlock.

"Do give my regards to whatever god of death actually awaits." Greg smirks at me.

"You can say hello yourself." Aggie's voice.

Greg's smile drops as a circle of black appears in his center. It widens, like he's paper being burnt away from the center out. It gets so large that I can see Aggie through it. She's got her face tensed, forehead creased and jaw set. Both her arms are out. She's beyond exhausted, and she's still managing to strip the stripper.

I want to tell her to stop. She's risking herself to save us. When I open my mouth, all that comes out is a groan.

The pain eases, my own burning dropping away as Greg is burned from the inside out. He's the one screaming now, and it's music to my ears. Somewhere overhead, I see a shimmering light above me, and when it sinks into my skin I could cry from relief.

I fall back. My legs refuse to cooperate when I try to push up and help the witchling. All I can do is kneel on the ground and catch my breath. I do manage to tilt my head far enough to see Jackal in a similar state. He's back in his fur, thank the moon.

A light is building around Greg's burning form, and instinct tells me I don't want to be close when this finishes. My legs won't move right. They're wobbling under me.

To my right, I see Todd, in his skin, scooping up Charlotte. He shoves the hyena and himself behind a tree.

I scream again as something sharp sinks into my arm. When I twist my head around, I see Jackal. The hyena is stumbling backward, dragging me away from Greg and Aggie.

"Wait. Aggie. Aggie!" I scream her name louder as the hyena pulls us away.

The warlock is almost gone, only one reaching arm remaining as Jackal tugs me behind a tree as well.

There's a percussive boom, followed by a wave of air so strong the tree shielding us creaks and leans.

Once the trembling branches go still, I chance a look back at the clearing.

Gregory is gone, and Aggie is lying on the ground.

24

HURTING & HELPING

My legs still feel like they want to tilt and spin underneath me, but I force them to cooperate as I rush toward the fallen witchling.

We've won. No Rizik. No warlock. No more accomplices, and as far as I know all the kids are safe.

But it's not a victory at all if Aggie doesn't make it.

"Aggie!" I yell for her as I fall to my knees, crawling the rest of the way and then clutching the witch in my arms. Todd lumbers up behind me. He's put on his fur, but he's moving slowly. Jackal is right behind him, yelping and still dragging one back leg. I've got no idea how he managed to pull me. Jackal yips at something behind him, and Charlotte stays back behind the trees.

Aggie's lips are tinged with a frightening blue shade. I lift her hands and see the same thing on her fingernail beds. I clutch her head and bring it close to my ear.

"She's breathing, but it's shallow."

"Put her on me. We'll make our way back to the others." Todd doesn't look strong enough to carry a leaf, let alone a witch.

"What about the cave-in? We'd have to go around and ..." And I don't know the way. The rest of the group hasn't found us yet, which doesn't bode well for our own chances for a speedy reunion. And besides, what are they going to do?

This isn't the first time Aggie has pulled too much from herself. She cares so much about everyone else, even when it's to her own detriment. In the past we've had a bear sleuth healer, potions left to us by Chrys's family and prepared by Elios, and the Sewing Circle witches around to help put her back together.

Now we've got three shifters all healing from their own stripping, and a child.

We're not what she needs, but I can think of one way to help her.

"Come on, come on." I squeeze my eye shut, focusing on the witch. The scythe appears in my hand.

"Shit!" Jackal scrambles away from me, and Todd immediately feels on edge.

"Never, are you sure? You're sure it won't hurt her?"

I've only used it once. And I've only tried to tap into some fate-changing power with Shiftress and with Danger. I killed Shiftress and couldn't save Danger, so my track record isn't great. Danger may be a goddess, but she's still dead.

What if all this Reaper power is good for is killing? That's what a Reaper does, isn't it?

I stare back and forth between Aggie and the scythe.

There's only one other way I can think of to get instant help. It didn't work with Danger, and I'm loath to consider the consequences, but I have to try.

Aggie is worth it.

"Don't make me regret this," I whisper as I tap my eyepatch twice.

B.R. doesn't make us wait. He solidifies from a pile of shadows within seconds.

"The witch." Visitor's blue eyes widen as he takes her in, his surprise evident. Then they slide to my scythe and he gasps.

"You were going to—"

I don't waste time on pleasantries.

"Fix her. Now, Bone Reader. And damn the cost. I know you said with Danger it wasn't possible, but—"

Visitor holds up a hand.

"Danger had been chewed up by zombies and was beyond help."

"And the witch?" Even after my demands, I hardly dare hope.

"Isn't facing certain death. Yet. But she's close. She's draining more as we speak."

Todd roars behind me, blowing some of my hair over my shoulders. Jackal doesn't even know her that well, but I can feel he's grown attached. Who wouldn't? The witchling is the level of selfless most of us only try to be, but never achieve.

I swear, if she makes it through this I'll wear all her ridiculous shirts on repeat for a year. Two years. I'll hand out hugs to every guest at the vampsion. I'd even be willing to give up caffeine.

"What do we need to do?"

Visitor frowns, the crease lines on his forehead marring the otherwise perfect features. He reaches down and clutches Aggie's fingers, pinching and squeezing one so hard she moans. I snarl, but B.R. doesn't feel antagonistic.

He's thoughtful. He's reading her bones, from inside her skin.

"She needs to strip someone. Her key doesn't drain her, and even though this stripper doesn't collect the powers she strips, it will be energizing to her. What she did to kill the warlock was like the opposite of stripping. Instead of ripping the power out of him, she supercharged his own until he combusted. It was the most dangerous thing she could have done. The antithesis of her key."

The witchling is a marvel, but she may have just doomed herself.

"She can't strip anyone in this state," Todd rumbles.

B.R. stares down at the witchling. Then back at me again. I let the scythe fade away. It's attracting too much of his attention.

B.R. sighs.

"I can jolt her awake. It will be painful. It'll be like shocking a heart into rhythm, and it won't keep her up long. Just long enough for someone to tell her what to do. Never, she trusts you and Todd the most. One of you will have to convince her very quickly to use her key, or she'll lapse back into unconsciousness and be even more drained from the attempt. At that point, she might be beyond even my help."

Todd and I are both nodding along.

"I'll tell her. She'll listen to me," I respond with certainty.

"Of that I have little doubt. She considers you her actual sister. But we have another problem."

I glare at him.

"The three of you won't be of any use to her. You're already drained as it is. If she strips any of you in your current states, you'd just be trading one life for another. The same with the smaller hyena. She's too young to survive it, not that I'd recommend such a thing."

Good to know he's got boundaries.

For a moment, Jackal wrestles with something. He's worried we'll offer him. He's the new guy, and I see where he'd make the assumption. I lean to where I'm blocking B.R.'s view of him, as well as Todd.

"I'll do it."

Visitor just huffs.

"I knew you'd say that, you foolish shifter. One trip to the Underworld wasn't enough?"

"You're the one who sent me to—"

"I know! I know I did, and I know you hate me for it, whether we're allies or not. Which is why I'm going to let the witchling strip me."

"What?"

What could possibly be gained from this? My intuition searches, but all I feel is a genuine desire to help. It's foreign, coming from him. Misplaced and uncomfortable. He's hesitant about what he's offered, but he's not changing his mind.

"It will weaken me significantly. Once it's done, I'll leave immediately. If there's any other help you were hoping for, you won't get it from me today."

Who knows how many deals he'll have to make to recoup this loss, or maybe not. From what he's told me, he's a good ten thousand years old and change. Maybe he's got power to spare.

Now's not the time to argue.

"Name your price. From me. Nothing from Aggie," I clarify, just in case he is thinking of trying anything.

"If I succeed, I'll name it afterward. You know how this works."

I do.

"Whatever the price. Do it. Please."

"Very well. Everyone move back. Now, I want to reiterate that what I'm about to do will hurt her. A lot. She's probably going to scream. She'll definitely be in pain. Do *not* lose focus and charge at me. Attack me, and I'll lose my hold on her. Your job is to convince her to strip me. When she does, do *not* look at me. That is one of the non-breakables of this deal. Look over here before the witchling has regained her strength and I have made my exit, and I'll make all of you wish you'd never set foot on this earth. Do you understand?"

"Clearer than crystal," Jackal quips, suspicion pooling in his gut as he takes in the Bone Reader.

Jackal guides his niece behind one of the trees. Todd and I

move back, keeping our eyes locked firmly on Aggie. Curiosity killed the cat; I'm not going to let it be the demise of the witchling. I don't see anything hit Aggie. There's no lights or colors, like with some magic. She just floats upward, her back arched. Her eyes flash open, and she starts to scream.

She screams like she's being broken from the inside out.

"Aggie! Aggie, look at me!" She twists her head in my direction, tears streaming down her face.

"Never. H-help."

I force my own tears down.

"Aggie. I need you to reach in front of you, and strip. Strip the Bone Reader."

Fear sweeps through her, along with the pain.

"I ca—"

"Yes, you can. You have to, Aggie. I need you to trust me. We don't have time. I won't let you get hurt." A lie. I'm letting her get hurt right now, but I barrel past it. "But you have to listen to me and do it now!"

She whimpers, but she lifts her hand. Her eyes flash, and the wind that accompanies her stripping flows out of her hand like a tornado set loose. B.R. grunts as it hits him, but I keep my eye on Aggie.

She lurches, then drops to the ground. The shadows the Bone Reader wraps himself in when he turns into Visitor are piling around us, obscuring everything. I couldn't see him if I wanted to.

"Keep stripping!" I yell at her, afraid of what will happen if she breaks it too soon.

"I can only see shadows!" she yells back, voice trembling in terror. We've seen the Bone Reader reduce a field of zombies to nothing. What could he do to a single witch?

"Keep going! Strip until those shadows are gone, but don't look at him. Close your eyes!"

She slams them shut.

The Bone Reader's emotions don't waver. He's focused on his goal. Through the shadows and wind, I hear his voice. It crackles like dry leaves about to blow away in the wind.

"Don't forget our deals, Never. Both of them."

He doesn't wait for me to say anything. Even without seeing him, I can feel his presence fade away. Aggie drops her arm and falls. I dive, throwing my arms underneath her.

"We're clear! He's gone!" I yell at the other shifters.

Todd and Jackal run over, Lottie trailing behind her uncle.

Aggie stands up. She's shaky, but stronger.

"Why did I have to do that?"

"To save your life. I can explain it later. How do you feel?"

Her color is back to normal. No more blue-tinged lips. Her eyes are vibrant seaglass green. Her hair even looks shinier.

"I feel great, to be honest."

I hug her, holding her close to me.

"What you did with Greg? That was one of the most impressive displays of magic I've ever seen. Please never do it again."

She just laughs.

"It's the type of thing you would do."

"Exactly. And I'm insane. Everyone says so."

"Maybe, but little sisters are bound to copy their big sisters at some point."

Reluctantly, I pass her off to Todd for a hug as she reaches for the bear.

The five of us start making our way around the hills, and we're not far when a dragon swoops overhead.

"Never! Thank goodness! Where's the warlock?"

I don't know whether to laugh or cry. Nahum's eyes spark; fog drips from his fangs. He's ready to roast a stripper.

"Someone's beaten you to it. The warlock has been disintegrated, courtesy of Aggie."

"And she stripped the Bone Reader," Jackal supplies.

Nahum's eyes flash.

"She what?"

He lands in front of us, and behind him Hugh comes running.

I'll tell you about it later.

Nahum's scanning the area around us like B.R. is going to pop out of a tree.

Did you have to make any other deals?

The price! B.R. didn't stick around long enough to tell me. I pat myself down. I've healed enough from the battle and Aggie's stripping that the outfit I get when I shift is back in place. In the pocket of my jeans, I feel a folded piece of paper.

Without looking, I know who it's from.

25

NO S'MORE PROBLEMS

Nahum and I lag at the back of the group as Hugh leads us on a rugged path through the hills and to the others. We're in no shape for serious exercise, but we do our best.

You can read it with me, if you'd like, I offer to the dragon as I unfold B.R.'s note.

Nahum doesn't respond, but he feels the same wariness he does when we're facing an enemy. It's hard for me to drum up the same sentiment after what the Bone Reader just did.

I'm not defending him to Nahum yet, though. Not until I see what his generosity is going to cost me. The letter is written in scrawling black ink that shimmers.

NEVER,

I'VE MADE *many decisions over my thousands of years of life, and I stand by each of them. I cannot regret what I tried to do by sending you to the Underworld, even though I know you want me to. I do, however, regret that it hurt the only individual I've considered a friend in a very long time. Perhaps ever.*

Maybe this will go some of the way toward making things up to you.

You've no doubt figured out by now that you are not a Rizik, as I'd hoped. I suspect I'll only be confirming what you already know, but you are a Reaper. What that means for not only you, but the supernatural world at large, is both important and dangerous. Your friends won't have all the answers, because Reaper powers were once well-kept secrets.

Before I call in your debt to me to face my siblings, I will meet with you to explain in person exactly what you are now. I can answer the questions about what you can do and why it's risky.

You will listen. Then, you'll use your new abilities to clear both our debts.

That is my price.

That, and one more thing.

Fixing the witch will have left me in a weakened state. I am doing something that, in spite of the name Rizik, I hate to do. I am taking a risk. I've been following the actions of my siblings closely. I think they're preparing for their plans, especially after this case with the kids. Even so, we still have some time. At least a matter of months. No time at all in the life of a Rizik, but long enough to heal.

In the meantime, I ask that if my work with the witch is successful, you think better of me.

I will contact you when it's time.

The Bone Reader

I stare down at the letter, nearly tripping over a tree trunk. Nahum offers me his arm and helps me over.

Can you believe this? I demand as I scan the words again.

When did he even have time to write it?
I wave the dragon off.

"That's not the part I find surprising. B.R. has all sorts of tricks up his sleeves."

Think better of me.

It's the part about Reapers I should be focusing on, but it's hard not to get sidetracked by what B.R. had to say about himself. I owe him my bones, and now I've promised him my respect by making this deal.

"It's a real deal, right? What happens if you can't change how you feel about him?" Nahum is doubtful at my side. Oddly enough, the dragon was the calmer one when we met, but ever since my trip to the Underworld he's been even less forgiving than I am. At least with anyone he perceives as having wronged me.

"He could have let the witchling die," I reason. "He didn't have to save her."

Nahum shakes his head.

"No. Because you'd have known he was lying. He did this for himself, no one else."

Did he, though? If I'd flat-out asked if he *could* save her and he'd said no, I would have sensed the lie. But I didn't ask that. I just asked him to save her, and he volunteered. He's smart. Sharp enough to manipulate most of the beings around him for years. He could have gotten out of things if he wanted. He could have demanded Aggie's servitude like he's demanded my bones, but he didn't.

When he stared down at that witchling, he was feeling real affection. And it might not just have been for me. He respects the stripper, and I'm not even sure he realizes it yet. I was pulled into my friendship with Todd, Lynx, Aggie, and Nadia unwittingly. Before I knew it, I was in too deep to escape with my heart intact. The Bone Reader is far older than I, and for all I know even more damaged inside, but he *does* feel. Maybe we can win him over without him noticing as well.

There's hope for him yet.

"Call me crazy, everyone else has, but I don't want to give up on B.R."

Nahum rolls his eyes at me, but he doesn't argue. He'll follow my lead with the shapeshifter. He's more open to forgiveness after I fill him in on all the details of our battle with Greg.

"After Mizor, you said you wanted me to go back to targets who weren't after me personally. Tell me, is this preferable?" I nudge him with my elbow.

He laughs as he throws an arm around me and pulls me close.

"I know what you're getting at. And no, it wasn't better. I don't like you risking your life, but I blame the villains. I suppose I'll just have to keep going along on these missions until we've gotten rid of them all."

"A lifetime of chaos, then."

"If that's what it takes."

WHEN WE REACH the rest of the group, Nadia is seated crisscross-applesauce with a bevy of children around her in the grass. She's shepherded all of them into the cover of some trees and far enough from the cemetery that they don't have to see it. They're riveted and wide-eyed as she relates a fairytale to them.

It's fairly benign as fairytales go. When I was younger they normally ended with lessons and morals relayed through gruesome and violent means. It's possible Nadia's keeping things calm for the kids, or maybe Colombian folktales are just happier than others. I catch a bit about a shepherd girl searching for a herd of lost sheep.

"And then what happened?" a small shifter with a twitchy nose asks, completely entranced. The little girl smells like a prey shifter. A rabbit? It will come as no shock that in the supernatural community, where strength is power, most shifters are predatory.

A collective gasp rings out from the group of kids as Nadia tells them the sheep were all found, but missing their tails. Perhaps it's a gruesome story after all.

"The Magikai are going to want to interview the children," Jackal whispers from my side, echoing my earlier thoughts. He's ushered Charlotte over to the group, and she scoots close to another shifter as Nadia continues her tale.

"And people say I'm the intuitive one," I mutter.

Jackal shrugs.

"Your body language. You were relaxed watching the kids; then when the small shifter spoke you tensed up. She doesn't smell like the rest of us. You're wondering what the warlock and Rizik wanted with her. You want to know if there was more to it than just targeting kids in general."

The story finishes as the shepherd girl manages to reattach all the sheep tails and everyone lives happily ever after.

"You're very good. You said you were a watcher for the other hyenas. Is that a full-time job?"

He grins.

"Just an elected position. I was keeping my actual job to myself, but I suppose there's no harm telling you now. I work as a private investigator. With what I do, you have to pay attention to people. Being an intuitive sure would come in handy."

I smirk at him. "It's a useful skill."

"After a while, I decided I liked being pickier with my clientele. There was more satisfaction helping good people than simply working for whoever signed the biggest paychecks."

"Noble, but it's not going to bulk up any bank accounts for you."

He shakes his head.

"Maybe not, but I've never been a high-maintenance guy."

"Why not tell the Magikai about your skills? They would have let you in on this investigation sooner."

He chuckles, the sound turning into hyena laughter.

"You're an enforcer, and I've heard about what you did with Amun. I can put two and six together. You don't like being under their thumb any more than I would. I didn't want them trying to procure my services on a permanent basis, and if they'd made that a stipulation of letting me help find Lottie, I would have said yes. I kept information about myself vague."

Smarter than even I'd given him credit for.

He still puts me on edge, but I can read now that it's his own penchant for wandering and not something sinister. He just doesn't feel truly at home anywhere.

"You know," I start, "if you're looking for somewhere to stay for a while that doesn't require a government contract, you'd be welcome at the vampsion. I've been thinking of striking out on my own anyway. It would be nice to have like-minded people in the group."

"I'll think about it. I'll have to take Charlotte back to my sister first, but I'll return and help out for as long as it takes to get all these kids back to their families. I can agree to that, at least."

After that? I can already feel he's ready to run. Maybe we'll change that, and maybe we won't. At least he'll have somewhere more comfortable than the Magikai training ground tents to stay in for now.

Nadia wraps up another story. This one centers on La Muelona, and she's changed it from the version she once told me. In that version, a woman with fangs sought revenge against men who fell in love with her. In this version, La Muelona is a protector of children and the innocent, and her fangs are used for good. When she's done, there's a round of applause from the kids.

I wave at her over their heads, and several of them turn toward me.

"How are we getting this crew home?"

Nadia smiles.

"I've already contacted the Magikai."

"And they're sending several dozen jets?"

She giggles, then rolls her eyes.

"Not in a forest. They're sending us buses that will drive us to an airport. The children's parents can meet us when we land back at Magikai headquarters."

I frown at that.

"And where will the kids be staying while they wait for their parents?" Some of these families will be coming from across the globe. Some packs and groups settle things privately, so it may take us a while to track down where these kids all came from to begin with. I didn't like the idea of a trained investigator roughing it at the training grounds. There's no way in hell I'm subjecting the kids to those sad canvas cots.

"I was told they could stay at the enforcer trainee quarters. The trainees are going to sleep outdoors or on the floor of the representative offices," Nadia admits guiltily. She doesn't like it any better than me.

Hugh clears his throat, stepping between us and waving a hand.

"Lady Never, Representative Nadia, if I might make a suggestion?"

"Go on, Hugh."

"Well, you do have two full casinos and a vampsion at your discretion. All three of which are filled with very comfortably furnished rooms. Perhaps, if we were to temporarily diminish our profits, we could house the children."

I stalk closer to Hugh.

"Hugh. Do I look like a babysitter to you?" I flash my teeth. "Because ... I'm more than happy to try it out for a few days.

What do you say, kids? Comfy beds with some snacks and movies?"

He lets out a sigh of relief as I approve the plan.

Quite a few of the kids are still too nervous, tired, or confused to answer. Can't blame them. There are many, though, who cheer and smile at the idea Hugh has pitched to us all.

Who would have thought vampire casinos would become a house for displaced youth, Nahum teases in my mind.

Temporary only, I assure the dragon.

Todd lumbers up, in his fur—I'm thinking, just because he can be again.

"We'll need more adults to watch all these kids. I'm going to take the bear cubs directly back to my brother's sleuth and make sure the triplets get to Lynx, but after that I'll help out."

I'm relieved to see the two triplets toddling along in their fur underneath him.

Feral joins us, clearing his throat.

"Do you know, I think several individuals at CoED might be interested in a short Vegas vacation."

Perfect. The Sewing Circle may not actually be old, but they will absolutely embrace the doting grandparent routine. I'm betting even Tom will like these children. The denture-wearing griffin is more lovable than he lets on.

"Let's reach out to the vamps and make the arrangements. And Hugh, they'll have to watch themselves around the kids. Some of these children may be wary of vampires; we need to make sure their stay at the casinos is positive," I warn him.

"I would not allow anything less," he assures me. I'm assuming he'll be checking in with Chrys when he calls home as well.

Nadia and Aggie pass out food to the kids. When I see what they've got, I march back over to Hugh, who has started making plans.

"S'mores, Hugh? And we've been living off of endless granola bars?"

He blushes.

"I saved the best for when we'd won."

I thump him on the back.

"Excellent idea!"

Buses on the way, no more evil forces, and s'mores. It's the type of day even I can't get upset about.

I just hope it lasts.

26

HOME IS WHERE THE BAR IS

Each adventure, I've missed my house in Sacramento a little less, not that I haven't dreamed of my comfy mattress.

But that's not what makes it home. Home is wherever the people I love are.

Which is why I'm not all that miffed when, only three days after our heroic rescue, we're back to business.

Several of us pile into a booth inside the Lusty Lute. The Magikai representatives have yet to arrive, and it's making me antsy.

"I almost wish I'd demanded a different meeting spot," I grumble as a round of drinks is tossed in front of us and Elios lectures me.

"Gone for weeks! Off running into the woods, searching for kids, and you didn't think to call me? The master thief who could surely have gotten you in and out with half the mess and better results?"

"What better results?" I snap. "All the kids are safe and all the villains are dead."

That shuts him up, for about half a second.

"And I could have helped! Now that I'm back to my glorious self, I've got quite a bit more strength. I need something to do with it." He's brimming with energy, now that he's in his half-satyr half-Fae form and no longer a cursed grandpappy. He's itching to do something more active than tossing cheap beers.

"You're also brimming with confidence, you conceited old goat. 'Glorious self.'" I roll my eyes. "Sounds like something I would say. It looks to me like you've had plenty going on around here with all the renovations."

He opens his mouth to respond with what I don't doubt would be something snarky, but Aggie cuts him off.

"I like the look of the place. It's really fun," Aggie compliments him.

Elios's cheeks go red, and he squeezes the handle of a beer pitcher, then gets into a discussion with Aggie regarding said changes being all Calypso's idea. After we rescued the supernatural who got him cursed in the first place, I wasn't sure how things would go. Even I was surprised that he's absolutely smitten with her. Not that he'll admit it, and I'm not going to be the one to blab. He'd cut off my cocktails.

"Pushy, that's what she is!" Elios accuses. The hippocamp in question just grins as she approaches the table and drops off a few more drinks.

"Shouldn't they be here by now?" I crane my neck and stare at the door.

When the Magikai representatives heard my plan for keeping the unclaimed kids at the casinos, some of them were less than enthused. They insisted on a meeting, and I insisted it take place somewhere other than their headquarters or one of their properties. The bar isn't entirely neutral ground, but I don't own it and Elios wouldn't listen to me anyway, so this is what we've settled on.

The place is huge. Per Elios, Calypso procured some nifty magical expansion spell to enlarge the space. Instead of a dimly lit bar with worn booths and tables on a dusty concrete floor, there's now also a whole section with pool tables and a foosball table or two. There's a back corner with a stage and karaoke setup.

"Only on Fridays!" Elios had insisted when Aggie wanted to get singing going.

Best of all, there is a private party room, which is where we're currently seated. Elios told me it's impenetrable to even shifter hearing.

A familiar face pops his head into the room. Calder. The each-uisge is in his horse form and flashes his spiny teeth at me in his version of a smile. Calypso slaps him on the shoulder as she walks by. As his sister, I'd guess she can get away with it.

"Waiting on someone?" Calder makes his way to the table, still flashing that spiny smirk.

He was more than willing to get back involved with the Magikai once his sister was taken care of. He and I have had our minor differences, but his presence means I have at least one ally in the room. For that I'm grateful.

Even more so when the remainder of the chosen Magikai representatives who head the various committees clamber into the room. Sky and Ji-hwan are back. Occam is behind them, with drooped shoulders and circles under his eyes. The three of them have brought along several unfamiliar faces. My intuition can already tell I'm in for a battle.

Maybe I should have brought along more backup. Feral, Nahum, Aggie, Nadia, and I are here. I left Hugh to help Chrys set up the casinos. The Sewing Circle showed up to help them out with babysitting duty. Todd returned the bear cubs and the remaining triplets personally. He and Lynx haven't returned yet.

Elios passes out drinks so we can get the debate started.

. . .

"I STILL THINK they all should have gone to the training grounds. What does it say about our authority that people can't depend on our property as a place to collect their kids?" demands a gnome representative an hour into the discussion.

I snarl at the word *collect*.

"I'm sorry, you'll have to reintroduce yourself. You see, I don't remember you, since you weren't involved in any way with this rescue and therefore have less say than a vampire choosing a beach vacation destination!" I finish, voice rising.

The gnome glares at me. Sky steps in, raising her arms so the feathers on her forearms shimmer.

"The children are all safe and accounted for. I'm sure we can all agree that was the highest priority. But yes, where the ones awaiting their families should go is one of the topics up for discussion today. If you'll all refer back to your agendas, you'll see—"

"The hell with the agenda. I vote we leave the kids under Never's care," Calder shouts from his spot down the table. He's still in his each-uisge form and managing to slurp whiskey from a trough-like tray Elios set out for him.

"Hear, hear!" Ji-hwan shouts, pumping a fist in the air as he seconds the opinion.

I might have worded it a bit differently. "Never's care" sounds so personal. Either way, at least I've got supporters.

Both of them grin at me, Calder dripping whiskey over his spiny teeth.

"Oh, who cares where they stay? Shouldn't their families be showing up to get them soon, anyway? What's the point of any of this without family?" Occam sniffles from his part of the table. He felt sullen when he entered the room, and his mood has done nothing but decline. I'm honestly surprised he's still acting as a representative at all, but I can feel this is the last tie he has to his brother.

"A lot of the children will be picked up right away. The

Sacramento bear cubs have already been returned," Nadia assures the warlock. "This is just a temporary measure to keep the kids comfortable and protected while everyone travels here. There's also two dozen kids we rescued who weren't reported missing. It will take time to look into that."

Feral raises a few fingers in the air, waiting for Sky to acknowledge him before speaking.

"Even the children with known families present some complicated cases. It will take those from other continents a matter of at least a few days to get here and retrieve their kids."

"He's right. And we have yet to determine whether the unclaimed kids were provided to the warlocks willingly, if they were threatened not to report the kidnappings in some way, or if the warlocks and Rizik murdered their families in order to take them," Ji-hwan tacks on.

"Plus. It's possible there's still some lone supernaturals out there trying to find their kids themselves. That's what Jackal was initially doing. You'll have to make some sort of public statement," Nahum adds.

"It's even possible some of the kids have come from Fae. We'll have to send someone through the portal to discuss that with the royals there," Nadia finishes.

"Not it!" I call out. There's a lot of things I'd do to help these kids, but I'll avoid another run-in with the Fae royals if I can help it. I got the sense on our visit that one or two were primed for defection from the royal family, but none of them are particularly fond of me.

"You do know the Weres who guard one of the portals from here to Fae. That could be helpful to us," Aggie reminds me.

I do. They were one of the packs in my family's territory before I lost everything and went from Were princess to Never, vigilante. They would help me if needed.

"We could send Elios. That'd really annoy the royals." Aggie giggles. None of us had a good time with the Fae royals, and with Elios being half-Fae and a royal to boot, you'd think he'd have the best negotiating ability, but they hate him more than us.

"Sure, send the Faetyr." He groans as I create the nickname for his species, and ignores the idea to send him as an envoy entirely.

In the end, it's determined that we'll divide and conquer. In groups. Nobody gets to run off on their own this time.

Nadia and Ji-hwan will approach the portal and try to go through Nico and the other Were portal guardians first. Hopefully they can get done what we need without involving the Fae royals at all. If that's not possible, Elios will go.

"We will supply the payment to enter the portal," Sky volunteers.

Do you know, you all never told me what you paid to come through and retrieve me. I had the coin to get back, but it cost you something to get into Fae, didn't it?

We don't know the price. Whatever it was, the Bone Reader paid it on our behalf, Nahum responds.

Interesting and even more interesting.

I'm ashamed to admit it takes me until this point in the meeting to remember there's also a missing harpy to deal with. I ask Sky if anything's been done about their missing representative.

She frowns.

"We flew a few enforcers out once you'd made the area safe. They found his remains."

Moon's hell. Another senseless loss.

Sky sighs.

"We have to focus on what we can do now. Those of us in the Magikai will work to identify the families of all the kids."

The rest of us are on nanny duty until each kid is retrieved.

"Then it's decided. Never and the Vegas coven will have

responsibility for the children until every parent is found," Sky concludes, finishing the meeting.

I might as well change the neon signs of the casinos to flash "Never's Nanny Service." The kids need help, though, and I'm not going to be the one to kick them to the curb.

I'll just have to ask Hugh to help me go shopping. We're going to need diapers. And toys. And moon knows what else.

Hell's bells.

Maybe I should have stayed in the woods with Shiftress.

27
PREDICAMENTS & PROCRASTINATION

What's the best way to get out of babysitting duty? Replace it with something you'd like to do even less.

There's no getting out of this task, anyway. A promise is a promise, and a deal is a deal.

Now that the kids are at the casinos, I can trust my friends to look after them. At least long enough to pay a visit to a certain shape-shifting entity.

My fur is already on, and I step into the Bone Reader's cave on full alert. I agreed to hear him out, but I never said I wouldn't be on the defensive. If I was useful to him as a Rizik, what might he do now that I'm a Reaper?

Feral tried to prepare me as best he could. He went by CoED and gathered any notes he had. Hugh scoured the vampire library, and Nahum made a trip to his island for any texts referencing Reapers. The three of them locked themselves into the vampsion library for a full weekend to try to give me some idea of what I'd be walking into.

While I appreciate their efforts, it all amounted to just a scant bit of information.

Reapers work for, or with, the gods. They carry a scythe. They kill people. They're intensely feared. The only new thing I learned is part of why. Any wound dealt by the scythe is enough to end a supernatural being. I could give someone a paper cut with the thing, and that would be the end of them. I've just acquired an invaluable weapon.

While the males were researching, I was busy practicing. In between drives to the casinos to check on the kids, I locked myself in the dining hall of the vampsion. I practiced calling the scythe to myself over and over. At first, it took several minutes per attempt. I had to get the emotions right. I need to center myself, and focus on a real belief that needing the scythe is a matter of life and death. Mine, or someone else's.

I also learned that while it disintegrated Shiftress, it cuts furniture in half like any other blade. I've ruined a number of chairs and knocked out a good chunk of the dining table. Elios came by to supply food and cocktails when one of the vamps grew worried and told him I was barely eating.

Nosy, involved old Faetyr.

He'd had to duck me when he walked in just as I was swinging a scythe. I'd taken out the top half of a solid wooden chair instead of him, and he'd dropped an entire tray of drinks.

After that, signs were put on the doors to leave me be, to keep me from accidentally murdering someone.

Once Nahum, Hugh and Feral had looked through every text they could find, they'd all encouraged me to come here, to B.R.'s dwelling. I'd just as soon have waited for every last kid to be claimed. After all, since we're still tracking down parents, it could easily have taken weeks.

And we all know how I love to procrastinate.

They weren't having it.

"If the Bone Reader is right, and something even more dangerous is coming, we need to know what you can do," Hugh had argued.

They were right. My avoidance was purely selfish. Nahum was the only one who supported me ignoring the Bone Reader outright. He'd actually offered to come in my place, but there wasn't any outcome to that scenario that I could picture going well. Thus, here I am instead. Keeping my word. Albeit reluctantly.

"ALL RIGHT, you wheeling, dealing being. I'm here! As promised!" My voice echoes off the walls of B.R.'s ice cave.

"There's no need to yell," his voices weave over one another, then fade to a single tone. Visitor steps from the shadows in the back of the cave, assessing me with his frigid blue stare.

He walks over to me, movements so smooth he might as well be gliding across the ice.

"You did come after all."

As if I had a choice. You can't renege on a Bone Reader deal. There could have been dire magical consequences for me, or worse and more likely, Aggie.

"I've no doubt your friends have been digging for information since I confirmed what you are. Tell me, what did you manage to find?"

Nothing gets by the Bone Reader. After a quick think, I can't come up with a reason to keep the information from him. I run through what the guys found out about Reapers. The whole spiel takes only a couple of minutes.

Visitor nods along until I finish.

"As I suspected, then. There's very little information out there about what you are. That's good. Maybe it means my siblings don't know as much as they could. Although I know almost everything about Reapers, and they're just as connected as me, so perhaps that's too much to hope for."

"They certainly are. Your sister was working with a stripper, a bunch of vampires, and more warlocks. Who knows what beings the others have aligned themselves with. I am assuming the remaining siblings hate you, and us?"

Visitor tilts his head, one hand going to his chin as his features begin to roll and shift.

"My remaining sister, and one of my brothers, will be against us for certain. It's possible Rumple hasn't chosen a side. He never was much for team sports. After the whole name-guessing incident, he became a bit of a recluse. I might be able to get him to help us, but it's a long shot. He lacks my empathy, and he's not entirely sane."

"Empathy? Sanity? You?"

He shrugs.

"I'm speaking about Riziks compared to Riziks. Not compared to the rest of the world."

"Two to three left, then. Well, I killed your sister,"—after we all almost lost our minds—"how much harder can two Riziks be? Maybe a third. Just get me close to them and—" I mime some slicing and dicing.

B.R. just settles back into his Visitor features and sighs, putting one hand over his face.

"I wish it were that simple, but I don't share your confidence. Shiftress was the most reckless of all my siblings. The others aren't as hands-on. They're content to pull strings in the background and remain hidden."

I clear my throat, pointedly, and he scowls.

"Yes, yes. They're more like me. I get it. That being said, it's going to work against us. Not only will they be harder to find and catch, but they're subtler. Shiftress was clumsy in her execution. You were on her trail before she'd done any real damage and—"

"*Real* damage? She kidnapped tons of kids! She and those vampires and warlocks slaughtered multiple enforcers and representatives. She almost had my mate and me turning on each other! Because of her and that warlock, Aggie almost died!"

Much to my annoyance, the Bone Reader waves me aside as though those are trivial matters.

"What's that phrase humans use? Small potatoes? Surely you can see how she could have done much worse with her abilities, if she'd kept quieter about things. My remaining siblings won't make her mistakes. I doubt we'll know exactly what we're up against until things have reached a serious threat level. That's why I want to talk to you now. I'm going to be traveling. I'll be using my own networks and calling in debts to find them and figure out what they're up to. And you will be working on controlling your Reaper powers, so that when they are out in the open we stand a chance."

I cross my arms, grumbling to myself, but can't come up with a serious argument.

"Get them out in the open. Kill them. That's all we need to do?"

His features shift again, and all the convolutedness of whatever he's planning rolls over my intuition, gliding across my skin like oil.

"It won't be a simple process—"

"Of course not."

"But that's the gist of our goals, yes. There will be more steps, but killing them is the end game."

Now I'm the one who waves him off. There's always more steps. I'm not here for what we hope to do in the future. I'm here to find out about myself.

"B.R., you wanted me to hear you out. You intimated you had something to add to this whole Reaper quandary. Care to share?"

Back in his Visitor form, he glides to me until we're face-to-face. He reaches out and grabs one of my hands, holding it between his. I flinch on contact, but there's no burn this time. That, more than anything, makes me pay attention.

"I have no doubt you figured out how pleased I am to have a Reaper on my side. You're more powerful than other supernaturals, and that includes Riziks. From what you shared, you've already heard the rumors. I can tell you they're true. The gods, sometimes directly and sometimes through assassins, killed the last Reapers off one by one."

"Why?"

Victims of crime always want to know why, and I'm no exception.

"Power. It's a boring answer, and I find it tedious, but there you have it. Reapers were feared and revered as much as the gods themselves, and it wasn't well-tolerated. The world does need balance, as much as I appreciate a good bit of chaos. You've no doubt realized we're severely unbalanced. No Reapers, until you, and precious few gods. They're not meant to be idols demanding worship. Gods were intended to provide support to supernaturals behind the scenes."

There's something else; I can feel it.

"You didn't drag me all the way up here to tell me how powerful I am. I'm a Rizik-killer; I get that. But what else?"

He drops my hands and turns away.

"You're going to have to trust me. When you need to know, I'll tell you."

I clench my fists and slam them to my sides.

"B.R., that is B.S.! What are you hiding from me?"

"Nothing you're ready to hear. You were satisfied being a Were, and now I've made you something beyond even my own imagining. Don't rush into knowledge you're not going to want. Just like my deals, everything extracts a cost. That's all I'll say for now. That, and keep practicing with your scythe."

Really glad I trudged all the way up to Alaska for this. I'm tempted to call it a waste of a trip. The information I've gotten amounts to precious little, but I am seeing a softening to the Bone Reader that wasn't there before. Personally, I'm as intrigued by that as I am by the Reaper information.

"If you have nothing else to share, I'll be headed home."

"I'd say we have a matter of months left, Never. Things are ramping up; I can feel it in my own bones. I have things to do, but so do you. I'm going to send you a gift, and I would ask that you and your friends give it your utmost attention."

And the regular Bone Reader is back. The being could host a master-class in cryptic statements.

I turn to head to the entrance of the ice cave, but spin around just before making my exit. It worked for Aggie; maybe it'll work for me. I'm on the Bone Reader's side no matter what, but it would be nice if he was on mine. Maybe, just maybe, that's possible.

I run for him before I can lose my nerve, throwing my arms around him. He tenses and dry-ice burn lights me up, but then it fades away. The Bone Readers feels comforted as I hug him, and the sensation wraps its own warm embrace around my intuition.

"I owe you my bones, but I would fight with you regardless. You're a morally questionable agent of chaos, but you are also my friend, and I have your back," I say before releasing him.

A very tentative and hesitant joy makes its way to my intuition. I can feel the Bone Reader's icy interior cracking, but before my intuition can pick up on whatever's underneath, the shadows consume him.

Maybe he was just in a hurry to get started with his side of our mission, or maybe warm and fuzzy feelings are too much for him. Either way, the Bone Reader has left me alone in his cave.

28

PEACE & CHAOS

When I walk through the doors of the vampsion, I'm hoping for peace and quiet. Don't ask me why; I know it's delusional. I'm not even two steps through the door when Hugh comes running out, hefting a large and ornate wooden box. It has brass finishes and an inlaid lock.

"Lady Vicious! This arrived not an hour before you, with explicit instructions that only you may open it. The note stated it's from the Bone Reader."

Feral is less hurried but just as curious as he follows Hugh to the entrance hall. He's spinning a large brass key around one finger and looking at me.

Nahum follows them both, and his emotions wash over me. A mixture of pure joy that I'm back, which I relish, and uncertainty over whatever B.R. has seen fit to give me.

Is this a real gift, or part of another deal? Even his voice is tense in my mind.

I don't know that the Bone Reader gives anything without strings attached, but he told me something would be waiting.

The halls of the vampsion have no shortage of ornate side

tables, and the entrance is no exception. Hugh plops the box down, and it wobbles, just a bit too large for the thin table. Feral reaches out to steady it with one hand and with the other gives me the key.

"No time like the present, I guess," I grumble as the three of them crane their necks to look.

The key slides in and turns effortlessly, giving no more resistance than an audible click. I pop open the box, and sitting on plush black velvet are three things I never expected to see in this lifetime.

"Shit on a shortcake," I gasp.

Hugh raises a nostril at my language, but his emotions are just as shocked. Feral is in a state of reverent awe, and the hand that held the key reaches out. He only just stops himself from grabbing the contents of the box.

"Somson orbs," Nahum supplies, still wary.

They're all three shining with swirling light inside. One an eye-catching silver, another midnight blue, and a third the same deep green as a forest at night.

I do a quick count. I already had three. One found on the Isle, one given as an apology from Sky, and one from Gladys when the Sewing Circle decided to take up residence at CoED. Feral has three of his own. Now that we have these from the Bone Reader ...

"Feral? Hugh? How many of these did you say the legends mention?"

I already know the answer, but I need it confirmed aloud.

"Ten," Feral responds.

"Sources differ, and they depend upon the area where the legends originated and the timeline, but all things being even ... ten. Ten is the most common answer." Leave it to Hugh to clarify.

"Nine down. One to go." Nahum is staring at all three with intensity. His emotions are at war—half believing the orbs could be a salvation of sorts in whatever the Bone Reader plans to drag us into, and half acting like the orbs are serpents that could strike at any moment.

"Never," he begins, "what did the Bone Reader tell you?"

By midnight, the three of them have run out of questions, although I'm certain more will be coming. They all had their minds half made up to go to Alaska themselves for clarification straight from the Bone Reader, but that's not possible. I relayed his message about traveling.

"To get the tenth orb," Feral had guessed.

That's got to be it. Otherwise, why give me these three? All I know is, if the Bone Reader thinks a Rizik and a Reaper aren't enough to handle his siblings and whatever they're planning, I'd be more than happy to accept a tenth somson orb.

I'M LYING under the sheets, curled up against the dragon, but my mind refuses to shut down. Beside me, Nahum's breathing gives him away as being awake as well.

I begin lazily running my fingers up and down his arm. He turns, facing me with one eye peeping open.

"Trouble sleeping?"

"Well, you all did subject me to a multi-hour interrogation," I tease.

He frowns.

"Sorry about that. We may have gotten a bit carried away. If you want, I can go back to my island and see if I can find anything else on the orbs. Maybe contact some of the individuals I buy rare books from?"

"Hmm."

"You don't like the idea?" He grabs the hand that's been tracing his muscles and brings it to his lips, where he begins kissing each finger.

"I don't like the idea of being separated from you again," I admit. "This whole thing sounds like it's going to be an immense clusterfuck. Even more than the regular clusters we manage to find ourselves entangled with. I was thinking that I should take advantage of our time together while we have it."

His chest rumbles with a deep laugh.

"Are you being sentimental?"

"Maybe. It's possible. I suppose you have grown on me." I squirm as he wraps his arms around me and pulls me tight against his chest.

I'm mated to him. I've agreed to marry him. It's not a lack of love for the dragon, it's just fear.

"You're worried about losing me. Of losing everything you care about. Again."

"Now who's the intuitive?" I shove against him, not really trying to get away. I just press myself far enough to be able to crane my neck back and meet his eyes.

"I may not be intuitive, but I like to think I'm becoming an expert on reading you. We've both been to the Isle. We both have complicated histories. Losses we can't recoup, and no family or friends we've gained since will replace what was taken from us. I promise, though, you will not lose me."

The certainty he feels in his words envelops me in a soothing cocoon. I won't point out that he lost a hoard, and I lost everyone I loved. No sense comparing grief.

I place one of my hands over his heart.

"We don't know what we'll be coming up against. You've said before that I'm the only one on earth who can kill you. Maybe I'll just be the one who gets you killed. We have a lot now. That means we both have a lot to lose."

Nahum runs a hand through my hair, thoughtful.

"When you went to the Underworld, there was a moment where I truly thought you were lost. I've been terrified of having to face something like that again, but we have no choice. Whatever comes, we'll handle it together."

"And everyone else?"

The dragon means the world to me, but I've gotten greedy. I don't want to risk a single one of the magicals I consider family. If I kept Nahum but lost Aggie, or Hugh, or Todd, or Chrys, or any of the rest of them, it wouldn't be a victory.

"I promise, Never, I will do everything in my power to make sure you don't lose anyone else you love." His fingers are tipped in claws now, and they send a pleasant sensation tingling down my spine as he continues to play with my hair.

It's not a guarantee, but it's everything he has.

And while it could take the Bone Reader months, or even years, no amount of time is guaranteed.

With that thought in my mind, I throw myself onto the dragon, my lips pressing against his. He responds with hunger, one hand reaching around my back to mold my chest to his, and the other tangled in my hair as his tongue dances across mine.

My own hands trace his arms, and then his chest. I savor the feel of his heart beating, taking not a single beat for granted. Nahum grabs onto my hips as I settle on him.

Within a few minutes we're rolling off the bed and in a tangle of sheets on the floor.

It is possible that when supernaturals get together, things can get a bit carried away.

BACK IN BED, with a comforter pulled over us, I survey the shredded sheets still mangled on the floor. A side table has been knocked over, and a vase of flowers the vamps left for me sits shattered on the hardwood. Hope they don't read into that. The one thing we were careful about was avoiding the piles of books Nahum has started accumulating here.

The dragon has one arm thrown behind his head and the

other around me. I've got my head on his chest. He's managed to actually fall asleep. I'm just faking it.

The dragon did his best to reassure me, and he certainly relaxed me, but even a dragon has a hard time competing in my mind against the potential end of everyone I love.

The stakes are high, and I don't even know exactly what I'm fighting.

There's one thing I can do, though.

What I've been doing so far is child's play. Starting tomorrow morning, real Reaper training begins.

Well, actually we need to go to the casinos tomorrow to check on project "kid reunification." So, I guess technically, Reaper training will begin at some unspecified time in the afternoon or perhaps even evening.

But the first way sounded cooler.

29

LOOSE ENDS & ELOPEMENTS

Chrys hangs up the phone behind the Vicious casino desk and waves me over.

"That was Jackal. Says he's got his niece returned, but he'd like to come back here and take you up on your offer for a while." She raises a brow at me.

"I promised him a room at the vampsion if he wanted to stay and help through the rest of the kid-returning and our upcoming Bone Reader–led disaster," I inform her. "Plus, he's a private investigator. I was thinking it's a gig I might look into."

"Hmm, a career change. Maybe that is something to think on," she muses.

The witch has filled all sorts of roles in our group. Defender, home security, vampsion babysitter, casino manager. I pay her a lot out of the vampsion funds, but I've never bothered to ask her which, if any, of her roles is something she'd like to keep long-term.

"Trying to find your calling?" I dig.

She shrugs, white spiral curls bouncing off her shoulders.

"A girl should keep her options open. At least when it comes to paychecks. I'm with whoever this hyena is, though; I'll stick with this crew until we find out what it is the Bone Reader has everyone so worked up about."

The others have all expressed similar sentiments. Feral called the rest of the remaining CoED members, including the other Founders, back to his castle in the woods. The Sewing Circle have been given official long-term rooms there, and suites at the casino.

"A battle to end all battles? Wouldn't miss it," Tom had quipped when they'd been informed of their options. In fairness, the griffin probably didn't sound quite so clear. Per Feral's recollection, Tom had his dentures out at the time.

Hugh runs up to us, clipboard in hand. He dashes behind the desk and wraps Chrys into a hug. He's turning back to me when she grabs him by the shoulders and pulls him back for what becomes an awkwardly long kiss.

She blows him another one and saunters off as he faces me. He's flustered, and blushing. He tugs at his shirt collar.

"Yes, well. Um, I came here for a reason. I'll just—"

I point to the clipboard.

"Right. Right-o. The numbers. That was it." He snaps his feet together and salutes like some overly formal soldier. "Lady Never, I am happy to report that we have only ten remaining children unclaimed."

"And their parents? Are we any closer to figuring out who they belong to?"

He sags.

"We have a lead on a young nagi. Nothing for the other nine. That leaves us a bear shifter not from the Sacramento pack, three wolf shifters, two sea-shifters and a hippogriff, a drake, and a young girl with twisting vines for arms who said she was a *vippery*. It's not in any vampsion book, and based on her description of her home, I'm thinking she's Fae."

He sighs. I put my arm around his shoulder.

"Buck up, Hugh. That's a lot of progress in a short amount of time. We'll get it done."

After all, it's not just us anymore. Nadia and Sky have the entire network of Magikai representatives putting out feelers. Feral asked the Founders to contact a few packs and groups on their way back to CoED, and Nahum even managed to get one of the supernaturals he buys books from to see what he could find out abroad.

The phone behind the desk rings again, and Hugh snaps it up before a passing vamp can reach the thing.

"Vicious Casino, currently booking—"

He hands me the phone.

"Nadia," he mouths.

I've been waiting for her call. During our last conversation, I mentioned staying with the Magikai 'for now,' and I could tell she had more questions. Since the leads on the remaining kids have fizzled, I'm guessing she's found the time to ask.

"You've got the leading lady herself," I quip as I pick up the phone.

She laughs on the other end of the line.

"Aren't you the one who has frequently insisted you're not a lady?"

"I am known to make that assertion, but it's a lady's prerogative to change her mind."

I'm one thousand percent certain Nadia is rolling her eyes at me.

"*A usted si que le falta un tornillo,*" she mutters.

Actually, I'm missing more than one screw, or at least I've got quite a few loose.

"Hugh's filled you in?" she asks. "All US-based kidnapping cases are closed, unless one of your kids turns out to belong to that group, but we have no more reported missing."

"They're not *my* kids. They're kids under my care, which technically means under the direct care of my friends and vampire staff and a few other stray supernaturals working for me that we picked up back when we broke up the Magikai's auction ring," I correct.

Another eyeroll, if I was a gambler.

"Whatever. I also personally coordinated with any South American cases, and there's no one else who's been reported as missing there either."

When she's done, I wait until the silence gets awkward. She sighs into the phone, and I prepare myself.

"Never, what you said about the Magikai ... are you going to quit? Is it because of Amun and everything that happened with the auction ring? Or the fact that you were pressured at best and threatened at worst to join in the first place? Is it people like Sky and Occam? Because I think I could smooth things o—"

"Wereling, slow your roll. The only reason I was still with the Magikai after all these years was because I'd grown complacent. Now that I've found myself again, thanks to all you pesky beings that wouldn't leave me to my misery, I want something else out of life."

She's half-ecstatic over my warm words, and half-crestfallen at the rest of them.

"And what about me? If I stay ..."

She leaves it hanging, but between my intuition and our relationship, I guess the rest.

"I will be incredibly proud of you. And I'll have a bit more confidence in the government as long as people like you are there. But don't tell the rest of the representatives, or my reputation as an anti-authoritarian will be in tatters."

She laughs on the other end of the line.

"I don't think anyone is about to accuse you of respecting authority."

"See, this is why you make a good sibling. You're full of

compliments. My only regret is that if I leave, I won't be seeing you nearly as often."

Nadia giggles.

"Oh I wouldn't say that. You might be seeing me sooner than you think. I'll talk to you soon, Never."

The phone is barely back in its cradle—yes, we have the old kind that plugs into a wall—when Nahum approaches me.

The dragon's eyes are hungry, and I suppress a giggle as he sweeps me off my feet, sets me on the counter, and kisses my neck.

"The people who work here might consider this unprofessional," I warn him.

"And the guests," he agrees, "but you'll notice the lobby has emptied."

I push him gently off, and sure enough he's right.

Hell's bells. I've been so engrossed with my conversation with Nadia that I didn't even notice.

He's so satisfied with himself that I give another playful shove and narrow my eye at him.

"You're up to something. You may be a dragon, but right now you're wily as a fox."

The gold flecks in his eyes shimmer.

"Maybe. You may recall that some time ago you made a deal with me. A deal to give me your hand in marriage, in addition to your heart as my mate."

"Maybe," I allow, drawing the word out.

He chuckles.

"You sound so suspicious, even when I'm trying to be romantic. It's part of why I love you."

"And we're counting my suspicious nature as a positive why?" I can't help asking.

"You love me. And I know it's not just because you think I'm handsome, or I'm a powerful supernatural with an astounding amount of money—"

"Books. A truly astounding amount of books. You'll recall I also have a very hefty bank account."

He rolls right on as if I haven't spoken. Something that would annoy me in most males, but in Nahum I let it slide this time. Because he's right: he is handsome and I do love him.

"—or because we trauma-bonded over our crappy past. I mean, we did, but that's not why you love me. You love who I am. And I know that, because you analyze everything. Everyone's statements, and behaviors, and emotions, and motives. I'd never have gotten past your defenses and into your heart if you didn't genuinely care for me."

"And what about you? What about your feelings for me?" Am I digging for compliments? Perhaps. But the dragon's on a roll. It'd be a shame to stop him now.

"My heart was lost to you the moment you left my island. You carried it with you on that boat. I just didn't realize it until it became clear you were my mate. After all those years thinking I was happy to be isolated, I couldn't envision spending my years without you. I would banish myself to a solitary existence if you needed me to, but I prefer my life by your side. Protecting you, supporting you, and trying to keep you alive even when you insist on frequently ensconcing yourself in trouble."

I have no defense for that last part, folks. Troublemaker. That's me.

"You're in a very romantic mood today," I note, pulling him in for another kiss.

The dragon's emotions go all mischievous, and elated.

"Well, this seemed like the perfect setting. You can, of course, say no if you're not interested, but I thought it was a great idea."

"Nahum."

"I mean, most of the people we care about were already in

the area, and the rest were more than happy to take the time to travel."

"Nahum."

I said the dragon was on a roll, and he rolls right over my interjections.

"I know you didn't want a huge, flashy wedding. Or the stress of planning something. I just thought, well, I mean, if you don't like it I'm happy to tell them all to get out."

I glance around the lobby and at the double doors that lead to an event space on the property. The minute my eye hits it, the dragon's emotions kick into hyperdrive.

I look back up at him.

"Did you plan me a surprise wedding? *Our* wedding? Are all our friends waiting in that room?"

His emotions are so wild I assume he'll be a mess, but instead he takes a deep breath and grabs my hands.

"Yes. Never, I don't know how much time we have before whatever the Bone Reader's got waiting for us. You're already my mate, but I'd be honored to have you as my wife as well. I figure we could all use some positivity at the moment. A wedding, and the inevitably wild reception, seemed just the thing. If you're up for it. If you'll have me."

I pull his head toward me until our heights match and I can rest my forehead against his.

"You crazy, good-hearted dragon. Of course my answer is yes. There's only one problem."

Worry swirls in his heart and buffets my intuition.

"And that is?"

"Whatever will I wear?"

The dragon laughs, and I pull back enough to stare into his eyes.

"I'd marry you in anything. Even one of Aggie's ridiculous shirts. Maybe she can find me one in the lobby gift store that says *Vegas Bride,* or something like that."

Someone clears their throat behind us.

"That won't be necessary."

Aggie is beaming. Next to her are three other witches—Chrys, Gladys, and Rose. All of them grinning like crazy.

Chrys steps forward.

"When Nahum told us his plan, we were only too happy to help. Why do you think the Sewing Circle rushed back here? Aggie is event security, and your maid of honor. I've wrapped extra defensive walls around the casino so nothing interrupts your wedding—"

"And we are supplying the dress! I didn't have a real suit and wedding dress on hand, but we won't need one. Stand here, please." Rose ushers Nahum and me into an open part of the lobby. Once we're in position she starts waving her hands around, and her eyes begin to flash while she uses her magic. I'd almost forgotten what an illusion-keyed witch could do.

In minutes I'm staring at Nahum dressed in a delectably handsome suit of dark slate gray. Looking down at myself, I see I've been put in a form-fitting dress that's smooth, creamy satin. It's a gorgeous and incredibly pale cornflower blue. I can feel that the back is open, dipping low.

"Not white?" I tease her as she admires her work, wiping away a tear. She swats me on the arm.

"As if you would have let me dress you in anything conventional."

"And I will be supplying the veil. You may not have had the best experience in Fae, but there's no denying the flowers are pretty. Hexia and I put this together. She even loaned me some from her own personal stash." Gladys pulls an intricately woven, floral veil from her pocket universe. Lucky witch, to be keyed with all that storage.

When we walked through Fae, the Easter-egg colored flowers were a bit much. As soon as I see the veil, though, I'm in shock. There are pale blue flowers, but also dried and preserved leaves, and a spray of small white and silver flowers as well.

"It's stunning," I say as she gestures for me to bend down so she can place it on my head. I can't think of a single snarky or snippy thing to say.

"I'm genuinely touched," I tell her. And it didn't escape my notice what she said about Hexia. The old dragon hoards plants. I'm one thousand percent certain these are just on loan, but the enormity of her allowing me to wear them isn't lost on me.

"We have good friends," Nahum whispers to me as the witches move back toward the doors and he takes my hand.

"We have a good *family*," I counter, placing my hand in his.

The witches stand two at each door, ready to pull them open as we approach.

"There is one thing I didn't plan for," Nahum admits.

"Hmmm?"

"The honeymoon." His voice rumbles a bit, sending a pleasant shiver running through me as he leans in.

I shoot him a mischievous smile.

"There is one spot. A private island a dragon I know owns. He makes a mean latte, and I've heard the property has an extensive library. There are some very pleasant hot springs as well, if you're into that sort of thing."

His eyes light up.

"Yes, that could be *very* nice."

The witches pull the doors open. I can see everyone gathered. Nadia shoots me a wink. She was right. I'm seeing her much sooner than I thought.

This whole scene is so sappy I would hardly be able to stand it, if my heart weren't so full.

I'm sure that, soon enough, everything will devolve into its usual state of peril and mayhem.

Until then, for once, I'm letting myself enjoy the moment.

EPILOGUE 1
FAMILY IS A MAZE

The Bone Reader
3 months After the Wedding

People think Greenland has only one natural forest. In truth, it has two.

Two forests, and one forest-hoarding Rizik.

Cycling my features has become second nature after so many years. It's a habit at this point, and requires less effort than breathing. As I step up to the edge of my brother's forest, I let out a deep breath and drop all illusions.

Unlike my other siblings, I would be very shocked to find Rumplestiltskin wearing anything but his own skin. Matching him might help remind him we're on the same team. At least we should be.

The barrier of the forest shimmers. I have no doubt I've got more than enough magic to force my way in, but that won't put him in any mood to give me what I want. Not that I've known my brother to possess a good mood in the last several centuries.

He was never the most cheerful among us, and, being truthful, he was never the most intelligent. He can blame bad luck for getting caught out on his name all he likes; he got careless. Now that he's a recluse, I don't even know how he manages to make the deals necessary to survive. I suppose it helps when his ability isn't reading bones, or manipulating minds. It's taking one look at someone and being able to determine their greatest want.

Another of my siblings can look at you and determine your greatest need. The two are actually quite different skills, but since most people who come begging for deals don't know any better, they both always had an easier time than the rest of us.

Now that there's video chatting and phones, it's highly likely he doesn't need to venture into society. He can just receive calls in whatever tree he calls home here.

I know he'll have sensed someone at the edge of his woods.

He makes me wait for hours. A power play. One I've used quite a lot. I don't let it show how much it bothers me. I don't pace, or sit, or move in any way. I just stand, staring at the magical shimmering wall while I remind myself over and over why this wait is necessary.

After a time that he must deem long enough, I hear Rumple's voice booming and echoing from the darkness of the woods.

"Why have you come to disturb me, brother?"

For just a moment, I'm tempted to yell back that he should drop the theatrics and let me in. Never has rubbed off on me more than I realized.

"I am here because I need answers, and you're the only one who has them."

If Never *were* here, she'd no doubt be bowled over by the satisfaction my brother undoubtedly feels at having his ego inflated. The words are too sweet in my mouth, but they have the desired effect.

"You have intrigued me, but I'm afraid you'll need to do better than that if you want entrance."

I can't quite suppress a sigh. Rumple was always caught up in riddles and tricks. I viewed life as a chessboard full of moves and powerful pieces. He viewed it as a joke that only he fully understood.

"Little pig, little pig, let me come in."

His tittering laugh echoes through the trees. Even after his downfall, Rumple always was fond of fairytales.

"Not by the hair of my chinny-chin-chin," he calls back, walking close enough to the magical border that I can see him.

For just a moment, he's a wizened old man with a long beard that reaches his knees. After a grin at me, there's a flash and he's presenting himself as the true Rizik I know him to be.

Our forms are part of our power, and I have no intention of sharing them with anyone outside my siblings.

He stares at me, and I finish his game.

"Then I'll huff, and I'll puff, and—"

"Oh, very well, then. No need to threaten me." He laughs, then snaps his fingers and the shimmering vanishes. He gestures toward the woods.

"Follow me."

I WAS right about his living situation. He has a dwelling built in the forest. Walls made of tree bark, leaves and dirt for a floor. I prefer my ice. It's clean and elegant. I sit in a chair cobbled together from branches and bark while Rumple putters around. I take the tea he offers and drink it, even though it's bitter beyond words. After I'm halfway through the tea, I judge it a good time to broach my real reason for visiting.

"I'm not sure if you're aware of what our siblings have been up to, but they're causing trouble."

He waves me off, as expected. What does he care?

"This is no trivial matter. They're plotting. Using their deals and schemes to build up forces and spells that could destroy everything we know. Wipe out the supernatural communities, not to mention humans. Wreck Fae."

Rumple keeps shuffling around, busying himself with odd jobs. He arranges a bunch of items on his wooden counter, then shuffles them all together again. They're ordinary things. Flowers, leaves, sticks. No magic to them. He's more addled than I'd thought.

"What do I care what they do? They can destroy what they like, and I'll make deals with whoever is left. I don't even need to leave the forest."

As I suspected. Long-distance deals.

"You will care if they achieve their aims," I insist, trying to balance persuasion with pressure. This has to be his idea. "From what I have seen, I think they're intending to overthrow the balance and set themselves up as the new gods. We've got a dwindling number already. What then? What if they bring back old sacrifices and worship? What if there's no one to make deals with you because they're only seeking out our siblings? What would happen then?"

His hands still, and he stares down at the cluttered counter under his fingertips.

When he turns to me, I wait. I think I have him, but I can't look too eager. He gives the smallest nod.

"That could present a problem. But what do you intend to do about it? Tell me you're not thinking of involving me. I've no desire to face them head-on."

He'd lose, but I don't say it.

"I have a plan. I have reinforcements. I'm only lacking one thing."

And I tell him. I tell him about Never's friends, and the Fates. I tell him about promising to make more gods. Why wouldn't I? They'll even the odds when it comes to whatever my siblings have up their sleeves. I tell him about Damien, and now Danger, already being added as deities.

"And this Never, when she came back, she was a Rizik as well? Are you saying I have a new sister to welcome?"

This part is trickier. If I want him to cooperate, I can't let him catch me in a lie. The only way to guarantee that is to be honest. Normally, I prefer to keep my definition of honesty flexible.

But I need him. I need what he has.

"She did not come back as a Rizik. I miscalculated."

Rumplestiltskin guffaws, sitting in one of his rickety wooden seats across from me. He nabs a crackling and crumbling leaf off the dirt floor and crushes it in his hands.

"My genius brother? Miscalculated? That must have infuriated you."

"Not really. She came back as a Reaper, so it's worked out for the best."

The remains of the leaf bits fall out of his hands. He freezes, then fixes me with a pointed stare.

"You? You created a Reaper? Then why come to me? She could eliminate either of us if she were so inclined. You'd better not have brought her here!" He looks left and right, as though the Were is going to materialize in the middle of his home. Foolishness.

"She poses no threat to us, *if* we remain on her good side." I don't bother mentioning that I'm only just now clawing my way back into her good graces. If I can defeat my siblings, and stop the chaos I have no doubt they'll unleash, that should fix things with Never.

"You've got my attention. If I help you both, what do I get out of it?"

"Are you saying you want to make a deal?"

It's not unexpected. Dealing with me won't gain him any

power, but it will give him the satisfaction of inconveniencing me.

"Of course I want to make a deal. Now then, get on with it. What do you want?"

I don't mince words.

"If I'm correct, you still have possession of a somson orb. The *last* somson orb. We've got nine. I need the tenth. Give it to me, and help us win."

His smile is far too satisfied for my liking. The brief thought occurs that I must come across like this to people who take my deals, but I push it away. I'm nothing like my brother.

He's completely out of touch with reality. My deals have a purpose.

"It so happens I don't *have* the last somson orb. I hid it. I couldn't have it falling into the wrong hands. But,"—he holds up a hand, palm out—"I would be willing to make a deal for revealing the location. You'd be responsible for retrieving it."

He tilts his hand to the side, ready to shake mine. My touch burns like dry ice, and I've been told it's unpleasant. His is worse. It feels like thousands of tiny needles embedding in the skin as we grasp hands.

"Fine. The location. I'll retrieve it, but you can't interfere with my collecting the orb."

"It's already got certain protections, but I won't add more," he agrees.

"And in return?" Now I wait.

The sides of his mouth curl up and he leers at me.

"I want something from you that I doubt you'll ever be able to find. All of you berated me when I lost the deal with that girl—"

"Because you didn't need to make it! You didn't have to give her a loophole with your name. That was—"

"I like my riddles! My deals are mine to decide. Don't worry though, brother, I won't leave any loopholes for you. Now then, as I was saying, you owe me for the somson orb's location. I want love. I want you to find one being you really, truly love. It can't be yourself. You have until you defeat our siblings to find such an individual, and then you will bring them to me. You said your little Reaper friend is an intuitive? She can verify for us, so I can be assured you won't lie. You know the repercussions if you fail."

I'm well aware. Breaking a Rizik deal is a death sentence. My brother has just tried to kill me.

Bargain complete, my brother wraps his arm around my shoulder, transporting us. I have my shadows, and he moves like a cloud. Small wisps of white that fade away.

We land on what should be an open field of ice. Instead, the horizon is dominated by a massive hedge maze.

The deal's done now, so I can afford to let a little of my impatience with him show.

"This is the sort of thing you're using your power for? Creating and concealing an entire maze?"

"Oh, brother, don't be so sour. It's fun. I got the idea from the minotaur. I have all sorts of intriguing traps and obstacles within. Even a few creatures I acquired through deals. I don't often use it, but when I need a bit of extra entertainment I enjoy sending people through it. It adds a bit of panache to the deals, don't you think?"

I wouldn't agree even if I weren't about to have to go through the thing. I've done many things, but I've never held live beings captive. Maybe I'll blow a hole in the side of the maze and neglect to repair it on my way out. I'm not a good enough person to take responsibility for any freed beings, but that would at least give them a fighting chance.

Rumple claps his hands together.

"I do hope you make it to the middle, brother. I'd like to collect on my end of the deal. If you don't, though, at least I'll have something to watch. Cameras all over the maze, you see.

That way there's no cheating. You can't just decimate every obstacle. You have to actually play the game. Otherwise, the orb will disappear and you'll never get your hands on it."

I'd like to hit him. Better yet, I'd like to let Never have a minute alone with him, but I still need the orb.

Instead of violence, I just stand in front of the maze with a blank expression, refusing to speak until my brother transforms back into a cloud and whisks himself away.

I roll my neck, and then my shoulders. As I do, my features change and cascade over one another again. It's comforting, having this series of masks back in place.

With that taken care of, I make my way into the maze.

EPILOGUE 2
TIME'S UP

Never
Four Months After the Wedding

The ends of my fur are iced over, and even in this form I bite back a shiver. It does me no good; my snout is shaking. The only warmth available is the air blowing out of my muzzle each time I take a breath. It's a particularly miserable day in the wilderness of Alaska.

You're sure this is what you want to do? Nahum asks.

It's not the first time. He's not in the habit of making me repeat myself, but his worry envelops me and I know it's because he cares. Relations with the Bone Reader are complicated at best, even after the events at the graveyard, but now I have no choice.

None of the representatives had any better ideas than we did. No alphas or kings or leaders have had a clue as to what to do. Even the Founders were stumped, and they're the oldest beings I know aside from our current quarry. That leaves the Bone Reader. Like it or not, this is probably connected to his siblings.

Agreement washes over me, even though the dragon doesn't like it. Nahum is in his skin, bundled up from head to toe. Even his eyes are covered.

Speaking of eyes.

Or eye.

Don't think I haven't tried a quick tap on my eyepatch to summon B.R. to me. I've tried it several times a day for nearly a month.

It hasn't worked.

Instead, we've had to fly all the way up here. After multiple cancellations due to unseasonably crappy weather, the Magikai had to lend us a personal jet. Even then they insisted on landing at an actual airport for the purposes of safety.

B.R. must know how mad it'll make me to have to trek across the ice. Before CoED I wouldn't have questioned it. It's part of the price everyone pays for the skills of the great Rizik. Now, though? I feel I'm owed some preferential treatment, to put it mildly.

I breathe a sigh of relief when I spot the entrance to B.R.'s cave through the icy winds.

"Almost there."

The moment we cross through the entrance of the cave, the sound of the whistling wind dies down, stuck outside. Inside, where we are, things are still ice, but there's nothing blowing or blizzarding.

"Neat trick," I muse aloud.

As I pad through the cave, it illuminates to its usual icy blue. I can see the goblet B.R. uses for most of his bone reading on a pedestal in the center, and the dark entrance leading to where he actually lives in back.

But no Bone Reader.

"Rizik! We have things to discuss. No use hiding!"

When he doesn't answer, and I can't feel any emotions either, I worry we've come all this way for nothing.

At least we can sleep here for the night if he's not here to kick us out, Nahum suggests.

"Yeah, but there's one more thing to try."

He hasn't responded recently, so there's no reason to think he will now.

For a moment fear squeezes my insides and works its way up my throat.

What if it's not his obstinate and stubborn attitude forestalling his appearance? What if he's hurt? He warned me his siblings made the other villains we've faced look like a baby kitten or something equally tame. After meeting Shiftress, I believe him.

What if they got to him first?

I reach up and tap twice with a shaky hand.

When black shadows swirl in front of the goblet, I can't decide if I'm more infuriated or relieved.

Even as Visitor solidifies in front of me, I haven't decided how to react.

"Abusing the eyepatch *and* breaking into my home? This must be serious." His voice lilts as he dusts off a grey sleeve.

I launch myself at him, punching him on his chest.

"You eyepatch-ignoring asshole! Where have you been? Do you have any idea what's been going on? Just popping out of existence with no explanation! You told me to start practicing Reaper stuff, which I did, by the way. But did you give us any guidance on what to do with that skill? No! You're off doing moon knows what while the world's been going crazy. Why weren't you home? I thought you might have been captured! You could have been dead!"

He doesn't move as I let out a lengthy tirade worthy of

Danger, a valkywolf with verbal spew that could impress even the most seasoned conversational interrupter. B.R. just stands there, staring down at me. Since I'm in my fur, he should be shorter, but I'm guessing he's given Visitor some added height to remind me who holds the power here.

"Are you quite finished?" he asks when my blows trickle to a stop. He raises one brow at me, vibrant blue eyes locked on my face.

Oh damn. I've got a tear running down my cheek. He reaches for it, but curls his fist closed at the last second.

"I'm touched. And here I thought you were still upset with me."

Wiping the tear away with the back of one hand, I present him with a scowl.

"Being upset with you doesn't mean I want to see you killed."

He laughs.

"So you do care."

"Where have you been?" I ask again.

"Out. Tracking clues. I did tell you my siblings were building up to something, and I think it's almost time for a grand finale."

"You think? In the last few months we've had an uptick in shifters going mad, whether they've lost mates or not. We've got supernaturals disappearing with no discernible patterns. We've had pixies attacking bear shifter sleuths and warlocks trying to capture a whole mess of drakes and all sorts of nonsense. We've had bodies mysteriously appearing. There's been a rise in break-ins or break-in attempts at almost every Magikai facility around the globe, and some have been successful. They've run off with magical items and objects I didn't even know the government had! And I can only imagine it's tied to your family tree," I finish, huffing and running a hand through my silver hair.

One of those break-ins was Jackal, paying back his debt to me. He stole me a sizable sapphire ring Hugh is experimenting with. It definitely has some sort of magic. Jackal said it was a wedding present."

B.R. nods, contemplative. He glances past me at Nahum, but the dragon doesn't say anything.

"My siblings are behind all of those things, but it's just the beginning. Things are only going to get worse."

"Worse? It can't get worse! The representatives are using every resource they have to keep the supernatural community under wraps and keep the headcount of the missing up to date."

"I know. We're going to need help. The friends you promised me in our deal, and my allies as well."

I scoff.

"You have allies? Aside from me?"

He raises a finger to tap on his chin.

"Perhaps. Even if that idea doesn't work, I've paid Rumplestiltskin a visit, and he—"

"Rumplestiltskin?" Nahum pipes up, and B.R.'s eyes slide toward him.

"Yes. My younger brother, by a couple thousand years. You've read the legend with the stupid gold thread and the name-guessing, I presume?"

"Yes, but I have another text that references him in my library back on the island. It's said he had a way of knowing your deepest desires and providing them to you."

B.R. grins.

"He can do so much more than that. At least, he used to be able to. I was at his residence, trying to convince him to part with an item of great value. As usual, his cost was high. It took me a number of weeks, but I had just gotten my hands on what we needed when you so rudely interrupted me." His attention is back on me again, and his emotions are turbulent.

B.R. must have gone through some sort of hell and back again to get whatever he's got, because he's harried and exhausted. I was too frustrated to pick up on it at first.

First he helps Aggie, then he endures some harrowing mission to help us. It's almost like the Bone Reader is growing a heart, but if he is, I'm not sure he'd know what to do with one.

I'm tempted to ask after that cost B.R. mentioned, but he reaches into a suit pocket that appeared flat moments ago and pulls out a glorious, shining white orb.

"You found it," I whisper, reaching toward it in awe.

"Is it the last one? Are there really ten?" Nahum questions.

The Bone Reader's eyes snap from me to the dragon again.

"There are indeed ten. The instructions on how to combine them and wield their power, without incinerating oneself and anyone in a multi-mile vicinity, is kept by three deities with whom you are familiar. That brings me back to the other portion of the plan ... allies."

He can only mean the damned Fates. Owners of my other eye. Bosses, in a manner, of my ex Damien. He may be king of the Underworld, but I've no doubt they're making the rules. Likely instructors of Danger, now that she's a deity as well.

They *would* be powerful allies, but working with them makes my skin crawl.

The eagerness in B.R.'s emotions makes me think I'll be meeting with them whether I want to or not.

"You're bringing the Fates. And I promised to recruit my friends. When I made that deal, just who did you have in mind?" I demand.

He shrugs, as if it's of no consequence.

"Everyone. Every ally you've ever had in this realm or any other. Any allies of those allies willing to put their necks on the line. I'm talking about anyone you've ever come in contact with who might have even a remotely favorable opinion of you. At the very least, anyone who would be willing to die to protect the supernatural community. Because that's what you'll be doing. Asking mere, regular supernaturals to face down beings whose power rivals that of the gods. You're all risking death. And this time, I have no plans to bring you or anyone else back."

"And you've already told me Riziks are tough. You wanted another Rizik, or a Reaper to fight them."

"Or a deity. A god could handle a Rizik," he informs us.

"My friends are none of those things. That means you or I will kill your siblings, or the damned Fates. If that's the case, why use the others?"

I've shoved my finger in B.R.'s face. He reaches a hand up and shoves mine aside. I ignore the dry ice burn as he speaks.

"You and I can't kill them if we can't find them. We need help to draw them out."

Of course he has a plan. He's always ten steps ahead.

"Why don't you clarify to me how we're going to do that," I insist.

"Very well. You, as you now know, are a Reaper. I hadn't even considered the possibility of your returning from the Underworld as one, since they haven't been seen in ages. The fact that you are here works to our advantage. My siblings and their spies couldn't have known, and so Shiftress couldn't have seen you coming."

"Yes, but if they're as nosy as *you,* it's very possible they know now. Someone could have seen us in the woods and gotten word back to them."

He nods.

"Undoubtedly, but my plan included a few key aspects. First, powerful allies. We've got that. Second, the orbs and a means to use them. A quick trip to the Fates and we'll have that as well. Last, and this is key because we need beings who can rival my siblings' power, I wanted more deities. Now we have a means to create those, too."

"How?"

Visitor's features melt away and he goes back to his rolling eye colors, hairstyles, and weaving voices.

"The Fates still had a few materials available for imbuing someone with godly powers. That's how I got you a weapon that would turn Damien, and sent you to the Underworld as well. Now, they're out of items. I made a deal with the Fates. I owe them more deities. That's where you come in."

My one working eye widens and I take a step away from B.R., and then another.

Never. I'm here.

The soothing presence of my mate gives me the strength to snap back with a response worthy of my snarky reputation.

"You'd better spit it out, Bone Reader. I've been training as a Reaper. I'm ready to kill for you, but that's all I know how to do."

His features freeze, half-changed. One eye green and one brown. Chunks of hair that are auburn, and some black. One cheek rounded and another sharp.

"Any fool can kill someone. That's nothing special. You are more, and better, than that. There was one bit of information I kept back from you before, when I told you about Reapers. You're not just controlling lives; you're controlling souls. Those struck down with the scythe will never see another plane. No Underworld, no continuation. Their soul simply ceases to exist."

Damn. I can think of a particular elf I'd love to have used this on. And a few other people.

"And?" I press.

"And you can do even more than that. Why do you think Reapers were on par with gods? You can end a soul forever, *or* you can save it. How do you think Danger managed to go from death's doorstep to a powerful deity? It had nothing to do with me, and it had nothing to do with something so silly as being Damien's mate. Surely you figured that out."

I can't breathe. B.R. leans in close, and lowers his voice to a whisper.

"Reapers have the power to create gods."

NOTES & ALSO BY

I want to extend an enormous THANK YOU to everyone who has followed Never's journey. We're almost to the finale, and I am so excited to share it with you all.

If you enjoyed this book and are able, I would be so appreciative if you would rate or review Never Mind wherever you look for new reads. This helps the visibility of the book so other readers can find and enjoy it as well! NEVER ENDS releases in 2025 and is available for preorder now.

For all who are wondering how the Bone Reader gets through the maze- I have a special treat I'm working on! There will be a short, free story available to all my newsletter subscribers later this year. To make sure you get the story when it's available, you can sign up on my website: nightlochpublishers.com

ALSO BY SILAS REAMES

Shifter Vengeance Series

Never Before: (A Shifter Vengeance Prequel Novella)

*The prequel can be read at any point in the series. It deals with what happened to Never prior to the Shifter Vengeance series.

Never (Shifter Vengeance 1)
Never Again (Shifter Vengeance 2)
Never Ever (Shifter Vengeance 3)
Never More (Shifter Vengeance 4)
Never Say Never (Shifter Vengeance 5)
Never Ends (Shifter Vengeance 7): You can preorder the finale now!

~

The Societies Trilogy
(Under Pen Name Sydney Reames)

-The Societies is a completed YA Sci-Fantasy series-
Assimilation (Societies 1)
Serpentina (A Societies Novella) -events take place between books 1 & 2
Alliance (Societies 2)
Ascension (Societies 3)

~

Connect With Me

To keep up with other projects and all things Shifter Vengeance related you can find me here:
Facebook: Silas Reames Author & Never's Vengeance Vixens Group
Tiktok & Instagram: @reameswrites
Website & Newsletter: nightlochpublishers.com

ACKNOWLEDGMENTS

The further I get into this series, the more people there are to thank.

A huge thanks is owed to my understanding spouse, who doesn't question me when I start muttering something about plot and disappearing into my office with no explanation for hours on end.

Thank you to Alyssa, who always offers the first round of enthusiastic responses to these books.

Doreen-you are owed the largest of thank you's for your editing magic. Ironically, this page will be the least put together because it's the only one you don't edit!

I want to extend an enormous thank you to my readers, and specifically to Jen, Angie, and Belinda. You all are rock stars. I really appreciate you jumping on to give feedback on an early copy when Helene messed up my typical beta reader plans! You guys made some last minute catches and saves that I'm sure readers will thank you for.

The biggest of thanks goes out to everyone who continues to read and buy these books. A tough, female Were book has been in my head for ages, and without all of you I wouldn't have been able to bring this series to life.

Milton Keynes UK
Ingram Content Group UK Ltd.
UKHW021909231124
451423UK00006B/628